"You okay?" Cal hustled over to the cash counter.

"Fine." Alana popped up from behind the counter, tugging at an evergreen wreath caught in her hair.

"Hang on." Cal went to her.

"No, it's okay, I can—"

Cal tried not to laugh. She looked both comical and adorable. "Stop and let me try." He gently loosened the strands of hair tangled in a large pine cone.

The silky tendrils slipped through his fingers, and he was so close that Alana's soft breath warmed his cheek.

"There you go." His breath stuttered, and he took several steps back.

"Thanks." She avoided his gaze. "You can go."

"I'll wait and walk you to your car. I don't want to leave you here on your own."

He didn't want to leave Alana anywhere. He hadn't wanted to leave her the first time, either. But he couldn't tell her why he had. He'd made a promise.

Dear Reader,

In *A Small Town Family Christmas*, I invite you to spend the holiday season with family and friends in Strawberry Pond, New Hampshire.

Second chance/reunion romances are one of my favorite kinds. In *A Small Town Family Christmas*, Alana Hansen and Cal Paquette were high school sweethearts, but a few years after graduation Cal unexpectedly left town, leaving Alana bereft. At Christmas, a season of hope, promise and magic, can they somehow find their way back to a forever love?

I've long wanted to write a Christmas romance, and this story captures my fondness for this special season. With a cute country tree farm, cookie baking, twinkling lights, small-town market and more, this book includes many of my own cozy holiday traditions. Alana's cherished ornament collection is inspired by mine, as well as those I've gifted my daughter annually since her first Christmas.

I enjoy hearing from readers, so visit my website jengilroy.com and message me there, where you'll also find my newsletter sign-up and social media links.

Enjoy!

Jen

A SMALL TOWN FAMILY CHRISTMAS

JEN GILROY

Harlequin
HEARTWARMING

Harlequin® HEARTWARMING™

ISBN-13: 978-1-335-60523-8

Recycling programs for this product may not exist in your area.

A Small Town Family Christmas

For questions and comments about the quality of this book, please contact us at CustomerService@Harlequin.com.

Harlequin Enterprises ULC
22 Adelaide St. West, 41st Floor
Toronto, Ontario M5H 4E3, Canada
www.Harlequin.com

HarperCollins Publishers
Macken House, 39/40 Mayor Street Upper,
Dublin 1, D01 C9W8, Ireland
www.HarperCollins.com

Printed in U.S.A.

1 2 3 4 5 6 7 8 9 10 HDC 29 28 27 26

Jen Gilroy writes sweet romance and uplifting women's fiction—warm feel-good stories to bring readers' hearts home. A Romance Writers of America Golden Heart® Award finalist and short-listed for the Romantic Novelists' Association Joan Hessayon Award, she lives in small-town Ontario, Canada, with her husband, teenage daughter and floppy-eared rescue hound. She loves reading, ice cream, ballet and paddling her purple kayak. Visit her at jengilroy.com.

Books by Jen Gilroy

Harlequin Heartwarming

The Montana Carters

Montana Reunion
A Family for the Rodeo Cowboy
The Cowgirl Nanny
A Rancher's Return

A Strawberry Pond Romance

The Hero Next Door
A Surprise for the Single Dad

Visit the Author Profile page at Harlequin.com.

For everyone who believes in the magic of Christmas

CHAPTER ONE

IF CHRISTMAS WAS the most wonderful time of year for Alana Hansen, Thanksgiving came a close second.

In the big dining room of the New Hampshire farmhouse where she'd grown up, she surveyed the long table ready to welcome their guests. Along with her mom's best dishes, part of every Thanksgiving celebration as far back as Alana remembered, the rustic pumpkin-and-twine centerpiece she'd spent the past several evenings sewing added a cute and cozy vibe.

"It all looks perfect." Joining Alana with a basket holding coloring sheets, pencils and other Thanksgiving-themed craft activities to entertain her four young grandchildren, her mom gave an approving nod. "This year especially, I don't know what I'd have done without you to help me get ready." In the November sunshine that streamed through the casement windows, the smile lines between her mother's nose and mouth were more pronounced than usual.

"It's my pleasure. You know that." Alana gave her mom's arm a gentle squeeze. "Now, more than ever, I'm thankful we're together for the holidays."

She'd always been close to her parents and two older brothers and their families, all of them living either in or near small-town Strawberry Pond in the Granite State's White Mountains. However, her dad's hip-replacement surgery a month earlier had made them an even tighter unit. Alongside her day job as the town's librarian, Alana had worked extra hours at her family's orchard, market garden and Christmas-tree farm so her dad wouldn't have to worry about the business when recovering. While every time of year was busy, the holiday season upped the pressure even more but Alana wouldn't have had it any other way.

It was a joy, Alana reminded herself yet again. Or it was supposed to be. She wanted to make people happy with Christmas trees and tasty, homegrown food. And Hansen Family Farms had a legacy stretching back three generations, with the fourth one waiting in the wings. While she didn't have a husband or children of her own, something she'd never envisaged back in high school when she'd had her head full of dreams of happily ever after, she was lucky to have the family she did.

Unlike some of her library patrons, she didn't have to be alone on Thanksgiving, Christmas or any other holiday. Still, for an instant, the pumpkin centerpiece blurred, and her heart gave a dull thud as she thought of her empty house in town. A house where she'd once hoped to host her own seasonal celebrations.

No, she mustn't let herself think about what might have been. Those wandering thoughts were only because her two closest friends had married within the space of less than twelve months. Since Alana had been a bridesmaid at both weddings, she'd gotten caught up in the idea of love and romance. She was happy as she was and that was the end of it. Now that her dad was doing so much better, she'd resolved to make this holiday season the best ever, a true hometown family celebration.

"Happy Turkey Day, Auntie Lana." A pair of arms came around Alana's waist to give her a hug.

"Where did you spring from, sweetheart?" Alana hugged her youngest niece, five-year-old Isla, back.

"Daddy said we should stay in the kitchen to surprise you and Gigi but I couldn't wait." Isla giggled. "It sure smells good in here." She sniffed the air and smacked her lips.

"That's because Gigi and me have been cooking and baking up a storm." Instead of the more traditional "Grandma," Alana's mom was "Gigi" to her grandchildren. It had a trendy, cool feeling that suited what, even in her mid-sixties, Alana considered to be her mom's perennial boho vibe.

"We sure have, honey." Her mom hugged Isla in turn. "Oh, there's the front doorbell. Alana, dear, could you go and see who it is? I told your dad I'd be right back up to help him down the stairs. He shouldn't manage that narrow turn on his own yet." Her mom peered out the window. "And there's the rest of the bunch pulling into the lane, five cars…no, six."

"Of course, Mom." As Alana spoke and headed for the door, more noise erupted from the kitchen, Lucky, her parents' golden retriever, barked, and Isla, still hanging on to Alana's arm, chattered about turkey, pumpkin pie and green-bean casserole.

Like every year, they'd have a houseful for Thanksgiving. In addition to their immediate family, her mom's brothers and their broods came from Conway, and her dad's sisters and all the cousins joined them from here in town. It was fun, though, and because everyone pitched in, Alana didn't mind the work. As her mom always said, the more the merrier.

"Did you make pecan pie, too? Auntie Lana?" Isla tugged on her arm.

"It wouldn't be Thanksgiving without it, would it?" Alana yanked on the front door. Not used as often as the one at the back, it tended to stick. "Hang on, Isla. Give me a minute. No, Lucky." She tried to shoo away the rambunctious dog. "Yes?" Finally getting the door open, she blinked in the sudden bright light. "Hey, Ted." The temporary farm manager they'd hired while her dad was out of commission stood on the doorstep. "Mom didn't tell you she left the food we made for you and your crew in the barn kitchen?"

"No," Ted Desmarais, a silver-haired man in his fifties, said. He was from Maine, and although he'd lived in town for a few years, Ted was still considered a newcomer. He shook his head. "Unless I missed a message, which is entirely possible."

"Don't worry about it. With those deliveries coming in late, it's not surprising. Mom may have forgotten, too. Anyway, now you're here, you can take a few extra pies with you. There's plenty." She leaned against the doorframe. "We sure appreciate you guys working today to be ready for tomorrow and didn't want you to miss having a Thanksgiving meal." She glanced beyond Ted to his truck parked by the nearest harvested field and to the other vehicles in the lane around which various other members of her family now congregated. "If you brought help, you can take that big chainsaw of Dad's you mentioned needing and save another trip."

"Sure thing. Got plenty of room in the truck bed." Ted shaded his eyes against the sun and glanced behind him. "Cal? Can you give me a hand here?"

The truck door opened and a tall figure slid out.

Cal. It couldn't be. It wasn't an uncommon name, but also not one heard every day, either. Alana stilled as Lucky, Isla, the other Thanksgiving guests, fields and distant mountains seemed to fade out and disappear as the man from the truck moved toward her as if in slow motion. That gait was familiar. The face shape, too, even though he was older. "Cal?" Her voice came out in a harsh croak.

"Yeah. New guy I hired, temporary for the season like you and your folks asked me to. Ex-military. Quiet but even though it's only his first day, already seems like he'll be a real hard worker." Ted nodded and smiled. "Hey, Cal. Come on over here and meet Alana. You two will likely be working a lot of shifts together, although technically, being the daughter of the farm's owners, I guess she'll be your boss." He chuckled and bent to pat Lucky.

Cal. It couldn't be, but it was, and now, he

was standing right in front of Alana beside Ted. Staring at his feet rather than her, like he used to whenever he felt awkward or embarrassed. Wearing work boots with steel toes. Still size ten and a half? Blue jeans with frayed hems and a white T-shirt beneath a blue-and-white checked work shirt peeping out from under a brown barn coat.

Alana's gaze traveled upward. Strong jaw, dark hair cropped too short but longer in the back. A military cut growing out? Deep-set gray eyes and a generous mouth that had once kissed hers.

"Cal. Cal Paquette." She made herself say his name, keeping her voice cool without even a hint of a tremble. "Long time, no see. Welcome back to Strawberry Pond."

"Yeah. Alana. Hey."

His voice was deeper now, more manly, and when Cal finally lifted his head and their eyes met, his gaze quickly skittered away again, back to his boots.

"Wait? You two already know each other?" Ted rubbed his gray-stubbled chin.

"From high school, so way back. Years ago." Alana held the doorframe in a death grip, and as reality returned, she was aware, as if in another dimension, that Isla was staring at her, wide-eyed. "Right. I'll show you where the hands left the chainsaw. It's over by the chicken coop. Isla, honey, can you go ask Gigi to pack up a few more pies for Mr. Desmarais?"

The child nodded and dashed away, taking the dog with her.

"Sounds good." Ted clapped his hands. "Wow, it's sure a small world, isn't it?"

Too small or maybe not big enough. In the blink of an eye, less time than it would've taken her to cut into one of the golden pumpkin pies cooling on the kitchen counter, Alana's plan to have "the best holiday season ever" had turned into what might become her worst nightmare.

ALANA HANSEN. AS TED and Alana walked toward the chicken coop in the Hansen family's farmyard, Cal following several steps behind, he kept darting furtive glances at her. She was still petite, "five foot nothing but sweetness," like he'd once teased, and no bigger than she'd been in high school. However, her sandy hair was now more brown than blond. It also barely grazed her ears instead of trailing down her back in thick waves.

Although coming back here, he'd expected to bump into her—Strawberry Pond was a small town—he'd never expected her family ran the Christmas-tree farm he'd be spending the next five weeks working at.

Even as Ted had driven the pickup truck up the bumpy lane, the penny hadn't fully dropped. Back when he knew Alana, the Hansens had been big into the orchard and market-farm business. They hadn't had anything to do with the local Christmas-tree-farm operation. Sure, he'd been to this farm many times, but when Ted said he had to stop by here to pick up a few things, Cal still hadn't put all the pieces together.

And now, he had. From the looks of things, Alana was as cool as that proverbial cucumber and he was a mess. Sure, he'd mumbled something in greeting when Ted had been about to introduce them, and then he'd closed his mouth fast, afraid something would spill out he'd regret. Including a promise—and a secret—he was honor-bound to keep.

What was it his second, but last, foster mom used to say? "Let sleeping dogs lie." That was it. All he wanted was to do his job, take some time to figure out his next steps and then he'd be gone again. Navy life was behind him and, although it might sound corny, new horizons beckoned.

"So what brings you back to Strawberry Pond, Cal?" Alana spoke to him over her shoulder as they walked across the tidy farmyard.

"The holiday season." When they reached the chicken coop, painted blue rather than the yellow he remembered, he saw a small tractor and attached trailer holding a chainsaw parked behind it.

He couldn't tell her that in a lot of ways, he was right back to where he'd started fifteen years ago. No longer a teenager but still determined to make something of his life. Back then, it was so he could be worthy of *her. Alana.* The girl he'd once thought hung the moon and shone brighter than an entire sky full of stars. One of the most popular girls in school and she'd chosen him. All along he'd thought it was too good to be true and, in the end, he'd been proven right.

"You remember my foster mom, Mrs. Barrett?"

"Sure, I do." When Alana bent toward the chainsaw, her cheeks pinkened.

That pink was the same color as New Hampshire wild roses in June. Not that Cal had a favorite flower, but if he did, it'd be that soft, subtle pink, almost but not quite a blush. "Well, you likely heard her husband passed a few months ago. Since both her sons are serving in the military and can't get leave to come home for the holidays, she was going to be on her own. Like I was. We've always kept in touch so when she invited me to come and stay, I couldn't rightly say no."

It wasn't as if he'd considered contacting his younger brother, Jesse, and suggesting they spend the holidays together. Despite Jesse only being in Boston, less than a day's drive away, he might as well have been halfway around the world. While they weren't exactly estranged, they also weren't part of each other's lives. It was just how things were. Lots of siblings weren't close, and Cal was happy on his own. Besides, Jesse had his own life with a wife and baby son. He didn't need Cal interfering. He'd said as much, hadn't he? So Cal had taken his brother at his word and backed away. And now, while he might be close geographically, his links with Jesse were tenuous. Rooted in the past, not the present or future.

"Mrs. Barrett must be so happy to have you join her." Alana's voice sounded as if it came from inside a freezer. "I still see her from time to time when she comes into the library. I'm the town librarian."

Cal nodded, not surprised about that, at least. Alana had always liked to read and she was smart. He used to joke, asking what a smart girl like her was doing with a guy like him, but she'd always laughed and said he was smart, too. Life smart as well as being able to fix pretty much anything mechanical. "Good for you. What about your folks and the rest of the family?"

"They're fine." She raised her head from the

trailer hitch. "My brothers are both married and have kids of their own."

"Say, Alana, do you have any tie-downs we can use?" From the other side of the tractor, Ted, who'd been studying the chainsaw, spoke up. "The ones you've got here are fine for this trailer, but I'd like something sturdier for the back of the truck."

"Sure. They're in the shed." She inclined her head to a small, gray-shingled lean-to that used to hold a lawn tractor in summer and a snowblower in the winter. "I'll—"

"No, no. It won't take me but a minute." Ted's jovial face creased into what, despite less than a day's acquaintance, Cal already guessed was an almost perpetual smile. "I expect you two kids have lots to catch up on. Even today, some of my best friends go back to high school. Those teenage memories are irreplaceable."

They were but not in the way Ted likely meant. Cal stuck his hands in the pockets of the barn coat that the staff at the Christmas-tree farm, half a mile up the road, wore as part of their work uniform. "So you're not married then?" He'd assumed she would be. A woman as pretty and popular as Alana wouldn't be single. He could almost picture her kids. A boy and a girl, like they'd wanted whenever the two of them had talked about their future together. There was a sour taste in his mouth, and he dug the toe of his boot into a half-frozen rut.

"No—no husband or children." Alana paused. Her light brown eyes were hard, not soft and gentle like he remembered.

"Look, I didn't know your folks owned the tree farm, okay? If I had, I wouldn't have applied for a job here. I saw the ad online, and when Ted interviewed me, virtually, he never mentioned your family." And then Cal had not yet had a chance to talk about it with his foster mom ahead of time. "You and me working together might be awkward, but we're adults, right? Water under the bridge."

"Awkward?" Alana's voice had a bitter ring, like a wrong note in an otherwise harmonious piece of music. "That's an understatement. However, to be fair, my family only bought the local Christmas-tree business six years ago when the previous owners retired. You couldn't have known. Not unless you'd asked around."

Which Cal guessed he'd have had to be here to do. All that time, traveling the country and then the world with the military, he'd kept Strawberry Pond firmly in his rearview mirror. It was his past. Except for annual Christmas and birthday cards to Mrs. Barrett and the occasional phone call or email, he'd kept the past and present, the kid he used to be and the man he was now, separate. He'd also made sure to never ask Mrs. Barrett about Alana.

While he hoped Alana was happy, he didn't want to hear about that happiness. It was the only way he could cope. But now, he was back, if not to stay, for the next five weeks.

And while it was true he couldn't say no to Mrs. Barrett, a woman who was like a mom to him, he'd still thought he could compartmentalize his life the way he'd done with Jesse. Which, in Alana's case, had been a mistake, because as soon as he'd driven up that lane with Ted, all the feelings he'd thought he'd buried deep had rushed back again.

Alana Hansen. First love but not forever love. Not then and not now.

"Okay, water under the bridge." Alana's voice drew Cal out of his reverie. "You're right, we're both adults and it was a long time ago. Here comes Ted back with those tie-down straps."

"Yeah, sure." What felt like an actual chainsaw was tearing up Cal's insides, leaving him open, vulnerable and raw.

"I should get back to my family." She gestured at the house, where the crowd had disappeared from the lane, presumably inside where they'd gather around a table to laugh, eat and give thanks. "I'll send someone out with those pies. Happy Thanksgiving. Enjoy the meal and thanks again for working today." Her voice was neutral, casual even. Like there had never been anything between them, let alone something so important Cal still wasn't truly over it and maybe never would be.

But like he'd done for the past fifteen years, and holiday season or not, he'd live with the regrets. It was for the best, and if he said it often enough, he'd make himself believe it.

CHAPTER TWO

AT EIGHT THE next morning, Alana parked her compact car in the still empty lot behind the store and office at Rustic Hearts Christmas Tree Farm. Surrounded by snow-dusted mountains with Christmas trees growing along their lower slopes, the white-frame clapboard, with its glossy black shutters and red-painted doors, could have featured on a holiday greeting card.

Usually Alana loved working here but not today. Not having to face Cal working here, too.

As she got out of the car and locked it, her stomach lurched. Yesterday, in front of Cal and her family, she'd put on a brave face and brushed off his sudden reappearance as if it meant nothing. But as soon as she'd returned to her quiet home—after enduring rather than enjoying what should have been a wonderful Thanksgiving celebration—she'd retreated to her bed and cried. She'd convinced herself and everyone else that she was over Cal but maybe she wasn't.

She certainly wasn't over how angry she'd

been when he'd all of a sudden told her he was leaving town and they'd broken up. As soon as he'd asked if she was married, that anger had spurted up again and burned white-hot. She'd expected to marry *him*. Expected they'd have children and grow old together like her parents and grandparents.

Alana had dated over the years, but honestly, she'd never given her whole heart to any other man. She'd wanted to but something had always held her back. More fool her. If she'd settled down and made a family with someone else, seeing Cal again wouldn't have gotten her so churned up. She'd simply have greeted him like an old high-school boyfriend and gone on with her life.

Instead, it had taken every ounce of inner strength to keep her feelings hidden for the brief time Cal had been at Hansen Farms. How was she going to work with him for the hours, days and weeks between now and Christmas? She'd checked Ted's online staffing schedule, hoping he'd been wrong when he'd said she'd be working a lot of shifts with Cal, but there was no mistake. Except for today, they were often the only two on duty.

Gripping the handle of her tote bag tight, she took a deep breath of the crisp, cold air. Although barely a half mile down the road from her family's farm, Rustic Hearts was a separate part of the Hansens' business and only open from Thanksgiving to Christmas Eve, and occasionally for other holidays throughout the year. As well as the Christmas trees that the previous owners had grown since the 1950s, they also sold fresh garlands, decorated wreaths, tree stands, holiday ornaments and other items, like locally made honey, jam and artisan wood products.

She unlocked the back door, took off her coat and hung it on a hook, then flicked on lights as she went through the office, staff kitchen and small workshop area into the store itself. She'd brew herself a mug of her favorite peppermint tea while getting ready for what was bound to be a busy day. From making wreaths to putting out flyers with tree prices and filling a green glass bowl next to the cash with candy canes, she had plenty to keep herself busy. In fact, now she was actually here and thinking more sensibly, she could plan her day so she'd hardly have to see Cal.

She stopped, rooted to the spot beside a life-size inflatable smiling Santa Claus that marked the side door leading to the tree farm itself. Was that a crunch of footsteps on the gravel path outside? "Hello?" Her voice reverberated in the quiet store, and she held her tote in front of her like a shield.

"Alana." The door opened and Cal came through it. "Sorry if I startled you. I was outside checking the tree lot like Ted asked me to."

"But I didn't see a car. I came in through the rear staff entrance. That door was locked." Beneath her white-and-red, reindeer-patterned sweater, Alana's heart pounded as if it was about to come clear out of her chest.

"My truck is in for a service so Ted dropped me off about twenty minutes ago." Cal held up a set of keys. "I came in the front way and he said I should… Hey, you're shaking. I guess I really scared you. Here. Take a seat." He pulled out one of the chairs by the door, where customers could wait and warm up while their tree was being bagged.

"I'm fine." She waved him and the chair away and backed toward the cash counter.

"No, you're not." Cal's familiar gray eyes studied her. "I know you, remember?"

"You don't know me—not anymore." The edge of the counter bumped against Alana's lower back, steadying her. "It's been fifteen years. We're both different people now."

Cal let out a long breath. "We are, but you always liked to be early for things. School, work, parties. Gives you time to settle. You also don't like being taken by surprise."

"Don't try to analyze me." He was right on both counts, but Alana didn't want to admit it.

Maybe that's why their breakup had hit her so hard. She hadn't seen it coming. One day everything between them had been like it always was, and the next, their relationship was over. In the midst of her heartbreak, she hadn't had any kind of closure so the pain and devastation had lingered for years.

"I'm not analyzing you. If anything, I could be talking about myself. That's why I got here before I expected anyone else to show up." His crooked smile tugged at her heart, as it once had. "Ted said you'll likely have folks lined up outside a good twenty minutes before you open. Even if he hadn't asked me to make sure everything was shipshape out there in the lot, I'd have wanted to, anyway."

Because like her, Cal paid attention to details. "Shipshape?"

Cal's smile broadened. "I left the navy but maybe the navy hasn't entirely left me. One of the older petty officers used to talk about making things shipshape. I guess I picked the expression up from him. He was a good man who kind of took me under his wing and mentored me when I was still a wet-behind-the-ears new recruit."

"How was it? The navy, I mean?" Alana

wouldn't let herself react to that heart-melting smile, let alone return it, but she'd sometimes wondered about Cal's life in the military. Had it given him what he'd wanted? All of a sudden, he hadn't wanted her. Or had Cal even known what he wanted? Before that terrible day, he'd never mentioned joining the navy or any other branch of the military.

Going around the counter, Alana tucked her tote in a cupboard and pulled out the bag of candy canes from where she'd left it earlier in the week. *Get a grip.* She could have a casual conversation with the man without letting herself be drawn back into the past.

"I liked navy life." Without her asking him to, Cal held out the green bowl for her to pour the red-and-green-striped candy into. "Although I didn't realize it at the time, serving in the military was what I needed. It gave me structure and discipline. I learned how to take responsibility. I also felt like I truly belonged somewhere."

Hadn't he belonged with her? Alana pressed her lips together so she wouldn't say something she'd regret.

Cal nodded as if warming to his theme. "Being a foster kid, it's hard to put down roots, but in the navy I made friends who became like family. I also felt I was making a difference. Along with the adventure of travel, of course."

"Of course." Alana emptied the bag of candy canes, and Cal set the bowl back on the counter. She'd never thought much about Cal being a foster kid. Mrs. Barrett, his foster mom, had treated him like one of her family. He'd mentioned his mom had died and his dad had been killed in an accident when Cal was hardly old enough to remember him, yet he'd never said much else about being in foster care. Or about any other family, either. Sensing he hadn't wanted to talk about it, Alana had never asked. However, back then she'd been a typical self-absorbed teen. She'd never really thought about "belonging somewhere" in the way Cal must have because Strawberry Pond had always been her home.

"I guess you've traveled the world?" Except for visiting family in Boston and Chicago, a few trips to Canada and a winter vacation in Mexico, Alana's only travel farther afield had been in the pages of books.

"Pretty much." Cal took a broom propped against the wall near the counter and began sweeping the pine needles he'd tracked inside. "Over the years, I was stationed at bases on both US coasts, and I also visited a lot of countries in Europe and Asia. Even made it to Australia. Took part in a joint exercise with their navy."

"That must've been amazing." While at first she'd asked him about his time in the navy more out of politeness, despite herself, Alana was interested. All the places he'd seen, the people he'd met and the work he'd done were so different to her life in Strawberry Pond. She'd never wanted to live anywhere else, but maybe she should think about traveling more. Except, whom would she go with? All her friends were married and most of them had kids, and her folks couldn't leave the farm for longer than a few days. Did she have to go with someone, maybe—

"In some ways it was great but in others not so much. Dustpan?"

Alana handed the dustpan to him from where they kept it behind the counter. "What do you mean?" This more introspective side of Cal was new and it intrigued her.

"That structure I mentioned? Well, the other side of it is unpredictability." He swept the pine needles into the pan. "In the job I did, you rarely had much notice of where and when you were going to be deployed. I left the service for more autonomy and to find a better work-life balance, but now, I have to figure out what to do next. It's a strange feeling, if I'm being honest. The folks in Human Resources call it 'transferable skills,' but moving from military to civilian life can be a big change, especially if, like me, you don't have a spouse or kids. And I—"

"Hey, Alana." One of the high-school students

who worked holidays and occasional weekends came into the store via the back way Alana had also taken. "You must be the new guy Ted mentioned. Cal? I'm Maddie."

"Yeah, I am." He introduced himself and returned Maddie's friendly greeting. "All set?" Cal glanced at Alana as Maddie scrolled to one of their seasonal playlists and a jazz version of "Jingle Bells" filled the store. "While we were talking, time got away from me. Lots of people coming in." He gestured toward the front window, where a line of customers stretched halfway to the main parking lot and more cars were pulling in.

"Ten minutes until opening." Time had gotten away from Alana, too, almost like it used to when she was with Cal. She hadn't even made her peppermint tea or got the cash float from the safe.

"I'll head out to the tree lot. Call me if you need anything," he said. "My cell number's on the staff list. The other guys should be out there by now as well. Ted said the whole crew would be here today." He stepped away from the counter.

Alana had already noted Cal's number on that list. Not because she'd been looking for it, but she'd needed to double-check that every staff member working today was contactable.

"Choosing a holiday tree the day after Thanksgiving is still a tradition in Strawberry Pond."

The small town was all about tradition, and when Hansen Farms had bought Rustic Hearts, her folks hadn't considered changing its name. Everyone knew the Christmas-tree farm as Rustic Hearts so there was no reason to alter it.

"Those traditions are nice." For a moment, Cal's gaze caught Alana's and held. "Gives a person a sense of permanence."

Was that what Cal had been about to say when Maddie interrupted them, and he'd been talking about the transition between military and civilian life? Just after he'd told her he didn't have a wife and kids. She'd suspected as much yesterday when he'd said he'd be alone for the holidays, but had he confirmed his single status for a reason?

No, she wouldn't let herself go there. All that mattered was despite everything between them, she and Cal had been civil to each other. Alana's expectations were still low, but if they could keep up that fragile truce, maybe having to work with him for several weeks wouldn't be as bad as she'd first thought.

"WE'LL GET THAT tree bagged up for you right away." Cal smiled at the blond woman and her husband, who'd chosen a tall balsam fir and waved to one of the other crew members to come give him a hand. "Happy holidays."

"You look kind of familiar." As her husband went into the store to pay for the tree, the woman studied him. It was the end of the day—dusk, and almost dark—but the farm had lights on either side of the paths, as well as red, green and clear white holiday lights strung at the entrance and around trees that weren't for sale. "Did you go to high school in Strawberry Pond? Played football, maybe? Even after I graduated, I still went to most of the games."

"I did." Cal handed the tree over to the guy who'd bag it and, if needed, carry it to the purchaser's vehicle. He'd lost count of how many trees he'd sold today, but it had been a lot. Like this woman, other people had also recognized Cal. "But my high-school days were more than fifteen years ago." Those years had gone by in what felt like a flash and now, Cal was back here again, older and hopefully wiser, but also in some ways just like where he'd started from. Still trying to figure out what to do with the rest of his life. "I'm Cal Paquette."

The woman smiled. "I don't recognize your name, but I'm Laura Sullivan-Kaminski. I'd have been six or so years ahead of you in school, so our paths wouldn't have crossed there. It must be from football games or seeing you around town.

I have a good memory for faces. Here." She took a business card from her purse and held it out. "I'm a real-estate agent so if you're ever looking for a property, give me a call."

"Thanks." Cal took the card and tucked it in his coat pocket. He'd always rented, and if he was ever going to buy a place it wouldn't be in Strawberry Pond. However, like the rest of the people he'd met today, Laura had an easy friendliness that was refreshing. "My foster mom, Mrs. Barrett, used to mention the Sullivan family."

"That'd be us." Laura's laugh mixed humor with resignation. "There's a lot of Sullivans here in Strawberry Pond. Anyway, welcome home. It's good to have you back."

"It's good to be back." Cal said it by reflex to be polite, but there was a part of him that meant it. *Home*. For those high-school years with the Barrett family, Strawberry Pond had been home, the only one he'd ever truly known.

The holiday music Cal had become almost oblivious to stopped, and Alana's voice came over the farm's public-address system, as it had several times throughout the day. "Rustic Hearts Christmas Tree Farm is closing in fifteen minutes. Thanks for shopping with us. Please make your way to the store to pay for your purchases."

Cal stilled as he'd done each time he'd heard her speak. He'd promised himself he'd focus on the present, not the past, but how could he when Alana sounded exactly the same?

"That's one of my friends, Alana Hansen. Her folks own this place." Across from him, Laura gestured toward the overhead speaker. "Hey, you must have been in school with Alana. I hadn't made the connection before. Alana's great, isn't she?"

"Yeah, she is." She always had been, and although Cal hadn't fully appreciated it at the time, breaking up with Alana had been the biggest mistake of his life. He'd done what he'd had to, though, and kept his promise to his mom to look out for Jesse. His real mom, a woman he'd only had for his first ten years but whom he'd never forget. "I need to help with closing up and—"

"No need to say anything more." Laura waved away Cal's explanation. "I can be too chatty. Anyway, there's my husband, Trevor, waving at me from the parking lot. Say, since you already know Alana, the four of us should go out for a meal. A welcome-back-to-town holiday gathering. If you want, I could invite a few others. It'd be like a mini high-school reunion. Most of us still live either in or near Strawberry Pond."

"Cal?" Alana stuck her head, now topped with a sparkly reindeer-antler headband, out the side door of the store. "How many customers are still… Oh, Laura. I didn't see you there." Alana's gaze darted from Cal to her friend.

Cal's face warmed. "Sorry."

"Don't apologize. It's my fault. I kept Cal talking. You know me." Laura looked from Cal to Alana, and then her eyes narrowed as if she was all of a sudden sensing there was more between Cal and Alana than simply being old high-school acquaintances.

"I *do* know you." Beneath the light that hung over the store's door, Alana's face looked pinker than usual.

"I'll go check the lot. Round up any last customers." Cal ducked his head to avoid looking at either woman. He and Alana had history. So did lots of people, especially in small towns. It wasn't a big deal. At least, that's what he'd tried to convince himself while spending half the previous night tossing and turning on Mrs. Barrett's guest bed.

It was a new bed, queen-size rather than Cal's narrow single one, and the room had been redecorated since he'd lived there. Instead of their previous bright blue, the walls had been repainted in what he guessed was meant to be a calming neutral off-white. And those walls held a few framed watercolors of flowers rather than Cal's football, hockey and band posters. It was a comfortable room and welcoming with its crisp linens and soft lighting, and a vintage rocking chair and blanket chest where the battered student desk and chair had once been.

Yet, despite not holding any trace of the boy who'd once lived there, that younger Cal still seemed everywhere—and impossible for him to escape.

"Let me know about getting together," Laura said. "My number's on that card."

"Sure." With a vague hand gesture that could have meant yes, no or maybe, Carl turned away.

He wouldn't call. He couldn't. Laura was Alana's friend. Even if Laura didn't know what was between him and Alana, she soon would. While it was mostly harmless, folks in Strawberry Pond had an appetite for gossip.

Cal had been foolish to come back here. If it hadn't been for Mrs. Barrett, a woman who'd given him everything, needing him, he'd walk out on this job tomorrow. Yes, it was only temporary, however, he stuck to his commitments and wouldn't let down Ted, or Alana and her family. Especially not with Mr. Hansen still recovering from what Ted had said was fairly major surgery.

No, he had to stick things out. He'd already let Alana down once. The one commitment he'd broken and could never make right.

CHAPTER THREE

SHOULD SHE TAKE the library's Thanksgiving decorations down today or wait until Monday? On Saturday morning behind the circulation desk, Alana considered the paper turkey at her side, and the pumpkins, fall leaves and other seasonal trimmings festooned from the ceiling and displayed on shelves. Since it was still Thanksgiving weekend, she'd leave them for today but refresh the book display. Many of their patrons enjoyed Christmas stories all year round. In the past week alone, she'd been asked about several recently published titles that she still needed to process.

Strawberry Pond's library, an imposing, two-story Victorian stone building complete with gargoyles, had only opened half an hour before. However, it was already busy with the usual mix of older people, teens and families with children. Some were looking to borrow books, while others were here for a kids' story and craft session.

"Can I help you find anything, Mrs. Ryan?"

she greeted the woman who approached the desk. Martha Ryan was her friend Josie's grandmother and a regular library visitor.

"Not in the library, no. I just want to check these out." She returned Alana's smile and set the stack of books in her arms on the desk. "However, since I'm here, I wondered if you could set aside a Christmas wreath for me? One of those heart-shaped ones with pinecones and red gingham ribbon? I saw them on your website, but I couldn't get out to the tree farm yesterday." She leaned closer and lowered her voice. "I want to give a wreath to Josie and Heath as a surprise."

"Absolutely, Mrs. Ryan. I'd be happy to hold one for you." Alana took each book in turn, a mix of cozy mysteries and Christmas cookie recipes, and scanned them. "I could even deliver the wreath to you later. I'm putting in a few hours at Rustic Hearts after I leave here so your place isn't far out of my way." When Josie and Heath had gotten married almost a year ago, Josie's grandparents had moved to a small property adjacent to their family farm, leaving Josie, Heath and Josie's two daughters to live in the farmhouse. Like Alana, agriculture was Josie's heritage, although unlike her friend, Alana also had a full-time off-farm job here in the library.

"That's so kind of you, dear." Mrs. Ryan

beamed at Alana, her face framed by soft white hair. Her eyes, the same blue as Josie's, twinkled.

"It's not a problem. We're keeping the Christmas-tree farm open two hours later most Saturdays. Last year, my folks found people liked to drop in either before or after having a meal in town. Kind of a date night, and it also helps the town get in the holiday spirit."

When her mom had told her about the planned "late-night opening," Alana had been all for it. It would help her savor the Christmas spirit, too, but despite her optimism of yesterday, today she'd be on her own with Cal. It wouldn't be so easy to avoid him with only the two of them working there.

"Tom and I'll have to come by soon. We still love our date nights, even though they're more often lunches these days." Mrs. Ryan chuckled. "I'll also pick up a Christmas ornament. Something special for Josie and Heath's first anniversary."

"That's a lovely idea." Alana's breath hitched. She'd collected holiday ornaments from childhood, always imagining she'd have a family to share them with and tell the story of each one. Instead, those stories, from Santa on a bike to mark when she'd learned to ride a two-wheeler, to a jolly elf in a car, the year she'd passed her driving test, remained untold. "Here you go."

She forced a smile and helped Mrs. Ryan put her library books in a quilted tote patterned with pumpkins. "Happy reading."

Josie's grandma made those bags and had given Alana one for her last birthday. Since her birthday was in April, Alana's tote fabric featured daisies and she used it often. She was thirty-four, almost thirty-five, and the thought of that upcoming birthday reminded her that she was now the lone singleton among her group of high-school friends.

"Laura." As Mrs. Ryan bustled away, Alana waved at her friend, who'd come into the library with Trevor's teenage nephew, Danny. He was now Laura's nephew, too, since Laura and Trevor had gotten married in June. In reality, since Danny had lost both his parents, Laura was more like a mom to him while Trevor was his dad. "I wasn't expecting to see you today."

Laura joined Alana at the desk as Danny made a beeline for the reference section. "I didn't expect to be here, but Danny needed one of those old local-history books for a school project. That meant he also needed a ride into town since Trevor had already left for work." She gave Alana a crooked smile. "Between Danny's figure-skating lessons and all his after-school activities, a lot of the time I feel like a taxi service."

"But you wouldn't have it any other way."

After Trevor and Laura had returned from their honeymoon, he and Danny had moved into Laura's house on a horse farm several miles outside Strawberry Pond.

Alana took one of the new books, a popular contemporary romance, and a plastic cover from under the counter and began preparing it for shelving. Unlike her, Laura had never wanted kids, but she'd sure become a great mom to Danny. And now, with Trevor, the three of them were a family.

"No, I wouldn't have it any other way than how it is." Laura's brown eyes were soft with love. "Whatever Danny needs, I'm there for him. He's only fourteen, but Trevor and I are already dreading him leaving for college." She chuckled. "But enough about me. What's with you and Cal Paquette? At the tree lot yesterday, I thought I sensed some…vibes." Laura raised her eyebrows and waggled her fingers.

"We went to high school together. And we… dated for a while." Alana smoothed the plastic cover into place over the book where a silhouette of a couple holding hands seemed to taunt her. "But Cal left town years ago so that was that. It's not important."

"Really?" Laura glanced around and lowered her voice. "As a real-estate agent, I've developed a good sense about people. You're also my friend. There was sure something going on between you and Cal. Why didn't you ever tell me and Josie about him?"

"There wasn't anything *to* tell." Only a heartbreak Alana didn't want to revisit. She found a "new" sticker from a roll and put it on the front of the book with more force than necessary.

"If you say so, but with Cal back in town, local gossip is that since the two of you are both single you might—"

"No." Alana's voice was sharper than she'd intended. It was natural people would talk. Cal had been well-liked here, and along with playing football for the high-school team, he'd worked at the garage, where pretty much everyone took their vehicles. "I thought you didn't pay attention to local gossip?"

"I don't, not unless it's about somebody maybe wanting to buy or sell a house but—"

"Leave it, okay?" Alana gripped the book, turning it face down so she wouldn't have to see the cover with its happy couple. "Cal Paquette means nothing to me."

"Okay, but he's just come into the library with Mrs. Barrett and is looking this way."

"What? Where?" Alana glanced around, and as if by instinct her gaze landed on Cal, who stood near the door by the cart that held used books for sale. A small smile tugged at the corners of his mouth as he spoke to Mrs. Barrett.

He hadn't heard what she said, had he? No, he couldn't have. He was too far away, and children and adults heading to the stairs leading to the story-and-craft session were between them, all talking at once. The story-and-craft session upstairs in the library's activity room, where Alana should also be. She fumbled for the picture book she'd chosen earlier.

"I have to go." She nodded to one of the teens who worked Saturday mornings to take over from her and came around the counter, keeping her head down.

"Sure. Enjoy the rest of the weekend." Laura took a step back. "Give me a call if you want to get together."

"Hey, Alana."

Cal's deep voice stopped her at the foot of the stairs. "Cal." She clutched the picture book tighter.

"Fancy meeting you here." His smile broadened.

That's what he used to say at school as a joke when they'd bump into each other, accidentally on purpose. Back when she'd been a silly, lovestruck teenager.

"I work here." She shrugged.

"Of course, you do." His voice cooled. "Mrs.

Barrett wanted to come to the library and then pick up a few groceries so I offered to drive and keep her company. It's hard for her with none of her own kids home on Thanksgiving weekend."

Cal had always been kind and thoughtful. Except when he wasn't.

"I'll see you later, I guess. At the tree farm." Now, his tone was formal, like an employee talking to his boss.

Alana nodded and, glad she'd worn her trusty book-themed sneakers, almost dashed up the wide, curving wood staircase.

Strawberry Pond was too small for her to avoid Cal. No matter how much she wanted to.

EARLY ON SATURDAY EVENING, Cal came in from the tree lot at Rustic Hearts. As he stamped his boots on the mat inside the door, he breathed in the lingering scent of pine needles mixed with the gingerbread candle burning in a tall glass holder by the cash register.

As much as he didn't intend to, his gaze drifted to Alana, who was currently showing a customer several different styles of tree toppers.

The overhead light shone on her hair, picking up blond glints in the brown. In faded jeans and a fluffy pink sweater patterned with Santas, she was cute and casual, an older version of the girl he'd loved in high school. Like when he'd spotted her this morning at the library, during his shift here he'd hardly been able to keep his eyes off her.

Alana had said she was a different person now, but some things hadn't changed. Her playful sense of humor for a start. Those purple sneakers she wore, printed with books and flowers, almost made him laugh out loud. He'd also watched how she treated library patrons and customers at Rustic Hearts, and saw how good she still was with people of all ages. Patient, kind and helpful but never a pushover.

"I can hold one of the tree toppers for you until tomorrow afternoon but not all five of them. We have limited stock, you understand." Her voice was polite but firm.

"I suppose the mirrored star looks best." The customer, who had curly brown hair, glasses and looked to be in her mid-forties, gave Alana an apologetic smile. "I want the first Christmas in our new home to be perfect."

"If you go for the mirrored star, we also have lights to mix and match," Alana said. "You could add them to the tree or wind them around a stair rail. There're lots of possibilities." Alana took another box from the shelf.

There was no such thing as a "perfect" Christmas. Like there wasn't a perfect life. Cal had learned those lessons as a kid. If he let himself imagine perfection at Christmas or any other time, he'd be setting himself up for disappointment. While he wasn't a Scrooge, he was a realist. Like Thanksgiving, Christmas was a holiday he tried to get through as best he could.

"What a good idea. I'll take the lights as well." The customer gave a soft laugh as she followed Alana to the cash. "And four of those snowflake pillows." She pointed to where they were piled on a rustic bench. "I love Christmas. This year, my entire family will be at our place for the holidays, all four generations of us."

"How wonderful." As she checked for the price on each item, Alana made small talk about people the two of them evidently both knew. "Cal?" Finally her gaze connected with his. "Would you please help Becca carry all these things out to her car? I can't leave the store, not with other customers here." She indicated a gray-haired couple whose tree he'd bagged and taken to their car earlier.

"Happy to." His face heated. He should have thought to offer to do that, but he'd gotten caught up in watching Alana. How she still talked with her hands, the gestures graceful and animated. The timbre of her voice, as sweet as Christmas candy canes. And how a stray piece of hair brushed the rosy curve of her left cheek. All the things he'd tried not to notice but couldn't help himself during the almost three hours they'd been working together. Earlier it had been so busy they hadn't exchanged more than a few words, but in this last half hour before Rustic Hearts closed, customer traffic had slowed. "Here, let me." He took the boxes with the tree topper and lights from Becca, leaving her with the two shopping bags with the pillows.

"My car's right outside the door." Becca indicated with her chin. "My husband's looking after our kids tonight so I'm trying to get some holiday shopping in. Say, aren't you the same Cal who was in Alana's year at school?"

"Yeah, I am." As they left the store, Cal answered the question he'd been asked too many times to count in the past few days. Ted, his boss, hadn't known who Cal was, but almost everyone else around here did. This morning in the grocery store with Mrs. Barrett, it had taken longer to get her shopping than he expected because of everyone stopping them to chat.

"So you're also the Cal who… Sorry, it's none of my business." Becca stopped as she unlocked the rear of her SUV and pointed to where she wanted her purchases stowed. "I'm a nurse. I remember you coming to the ER with football injuries. Alana drove you to the hospital a few times, that's all."

"That would've been me." Cal muttered something else noncommittal and then stepped away. People here either had long memories or believed nothing much exciting happened. Probably a bit of both, but there was also something nice about how folks cared and looked out for each other. In his years away, he'd forgotten what small-town life was like. Or maybe he'd made himself forget because the memories were too painful.

With Becca's cheery "Happy holidays" ringing in his ears, he returned to the store, brushing past the gray-haired couple. The man was now carrying one of the store's decorated evergreen wreaths.

"No, no." The man waved away Cal's offer to assist. "It's near closing. You'll be wanting to get home yourself."

Cal would be if not for returning to an empty house. Mrs. Barrett had gone out for supper and bowling with friends. Although she'd offered to stay home, Cal had insisted she go. He didn't currently have a social life, but that didn't mean she needed to sacrifice hers. Like he did most Saturday nights, he'd be fine getting takeout and watching a movie.

"Want me to turn the sign on the door to say we're shut?" Cal asked as he paused on the doorstep. It was fully dark, and the air was cold and crisp. Growing up in these mountains, he'd have said it felt like snow, but he'd been away too long to predict the weather or anything else.

"Alana? Closing time?" he asked again, raising his voice over Mariah Carey singing "All I Want for Christmas Is You."

It was only a song, and so what if this was the fifth or sixth time he'd heard it since starting work here. All Cal wanted for Christmas was to figure out his next chapter. Was that too much to ask?

"Yes, close up." Alana's voice was muffled.

"You okay?" He flipped over the sign, locked the door and then hustled back to the cash counter.

"Fine." Alana's head popped up from behind the counter, and she tugged at a heart-shaped evergreen wreath seemingly caught in her hair.

"Hang on." Cal went to her as she stood.

"No, it's okay, I can—"

Cal tried not to laugh. Between the wreath and her embarrassed expression, she looked both comical and adorable. "Stop and let me try." Leaning over the low counter, he gently loosened the strands of hair tangled in a large pine cone.

The silky tendrils slipped through his fingers, and he was so close that Alana's soft breath warmed his cheek. Mixed with the gingerbread scent of the candle, he could also smell something floral. Her shampoo, maybe?

"There you go." His breath stuttered, he took several steps back and then shoved his hands into his coat pockets.

"Thanks." She avoided his gaze. "You can get going. I have to deliver this wreath on my way home."

"I'll wait and walk you to your car. I don't want to leave you here on your own."

She nodded and began to wrap the wreath in cellophane, while Cal went to lock the door to the tree lot, sweep up and turn off the outside lights.

He didn't want to leave Alana anywhere, not just tonight in the store. He hadn't wanted to leave her the first time, either. But he couldn't tell her why he had, even if he wanted to. He'd made a promise and it wasn't his story to tell.

CHAPTER FOUR

ON SUNDAY AFTERNOON, Alana smiled at her mom, who sat across from her in a booth for two at the Strawberry Spot Diner. Between the after-church crowd, as well as visitors getting a bite to eat before heading home at the end of the Thanksgiving weekend, the popular eatery on Main Street was packed. Although Alana always enjoyed getting together with her mom and did so several times a month, today was different. Now, she worried that her mom would mention Cal. The one person and subject Alana didn't want to talk about.

"It's great Dad's doing so well." So far, Alana had kept the conversation about family, friends or the library. Last night, Cal untangling her hair from that wreath had felt almost intimate. And when he'd walked her to her car like a perfect gentleman, a hint of familiar attraction had vibrated between them. Had he felt it, too?

"Your dad's making wonderful progress, but he's still itching to hustle around like he used to. The doctor says he'll likely be able to return to work in mid-January, but he might be able to help out at the Christmas store earlier." Her mom shook her head at the server to decline a coffee refill. "If he makes it to the store—and that's a big *if*—he can only do light duties. Sitting behind the cash register when it's slow or pricing stock. Still, it would be a break from watching movies, reading and playing board games with me."

Like Alana, her dad was happiest when he was busy, so it must be hard for him to be stuck at home. Her parents were devoted to each other, but along with the worry, the change in routine must also be hard for her mom. The two of them had always been active, and her mom was as big a part of the market garden, orchard and Christmas-tree business as her dad and worked long hours in the greenhouses, barns and fields.

"Don't worry. I'll keep an eye on Dad and mention it to the rest of the staff."

"I know I can count on you, Alana." Her mom's dark brown eyes were loving. "Ted's a big help, but for your dad it's not the same as watching over the business himself." Her mom ate the last forkful of her piece of maple pumpkin pie, one of the diner's seasonal specialties. "Ted called me earlier. He said it's been a busy weekend at Rustic Hearts, and the store and tree lot are still steady today."

Alana nodded and focused on her apple crisp, comfort food in a bowl and made with apples from Hansen Farms, one of the diner's suppliers. Even though she didn't usually work at Rustic Hearts on Sunday, because of Cal the place still hadn't been far from her thoughts. "Late-night opening seems popular."

Her mom set aside her plate. "It does, but what about you, honey? Working with Cal? I was as surprised as anyone to see him again. If you want your dad or me to have a word with Ted about rearranging your work schedule, we'd be happy to do it."

Cal. He wasn't here in the diner with them, but in Alana's world he was nevertheless larger than life. "It's fine, Mom." She manufactured a casual, *doesn't-matter* kind of face. "We're co-workers. Like you said, Rustic Hearts is busy so we don't have a lot of time to chat." They still had time to look at each other, though. Stolen glances laden with meaning.

"Even so..." Her mom leaned closer. "I don't want you to be hurt again. When Cal up and left, you were heartbroken."

As if Alana needed the reminder. She swallowed a mouthful of apple crisp, and the oat topping stuck in her throat.

"Cal was almost part of our family, and I thought… We all did… And now, he's back in town, well, we're all on your side, sweetie." Her mom's tone was both caring and decisive. "Your dad was set to fire Cal, but I told him he couldn't. Not without cause, anyway. It'd only make more talk, and we do need the extra help."

"I know." Alana drank some water. Her mom didn't have to say she'd expected it was only a matter of time until Cal and Alana said "I do" at the church where several generations of the Hansen family had married. Alana and everyone else had expected the same thing. "Don't worry about me. You've got more than enough to deal with. Cal won't be in town long."

And when he left again, Alana's life would go back to the way it was before. She wouldn't have this perpetual uneasiness and sense of being on edge and off balance.

"I always worry about you—I'm your mother." Her mom reached for Alana's cold hands and clasped them in her warm ones. "As for any gossip, it'll soon die down. There's an initial flurry, that's all, but after a few days folks will turn to something else. None of the talk I've heard has been malicious. Folks are concerned for you because they care. How Cal left so sudden wasn't natural. Before that ruckus he was well-liked here."

Alana blinked back the burn of tears. It would be easier if Cal hadn't been so well thought of and such a good guy. "Even if you think you do, I guess you can never know someone, not really."

"Oh, sweetheart." Her mom squeezed Alana's hands tight. "You mustn't think such a thing. People are complex, true, and while your dad can still surprise me, we understand each other. I know he'd never let me down. Maybe if you tried talking to Cal—"

"No, it's too late." And Alana wouldn't open herself up to that kind of hurt again. "You and Dad are lucky." Her parents were teenage sweethearts whose love was strong and true, destined to last a lifetime.

"We *are* lucky, but like all couples we've had our rough patches and had to figure out how to work through them." Her mom studied Alana. "That's what marriage is about, but it's not too late. The right man's out there for you."

"Sure he is." Alana made herself sound more confident than she felt. "But at the moment, I'm not looking."

"That's often when love sneaks up and finds you." Her mom chuckled and with a final squeeze released Alana's hands. "However, it doesn't hurt to keep an open mind, and Christmas *is* the season of miracles."

"You've watched too many holiday movies." Alana rolled her eyes.

"Yes, and we've watched a lot of them together," her mom teased back. "There's a reason those movies are popular. They give people hope and are a comforting escape from the hard parts of real life."

But they weren't real life and never would be. Alana had accepted that fact long ago, so she could enjoy feel-good movies and romance books for the escape they were without expecting anything else. Unlike her mom, she wasn't a romantic. Not nowadays. Talking to Cal about anything but work or ordinary daily life would be pointless.

"WHAT ABOUT HERE? We should have a good view of the holiday tree lighting." On the first Tuesday evening of December, Cal let go of Mrs. Barrett's arm and gestured to a spot on the library side of Strawberry Pond's town green.

Warm yellow light spilled from the library's windows, and an inflatable Santa Claus, like the one at Rustic Hearts, sat outside its front entrance. Was Alana inside? Her shifts hadn't overlapped with Cal's on Sunday or Monday and he'd missed her. Which might make him a fool but he couldn't help how he felt.

"This spot's perfect." Mrs. Barrett beamed as

Cal unfolded the camping chair he'd brought for her to sit on and then, when she sat, arranged a blanket over her knees. "You're so kind, but I'm not elderly or infirm."

"No, but it's cold and with that light dusting of snow we got it's icy. I want to look out for you." Like Cal would've looked out for his own mom. She'd been gone for almost twenty-five years, but he still thought of her every day.

"You always were a good boy." As Mrs. Barrett nodded her head, the red pom-pom on her winter hat bounced up and down, the bells she'd attached to it making a cheery jingle. "And you've grown up to be a fine man who served his country with bravery and distinction. I'm as proud of you as if you were one of my own sons."

Cal ducked his head. He'd never accepted praise easily, and until he'd come to Strawberry Pond, as a foster kid with a brother who was often in trouble, he was more used to people thinking the worst of him than the best. Guilt by association because of what Jesse had gotten up to. Shame, too, which was why only Mr. and Mrs. Barrett knew about Cal's brother and he'd never mentioned Jesse to Alana or anyone else here. However, that was years ago, and it was time he accepted that against the odds he'd made something good out of his life. Something he could also be proud of.

"I mean it." Mrs. Barrett patted one of Cal's gloved hands. "I hope you believe it."

"Yes, ma'am." He grinned and adjusted his hat over his ears. Had the temperature dropped? "Do you want a hot chocolate?" He gestured to a table set up in front of the post office manned by elves in red-and-green pointy hats and green tunics over their parkas and leggings or dark jeans. The group dispensed drinks under a banner that read Happy Holidays from the Town of Strawberry Pond.

"I'll never say no to anything chocolate." Mrs. Barrett smiled back. "Those elves are members of the town council." She chuckled. "As you may remember, we go all out for the festive season here."

Cal did remember, and warmth curled around his heart. Usually, he worked over the holidays so service members with families could have the time off, but this year would be different. Mrs. Barrett had taken it for granted he'd want to come with her to tonight's official light-up ceremony, and maybe it'd be fun to embrace the joy of the holiday season.

"I'll be right back." He made his way to the hot-chocolate stand, greeting a few people he recognized as having bought trees at Rustic Hearts over the past few days.

Seasonal music spilled out from overhead speakers and Cal swayed in time to "Jingle Bell Rock" as he joined the short line behind a woman with two young girls. All three of them wore headbands with multicolored flashing Christmas lights atop winter hats.

"Alana will be here soon, Lottie." The woman gave the younger girl a one-armed embrace. "She just texted me she's leaving the library."

Cal's heartbeat sped up. There could only be one Alana who worked at the library. It made sense she'd be here tonight, and in a part of him he couldn't let himself fully acknowledge, he'd hoped they'd cross paths. Although he couldn't turn back the clock, even a glimpse of her made his day brighter.

"Yes, get a hot chocolate for Alana as well, Bella." The woman spoke to her elder daughter, who'd reached the head of the line and had been joined by a tall, dark-haired man. "Heath, you made it. I worried you'd get stuck on that work call." The woman gave the man an exuberant hug.

As Heath returned the hug, Cal's stomach knotted. The four of them were a family. The kind he'd thought he'd have one day. As he gave his hot-chocolate order to one of the elves, the girls talked excitedly to their dad, telling him about their day at school. It was an ordinary conversation, not about anything special, but to Cal it seemed like everything. "Thanks." He took the two cups from the elf and headed back to Mrs. Barrett.

"Cal?" Alana's voice stopped him.

"Hi." He greeted her, for an instant oblivious to everyone around them. She stared at him, the perfect oval of her face framed by a white hat dotted with tiny silver sparkles. A matching scarf was wrapped around her neck atop a dark blue parka.

"Alana!" The girl called Lottie ran up to them, the rest of the others close behind. "Mom says the lights are going on soon. We got you hot chocolate."

"Hey, kiddo," Alana greeted her, then thanked the girl.

Cal's heart seemed to skip a beat.

"Meet Cal. He's a new staff member at the tree farm. He went to high school in Strawberry Pond but left years ago." Alana hesitated. "We were in the same year. Cal, these are my friends Josie and Heath. And their girls, Bella and Lottie. They live on a farm near town." She took her hot chocolate from Bella.

"Great to meet you." Heath's handshake was firm. "Want to join us? I'm somewhat new in town myself. Moved here from Boston almost eighteen months ago."

"Thanks but I'm already with—" He glanced toward Mrs. Barrett, now chatting with a couple who appeared to be in their eighties, who'd set up their own folding chairs next to hers.

"It looks like we're watching the tree lighting together." At Cal's side, Alana's voice was low. "Those are Josie's grandparents with Mrs. Barrett. There's some connection between the Ryans' and Mrs. Barrett's family way back. Small-town life. It's like old home week all year round."

Cal's breath got short. The tree lighting was a public event, and he and Alana already worked together at Rustic Hearts. "It's not a big deal." It wasn't a date. They'd become part of the same group by chance.

"No, it's fine." Alana kept her gaze averted.

Was she remembering what Cal was? Back when this tree lighting *had* been a date? Their first official date after he'd finally plucked up the courage to ask her out their freshman year. The pretty and popular girl who sat next to him in homeroom and whose locker was two down from his. The girl he'd thought wouldn't look at him twice, but then she had and changed his life forever.

"Hel-l-o-o-o, Strawberry Pond!" A female

voice came over a loudspeaker welcoming everyone.

After giving Mrs. Barrett her drink, Cal shuffled into place behind her chair.

"That's the mayor speaking." At Cal's other side, Alana cradled her own drink between mittened hands. "She was six or seven years ahead of us in school so you likely wouldn't have known her."

Cal nodded. He hadn't crossed paths with the mayor but there were lots here he had. Kids who'd been born and raised in Strawberry Pond and who were now raising their own families in the same space. Although he hadn't recognized it back then, this tree lighting was a multigenerational event for folks who had deep roots in what locals called "the Pond." He'd forgotten that nickname, but he'd used it. Once, it'd made him feel like he belonged, and that's what he'd wanted more than anything.

"Ten, nine, eight…" The mayor, who held the leash of a Bernese mountain dog with a red bow tied to its collar, began the countdown with Santa Claus, and the crowd joined in.

"Three, two, one." Cal's voice mingled with Alana's as Josie and Heath's girls squealed and jumped up and down.

Holiday lights strung across Main Street and the square, and what looked like every available tree, lit up the darkness to dazzle Cal's eyes. Vehicle horns sounded, clapping and laughter broke out, and more music, this time "A Holly Jolly Christmas" came through the sound system.

"I still like Michael Bublé. That's who's singing." Mrs. Barrett turned to Cal as she clapped along. "Do you remember giving me a couple of his albums one Christmas? I still have them. Play those CDs all the time."

He'd forgotten, but he'd always tried to choose gifts that would please his foster mom, saving money he earned at his after-school and Saturday job to give a special present to everyone he cared about. Alana, especially.

He darted a glance at her, dancing with Josie's girls and several other kids and gesturing for Josie to join them.

He'd given up the right to dance with Alana, give her presents and everything else. Not even if right now it felt like the years had slipped away and the two of them were teenagers again. The past was still between them, and unlike that pine cone that'd gotten caught in her hair, it couldn't be untangled so easily. Or at all.

CHAPTER FIVE

AT THE START of her Friday evening shift at Rustic Hearts, Alana set a box of decorated holiday sugar cookies on the table in the compact staff kitchen. Since she hadn't had time to bake, she'd picked up the treat at the bakery in town. It was a way of showing the staff their hard work was appreciated, something she and her brothers had learned from their parents.

Nowadays, her older brothers, Jordy and Ben, focused on the agricultural side of Hansen Farms and rarely came to the Christmas-tree farm and store, or dealt with their commercial customers. Even though Alana pitched in when she could, the outward-facing part of the business still rested on her parents' shoulders. What would happen when they wanted to retire? It was something she didn't like to think about but she had to. They all did.

"Cookie?" When Ted, their temporary farm manager, came into the kitchen, she gestured to the box.

"Don't mind if I do." His weather-beaten face creased into a smile. "One for the road until I get home for supper. I can almost smell my wife's chili cooking from here. Cal's out in the tree lot, and Maddie's still in the store. Her mom's picking her up real soon."

Alana nodded as Maddie rushed in to grab her coat and backpack. Once she and Ted left, Alana and Cal would be here alone until closing.

It would be fine. Cal was a colleague, nothing more. They'd gotten over the initial awkwardness, and even watching the tree lighting together a few days before had been okay. However, she hadn't missed how Mrs. Barrett had looked at the two of them standing side by side. Once, Cal's foster mom had been an important part of Alana's life. However, after their breakup, Alana had distanced herself from everyone and everything that reminded her of Cal, including kindly Donna Barrett.

After saying goodbye to Ted and Maddie, Alana locked the back door and went into the empty store, taking the cookies with her. If it was quiet, she could catch up on paperwork, and tidying and restocking shelves.

"It's getting wild out there." Ten minutes or so later, the side door opened, and Cal came in from the tree lot bringing a blast of cold air and snow with him. "I'd forgotten how fast storms can come up here." He shook snow off his coat.

"I left the library late and didn't check the forecast." As Alana spoke, a gust of wind buffeted the building and sleet pinged against the windowpanes. She went to the nearest window and peered into the darkness and swirling snow. "Given this weather, there likely won't be anybody coming by. We should close up and get home while we still can."

Mentally, she berated herself. Born and raised in the White Mountains, she always looked at the forecast before heading out, especially in winter. Despite only having to travel a few miles, on a winding and icy mountain road even a short distance could be treacherous. But the library's budget-planning meeting had run late, and in her rush to leave town she'd been distracted. Although she didn't like to admit it, she'd also been distracted by the thought of seeing Cal again.

She'd believed she could steel herself against him, but somehow he had her all churned up and remembering things she shouldn't. And here, working together, she couldn't avoid him as much as she wanted to. Even when he wasn't actually in her physical vicinity, his presence seemed to linger, swirling around her like a soft caress. And when she did see him, she was drawn to him as if by some invisible force.

"Good idea to close up. Pronto." Cal found the keys to lock the outside gates and, as the lights flickered, he grabbed one of the big flashlights they kept by the door. "Whoa." After opening the door a crack, he slammed it shut again. "In less than five minutes, it's become a regular blizzard out there. Trust me, Lanie, you don't want to drive in it."

"Don't call me *Lanie*." The pet name only Cal had ever called her was another blow to her battered heart. "And don't talk to me about trust, either. Forget the gates. I'll take care of them. Go and—"

"No, I won't go. Not this time." Cal's eyes darkened as he stared at her. "We need to—"

On her way to make sure the generator was on standby, all the old hurt, frustration and pent-up anger at Cal's leaving surged through her.

Returning to the store, Alana's cell rang, and vehicle headlights sliced through the darkness out front. Finding the phone in the back pocket of her jeans, she recognized Jordy's number. Heart pounding, she hit Answer. "Hey."

"I've got the four-wheel drive and me and Ben are here to pick you up." Jordy's familiar voice brought Alana back to the present. "We were only a quarter of a mile down the road when the storm blew in and were already on our way when Mom called. Snow's drifting bad. Your little car won't make it."

"Thanks." Alana ended the call and put one hand on thc counter to steady herself. "My brothers are out there. They'll give me a ride home." Whether to the farm or her house in town, they were both places where she'd be safe. "You should come with us." No matter what she thought of Cal, his small pickup wasn't suited to this weather, either. He'd be almost as likely to spin off the road as her.

He glanced from her to the swirling snow. "I've got winter gear but not like your brothers must have, and my truck bed's empty so with a two-wheel drive and not enough rear weight…" His voice trailed away. "If you're sure?"

"I don't want you to have an accident or get stuck in a snowdrift and freeze to death." Alana avoided his gaze as she closed out the cash register. "I wouldn't want that to happen to anyone."

"Good to know." Cal hesitated as if he wanted to say more.

"Can you deal with the gates? I'll meet you at Jordy's truck once I've put the bank deposit in the safe." Alana waved Cal away. "There's Ben coming to help." A dark shape hovered in front of the window. "Jordy's likely keeping the truck running and warm."

"I didn't mean to upset you. Before." Cal's

mouth worked, and he shifted from one foot to the other.

"You didn't." *Liar.* She pressed her lips together tightly. Cal had upset her more than she'd expected. More than she wanted him to guess. "It's nothing."

"To me, it was everything." Cal's gray eyes darkened, looking almost black.

Alana shrugged. It—them—had been everything to her as well. "Once trust is broken, it's gone."

Forever. The word she didn't add hovered between them.

"I'LL HAVE A meal on the table for you in no time." Half an hour later, Alana's mom moved around the big country kitchen at the Hansen farmhouse, which was almost the same as Cal remembered. "Nothing fancy. Only my cheeseburger casserole and a tossed salad. Leftovers."

"That'd be great, thanks." He sat at the long wooden table where Mrs. Hansen gestured.

"Is Donna Barrett doing okay?" She spoke with her head half-inside the fridge and then brought out various covered dishes and a big block of cheese.

"Fine." He'd called his foster mom a few minutes earlier, using the Hansens' landline since cell service was patchy here. "Like you, she's got a generator."

"That's smart. You can bunk in with the boys in their old room. I already had an extra bed in there for Thanksgiving. I'm sorry I can't give you the guest room, but Mark's still sleeping there owing to needing extra space and being so restless after his surgery." Mrs. Hansen nodded as Jordy, Ben and Alana came into the kitchen, their dad, Mark, and a golden retriever following behind.

Mr. Hansen's hair, which Cal remembered as being pale blond, was now snow-white. He also moved more slowly than he used to. Likely that was because of his surgery, but he also seemed more stooped. However, his penetrating blue gaze hadn't changed, and when it zeroed in on him, Cal forced himself not to flinch.

"Cal," Alana's dad greeted him before taking his place at the head of the table. "No, Lucky. Go to your bed." He waved a hand at the dog, who'd veered to greet Cal, gesturing to a pet bed near a window.

"Good to see you, Mr. Hansen. Thanks again for taking me in." While it couldn't hurt to express appreciation, Alana's family hadn't had much choice as the weather had worsened. Despite the four-wheel drive, and Jordy's skill behind the wheel, they'd never have made it to town. Jordy and Ben couldn't even make it home to their wives and kids. So like the rest of them, Cal was at the Hansen family home, where notwithstanding the outward pleasantness, the hair on the back of Cal's neck quivered and he couldn't let himself relax.

Mr. Hansen shrugged and then beamed at Alana, who slid a steaming cup of coffee in front of him. "We look out for folks around here. Stranger or friend." His gaze swiveled back to Cal. "Always have."

Which category did Cal fit into? He wasn't a stranger, but he wasn't a friend, either. Best not to pursue that train of thought. What could he talk to Mark Hansen about? Like Alana, Jordy and Ben were giving their mom a hand with the food, and their cheerful voices and sporadic laughter contrasted with the silence at the table. "Strawberry Pond hasn't changed much." Was that a sufficiently neutral topic?

"We like it that way." Mr. Hansen sipped some coffee. "You settling in all right?"

"Fine, but I'm not actually settling. I'm only visiting for the holidays." Surely Ted or Alana must have told him Cal's stay here was temporary?

"So what *are* your plans?" Mr. Hansen set his coffee mug on the table with a thud, which, albeit soft and light, nevertheless sounded a lot like a warning.

He didn't have any plans, not yet, but he couldn't say that to a man like Alana's dad. A guy who'd probably had his life planned out before he even started kindergarten. He was part of a family, and that family came with a legacy. All the pieces would have slotted into place as neatly as in one of the wooden puzzle toys Cal had spotted in a basket by the kitchen door, undoubtedly for the Hansens' grandchildren to play with when they visited.

"I haven't made any final decisions yet. I'm still considering my options." In truth, he was trying to find options, but that was okay. The career counselor he'd talked to when leaving the military said it often took people a while to find a good fit. Unlike his younger brother, who'd decided he wanted to become a firefighter long before he'd left the military, Cal's path had never been as clear.

Mr. Hansen made a harrumphing noise. "I'd have thought you'd be wanting to do something mechanical. With cars or other machinery. You used to be able to fix most anything. From what I heard, you'd made a good start there at Strawberry Pond Automotive."

Cal had loved that job. Before he left town. Had to leave, although he couldn't say so to Mr.

Hansen or anyone else. Thanks to the navy, he'd taken specialist technical training, and while related to ships and aircraft, some of those skills would be transferable.

"Don't try to organize Cal's life for him." Mrs. Hansen put a steaming plate of food in front of Cal and another one across from him. "You have enough to think of with our own family."

"Except for the grandkids who are too young, our kids and nephews and nieces are all settled and living upstanding, productive lives." Mr. Hansen accepted a piece of apple pie from Alana, while Jordy and Ben carried their own plates to the table and sat on either side of their dad.

"Dad." Alana shook her head and, like she used to, sat across from Cal. It was the only empty place so she hadn't chosen to sit there. Still, it reminded him of old times. "I'm sure Cal lived an upstanding, productive life in the navy. Now, he's transitioning into civilian life. I expect it'll take time."

In the midst of picking up his fork, Cal almost dropped it. Alana had stood up for him. She'd also listened to and remembered what he'd said that first day they'd worked together at the tree farm about moving from military to civilian life. Was a part of her still concerned for him? She'd always been kind and caring, but he hadn't thought that would still extend to him except in a general way. Like when she'd said she wouldn't want anyone to have an accident or freeze to death in this blizzard, him included. For an instant, it was like the mask Alana usually wore had slipped, giving him a glimpse of the real woman.

A woman who was hurting. The way she'd lashed out at him had told Cal that. He was hurting, too.

"Sorry, what did you say, Mrs. Hansen?"

"I said dig in while the food's hot. Mark and I ate earlier so you go ahead." Her smile, while guarded, nevertheless reached her eyes. Alana's eyes. "While I'd never welcome a bad storm, it's sure nice to have a bunch around this table again. I guess there's always a blessing if you look hard enough for it."

Mrs. Barrett often said something similar. She even had a fridge magnet with a phrase about looking for the positives and counting your blessings where you found them. The way he'd grown up, Cal had been conditioned to expect the worst. His parents' deaths. Bouncing around between foster homes and schools. Trying, unsuccessfully, to keep his brother in line and out of trouble. Jesse had been the reason for all those moves until he'd been sent to a juvenile detention center, and Cal had come to Mrs. Barrett's alone.

Cal swallowed guilt along with a mouthful of the delicious casserole. Jesse had a life in Boston with his wife and son. He was an adult who didn't need Cal any longer, and he hadn't for years.

In some ways, it might have been easier if they'd had one big argument and become fully estranged. Instead, once Jesse had gotten on a better path for himself, and even when they were still both in the military, they'd drifted apart. Different bases in different parts of the country. Different jobs. And two boys who'd always been different in terms of personality had grown up into two very different men.

Their calls, emails and texts had become more infrequent until they'd almost stopped entirely. They each had their own lives was how Cal tried to rationalize it, but along with guilt for not trying harder to keep in touch with his brother, there was also hurt and regret.

If he and Jesse were truly brothers, they'd be spending the holidays together. However, they weren't, and Cal had to make the best of it. Like he'd done his best for Jesse as he'd promised their mom.

Jordy passed a salad bowl, and Cal helped himself. With thick blond hair, blue eyes and a brawny frame, Jordy Hansen looked like his dad, whereas Ben and Alana favored their slighter, more delicate-featured mom. The same way Cal resembled *his* mom, and Jesse took after their dad. Or how their dad appeared in the few photos Cal had. Ones he kept in an old-fashioned pocket album with plastic photo sleeves.

The school pictures Alana had given him were in that album, too, as well as more informal shots. The two of them hugging and smiling for the camera in a pumpkin patch. At senior prom gazing into each other's eyes. Joking around wearing funny Christmas sweaters and Santa hats. Behind a cake at Alana's sixteenth birthday party.

Back then, most teenagers didn't have smartphones so Cal kept his memories in his heart and what were now faded snaps in a cheap album. But no matter where he went or what he did, those memories of his family and Alana had gone with him.

As the conversation swirled around him, ranging from farm business to a holiday concert at the elementary school Jordy's and Ben's kids were taking part in, Cal thought about what Alana had said.

Trust. Did it have to be broken forever? Or could it somehow be rebuilt? Cal wouldn't know unless he tried. For the first time since he'd left town all those years ago, something that felt a lot like hope nudged at his guarded heart.

Was he only looking for a fresh start in terms of work, or one with Alana, too?

CHAPTER SIX

"OKAY, IT WAS AWKWARD." On Saturday at midday after Jordy had brought her home, Alana glanced between Laura's and Josie's smiling faces on her laptop screen. Owing to the blizzard, and her friends not being able to get into town from their farms, they'd deferred their Saturday-morning breakfast at the diner and were getting together online instead.

Having Cal eat at her family's kitchen table and spend the night under the Hansens' roof had also been weird and uncomfortable, but although Alana couldn't admit it to anyone else, it had somehow been strangely right. Once, her family had been like Cal's family. Seeing him sitting in the same chair he always had for a casual family meal had brought back a lot of memories. Ones she'd done a good job of trying to forget, she reminded herself.

Was that why she'd stood up for Cal when her dad had asked him about his future plans? Sensing Cal's discomfort, and recalling what he'd said about the challenges of moving from military to civilian life, the words had popped out of her mouth before she'd thought. She'd have done the same for anyone. Or would she?

"So, you and Cal." Josie leaned closer to her camera and even through the screen Alana didn't miss the curiosity in her eyes. "I didn't remember him at all until Laura filled me in. Despite everything, any sparks with the old boyfriend?"

"Not the kind you're thinking of." Alana shuddered, even as awareness of the lie jabbed at her. There were indeed lots of those sparks between her and Cal, but she wouldn't let herself act on them. On the bright side, if Josie, who'd also been ahead of Alana in school, hadn't remembered Cal, there were also likely others in town who didn't. Alana was getting paranoid, imagining everyone was talking about her. "Last night when we were working together at the store, Cal said something about 'trust,' and I kind of lost my temper."

"Only kind of?" Laura made a sympathetic face. "From even the little you told me about how your relationship ended, it sounds like you have a right to be mad at him."

Alana did, but during the largely silent ride in the snowstorm to the Hansen farm, and then when they'd gathered around the table to eat, that anger had gone out of her like air from a burst balloon. Instead, all she felt was sadness and regret. Her mom and dad had been hospitable, as they would to anyone who needed shelter, and her brothers hadn't teased, but all four of them had kept darting anxious looks at Alana. She knew what those looks meant. They thought she wasn't as "over" Cal as she professed to be, and they were right. When it came to her family and maybe even her friends, she couldn't hide her feelings as well as she thought she could.

"Oh, honey." Josie's tone sounded as if she was speaking to one of her daughters. "It'll all work out somehow. Cal's only here for a few weeks. He'll be gone before you know it."

Alana should be grateful Cal wouldn't be in town long, but in only a few days everything she'd thought she knew about herself and what she'd once felt for him had gotten confused with the reality of him now. Parts of him were the same, but he was also different and way too attractive.

"Before I was aware of what happened between the two of you, I talked about some of us from high school maybe getting together. I gave him my number." Laura's voice was pained. "If Cal calls, I'll say I'm busy. That's the truth, but I'm on your side. I wouldn't think of socializing with him."

"We've both got your back." Josie gave a decisive nod, and several red-blond curls, which had come loose from her ponytail, bounced around her face.

"Enough about Cal. What's new with you two?" Alana made herself give a neutral smile. A few more weeks. That's what she had to focus on. At this time of year, there was also a lot going on to keep her busy and distracted. Yet, as the three of them chatted about their holiday cookie-making evening, which Alana was hosting this year, and Strawberry Pond's upcoming tractor parade of lights, her thoughts wandered.

Cal had once meant everything to her, and Alana had been sure he felt the same way about her. The more time they spent together, the more she was reminded of those old feelings. Before he came back to town, she'd hardly given him a second thought and that was as it should be. It was only because she was now seeing him on almost a daily basis that she'd fallen into what an article she'd read about getting over your ex called thought traps. Times when she caught herself wondering how her life would've been different if she and Cal had stayed together. And she got caught up in the past instead of living in the present.

It wasn't productive and she had to stop. She *would* stop.

"Sorry, Laura. What'd you say?" She forced herself to pay attention to the conversation.

"We're still snowed in out here, so I won't be able to make it into town to volunteer at the Pond Pantry and community kitchen at suppertime tonight. I feel extra bad because it was my last shift at the food bank before Christmas, and one of the service clubs is hosting a special holiday meal." Laura shook her head. "Trevor cleared part of our lane, but with first ice and then snow, both it and the side road are a mess. From everything I've heard that storm hit us harder out here than you guys in town. I can't risk driving anywhere."

"Same here," Josie said. "I had to use the snowblower to get to the barn to milk and you know how close our milking parlor is to the house."

Alana looked out the window of her cozy den. Although the branches of the maple tree in her side yard were cloaked in white, the town's streets had been cleared and the sun had come out to make rainbow sparkles against the fresh snow. The family who lived next door were building a snowman, with mom, dad and their two kids dressed in colorful parkas, snow pants, boots, hats and mittens. The same winter gear Alana had in her own closet.

"I can handle your food-bank shift." That

magazine article had also said a good way to shift focus from an ex was to do something to help others. Ordinarily, Alana would've been working at the library or tree farm today, but since they were both closed, it wasn't doing her any good to be stuck at home brooding. "The Pond Pantry is only a few blocks away so I can walk. I volunteered there in high school and have an idea how it works." Her folks also made regular donations of seasonal fruits and vegetables, all grown on their farm, to the food bank, and Alana had occasionally handled those deliveries.

"That'd be great." Laura's voice held relief. "I'll let the organizer know you're taking my place and email you the details. It's my Aunt Anne who'll be in charge today, so look for her when you get there."

"I'm happy to pitch in." Alana straightened in her chair. Anne Sullivan was friends with Josie's grandmother and another regular library visitor. Along with doing something practical for those in need, it would be fun to work alongside such a cheerful and good-hearted woman. "I'll whip up a batch of chocolate-chip cookies to bring with me as a treat for the volunteers." She'd taken the sugar cookies she'd bought for the staff at Rustic Hearts to her parents' home, where her brothers and Cal had made short work of them.

Cal. Even when she was determined not to

think of him, he still popped into her mind. That was the last time today, though, because she had cookies to make and a new audiobook to listen to. Then she had a food-bank and community-kitchen shift to get ready for.

She'd built a busy, full and fulfilling life without Cal, and she wouldn't want it any other way.

ALTHOUGH THE SIMPLE white clapboard building that housed the Pond Pantry almost blended in with the surrounding snowdrifts, Cal still recognized it right away. He'd come here after school every Wednesday afternoon his junior year as part of a community-service activity. Mrs. Barrett was big on volunteering, and she'd encouraged her sons and Cal to give back in whatever ways they could.

While he'd never given his foster mom a reason, he'd chosen the food bank because when his own mom had gotten sick and couldn't work, she'd needed to rely on a local food cupboard to feed herself and her kids. As a high-school volunteer, he'd only unpacked boxes and shelved donations, but it was still a way of trying to pass on some of the goodness he'd been grateful to receive. Today, he'd joined Mrs. Barrett to do more of the same, having dropped her off first before parking his truck.

He opened the outside door and came into a

small entryway, then hung up his coat and left his boots on a mat to change into the sneakers he'd brought with him. Then, he followed the sounds of voices and clattering of dishes, and smelled the tantalizing scent of meat cooking, into what had once been one big room, but now had several folding dividers down the middle.

This area must be for dining, new since he'd been here last. He took in the long, paper-covered tables lined with chairs on either side. Mrs. Barrett had mentioned that thanks to a big corporate donation, the food bank had expanded, and, with the community kitchen, was able to serve home-cooked meals several times a week.

"I'm Anne Sullivan, and you must be Cal. Please call me Anne. Donna said you were joining her." A gray-haired woman in her late seventies or early eighties came over to him. She held out a red-and-white-checked apron, and Cal took it. "I'm so glad you're here. We need all the help we can get today. Because of the bad weather, lots of our usual volunteers couldn't make it in."

As Cal put on the apron, he returned Anne's warm smile. "Put me to work."

"Go on into the storeroom. It's off the kitchen." Anne gestured. "We're already covered when it comes to cooks, but I could use a hand putting together prepacked grocery baskets. They're a selection of basic essentials to which folks can then add a few things according to their individual preferences."

Cal nodded. It'd been the same when he'd volunteered here.

"When our guests arrive, you'll be serving as well. It's spaghetti with a meat or vegetarian sauce, garlic bread and salad. Fruit and chocolate bread pudding for dessert. Comfort food that's warm *and* filling." With another smile, Anne went to speak with a middle-aged couple setting vases filled with seasonal greenery on the tables, leaving Cal to make his way to the storeroom alone.

Passing through the kitchen, he waved at Mrs. Barrett, who stood at a sink washing lettuce. It was nice to be part of a community-service activity again. It would also take his mind off having had to spend the night at Alana's family home, which had been more than a little uncomfortable.

He'd been relieved when Ben had gotten up early to clear snow and, since the storm had stopped, had also offered to take Cal back to Mrs. Barrett's. While everyone had been polite, facing the whole family again at breakfast would've been too much. When Mr. Hansen had asked him what his plans were, he hadn't known what to say. Although Alana had unexpectedly stood up for him, it was one more reason Cal had hardly slept and wanted to leave as soon as he could.

"I'm Cal, reporting for prepacked grocery-basket duty." As he made a joking salute, the words died on his lips and he dropped his arm. "Alana. What're you doing here?"

"Filling in for my friend Laura." Wearing a matching apron to his over dark jeans and a loose-fitting red sweater, she took a package of rice from a shelf and added it to a box. While they'd both volunteered at the food bank in high school, their shifts hadn't overlapped. Cal didn't have any memories of her here, but once again it was as if fate had thrown them together. "You met Laura at the tree farm. She lives outside town, and the roads are still too bad for her to come in."

"Yeah, I remember her." Cal had seen Laura in town a few days before but at a distance. Given her close friendship with Alana, he was glad to be able to avoid her. He also wouldn't think of calling to follow up on that high-school get-together she'd mentioned. "Look, I know things are strange between us, but until last night at the store, I thought we were doing okay." Before he'd opened his big mouth and started talking about trust. Bad choice of word but it had been an accident, as had calling her Lanie. If he could take back what he'd said, he would, but since he couldn't he had to try to smooth things over.

Alana added cereal to the box. "Right. I overreacted. Water under the bridge, remember?"

Except that water was foaming and bubbling like a cauldron, and each time Cal and Alana crossed paths, it got stirred up a bit more. "Okay, but I'm sorry. When I said for you to trust me, it was an expression, nothing more. Of course you can't trust me, not really."

"No, I can't." Alana indicated where Cal could find a box and gave him a list of prepackaged items to fill it with. Then they worked side by side at the counter, taking items in turn from the shelves that lined the storeroom's walls. "I don't mean I expect you to steal from my family's business or anything like that. You were always honest."

Except for when he couldn't be. Cal's stomach knotted, and all of a sudden, he felt sick. While he hadn't stolen money from her family, had he been a party to something even worse?

Mr. Hansen had also never thought Cal was good enough for Alana. He'd said so. Oh, not in Cal's hearing, but a few days before Cal left town, he'd brought his car into the garage where Cal worked. That's when Cal had overheard him say he "wanted the best" for his daughter. It made sense, since any parent would want the same, but it was nevertheless clear. Cal wouldn't be "the best" for Alana, and the sooner he accepted it, the better.

"Of course, I'm not a thief." His face burned. Although back then his brother sure had been. Minor offences, shoplifting and breaking into cars and outbuildings, but along with everything else, it had been enough to get Jesse sent first to that juvenile detention center, and then other community-care facilities and programs. Where Cal couldn't look out for him. His stomach and chest grew so tight he could hardly breathe.

"Let's drop it, okay? For the next few weeks, we can surely manage to be friendly coworkers. Yesterday was a blip. From now on, I won't go looking for slights in every small thing." A piece of hair Alana had tucked behind her ears fell forward to half cover her face. "No big deal, right?"

The shorter haircut suited her, but it was another reminder that she wasn't the Alana he'd known and loved. Friendly coworkers but not friends, and certainly nothing more. While Cal had expected as much, he hadn't expected how much it would still hurt. Seeing Alana, working with her and feeling so lost and empty inside.

"Right. No big deal." His voice rasped and he cleared his throat against the traitorous emotion. "Friendly coworkers."

She stared at him, her eyes hard. "Good. We understand each other."

Did they? Cal didn't understand himself, let alone her. He manufactured a smile.

"Cal?" Mrs. Barrett popped her head into the storeroom. "Folks are arriving, and we're getting ready to serve. Anne says you'll be dishing out the meat spaghetti sauce and… Oh, Alana." She darted a glance between the two of them. "I didn't know you were in here. If you can look after garlic bread, we'll be all set."

"Of course, Mrs. Barrett." Alana smiled at Cal's foster mom with the warmth she'd once directed at him. "Whatever you and Mrs. Sullivan need. Don't forget I left cookies for the volunteers in the tin by the fridge."

As she passed him in the narrow space, Alana's arm brushed Cal's. Even with her sweater and his shirt between them, the brief connection had felt like a special spark.

"Friendly coworkers" was a step up from mere coworkers. However, it wasn't enough, and now, Cal knew it never would be.

CHAPTER SEVEN

"OH, NO." AT FIVE minutes past nine on Tuesday morning after what people were calling "the big storm," Alana spoke into the desk phone at the library. She glanced around her cubby of an office, where coloring sheets, books, small prizes and treat bags for the library's holiday party for preschoolers were stacked on every available surface. "I'm so sorry and hope you heal soon. No, don't worry, I'll find someone else."

As she ended the call, her heart sank. She'd hired a Santa Claus from a town over the mountain from Strawberry Pond because the kids might guess the identity of any of the local men. They were still small, and she wanted the children to be awed and caught up in the magic of Christmas for as long as possible. But what was she going to do? The party was in an hour, and that call had been from the Santa she'd booked telling her that when leaving his house he'd slipped on ice and broken his arm.

Although she hadn't wanted him to feel any

worse than he already did, saying she'd find someone else was one thing. Actually doing it at such short notice was another, much bigger problem. Josie's gramps, maybe? Tom Ryan had played Santa in several town parades, and he was good with children. No, on that video call, Josie said her grandparents had gone to Montréal for a few days. "A romantic break," she'd called it.

Who else was there who might be suitable? Nobody Alana could think of who wouldn't either be at work or too recognizable. She dropped her head into her hands, panic rising and thoughts whirling. She couldn't disappoint the children, and it wouldn't be much of a party without Santa there.

She found her cell phone and scrolled to the farm's online staff-scheduling calendar. Was anyone who worked for Hansen Farms off today who she might convince to come and play Santa? Most of the guys were dads and even those who weren't would understand the urgency.

"No, no, no." She muttered the words under her breath. *Cal.* Apart from the high-school boys who'd be at school and were also too young, Cal was the only male who wasn't working this morning. Could she ask him? She didn't have a choice.

Taking a deep breath, she scrolled to his number and waited. *Friendly coworkers.* She was the one who'd said that's what they should be, so this was a friendly request.

He picked up on the first ring. "Alana? What's up? Is there a problem at the farm?"

"No, the problem's at the library." She briefly explained what had happened. "Luckily, I already have the Santa costume here."

"Sure, I'm in town so can be there in a few minutes. I often played Santa for holiday parties on the base. Being one of the few without kids, I guess I was an obvious choice."

Was that regret in his voice? "Thanks, I really appreciate it."

With anyone else, she'd have said she owed them, but this was Cal. If anything, he owed her. No, she couldn't let herself think that way. It wasn't a matter of "owing." Setting aside how things had ended between them, she knew in her heart that he was still a decent, kind and all-round good guy. How he cared for Mrs. Barrett proved it. It was also in what the other farm staff said about him. Ted, Maddie and the rest liked and spoke highly of Cal.

"Hang in there. It'll be fine. We can't let the little ones down."

For the first time in the past fifteen minutes, Alana breathed normally. Like "trust," that "we" was a figure of speech. She and Cal weren't a "we" in any sense of the word, but this time when she'd needed him, he'd come through for her. It was a start, and it was about the kids. That's who she'd be focusing on, not him, and now, she had to finish decorating before the library opened and her part-time staff member came in.

Two hours later, Alana clapped and sang along to the holiday music playing over the speaker system in the library's upstairs activity room. Despite the last-minute panic, the party had gone off without a hitch. Now, twenty excited preschoolers clustered around Cal, who was answering their questions and giving out treat bags like the experienced Santa he was supposed to be.

"Santa Claus *did* come to town." Anne Sullivan, here with two of her great-grandchildren, gave Alana's arm a reassuring squeeze.

"You heard?" Alana hadn't told anyone about the change of plan, deciding that since the crisis was over it wasn't important.

"The original one's my third cousin once removed. His wife called me from the hospital." She chuckled. "His replacement's been a good sport about it all. Wonderful with the children as well." She nodded toward her great-grandson, who clung to Cal's neck. "No, Emmett. Santa isn't a climbing tree." She darted to Cal to entice the boy away.

Alana picked up several holiday sticker sheets that had fallen to the floor from a craft table and gave a wry smile. Cal had always been wonderful with children, often better than he was with adults. He'd never talked to her about his own childhood, and whenever she'd asked, he'd brushed away her questions. Growing up in foster care must have been tough, though, and as an adult she had a new understanding of what he'd gone through.

"Come, too, Miss Alana." A red-haired boy tugged on Alana's hand to draw her into a conga dance led by Cal.

She looked around, puzzled. Cyndi Lauper's "Christmas Conga" hadn't been on her music playlist.

Cal held up his phone and grinned behind his fake white beard. "Merry Christmas. Happy holidays. Ho, ho, ho." Bouncing to the music, he was like a big kid himself, and Alana had to smile back. He'd even gotten the moms, dads, grandparents and other caregivers to join in. For the most part, they'd stayed on one side of the room, chatting among themselves while Alana had led the kids in games, a special story time and making Christmas trees out of paper plates before Santa's visit.

By getting everyone up and dancing, he'd also gotten them heading toward the door and on their way home. Since Alana needed to clean up the room before the mindfulness coloring group arrived, she needed as much time as possible. In a bigger town's library, there'd be other staff to help, but here, except for a few part-timers and a custodian who came in at night to clean the whole building, she handled most of the jobs herself.

"Thanks for coming. Glad you had fun. Don't forget your mittens." She waved a pink-and-white knitted pair shaped like a rabbit at one of the girls who held tight to Cal's jacket sleeve. "All right, Harper?"

The girl nodded. "I *love* Santa." Her mouth curved into a cherubic smile.

As she took her mittens and followed her mom and twin brother out of the party room, Alana's heart squeezed. She'd loved Santa, too, but he hadn't been Santa then. He'd only been Cal.

After storing the sticker sheets in the craft cupboard, she found garbage and blue recycling bags and began collecting juice-box containers, candy wrappers and stray paper plates. The decorations could stay up, as they were seasonal rather than specific to the preschoolers, but she needed to gather the party detritus and put the chairs and tables back where they belonged.

"I'll give you a hand." Cal's voice pulled Alana out of her musing.

"No need. I've got it." With only the two of them, the room somehow felt smaller. More intimate.

"I *want* to help." His gray gaze locked with hers. Although he still wore the Santa costume, he'd removed the wig, hat and white beard, and his own dark beard stubble shadowed his face.

Alana felt herself flush. At the tree farm, he was always clean-shaven, but today that hint of beard outlined the planes of his face and made him look rugged and manlier with no hint of the boy she remembered. "Okay, but I thought you'd be busy."

"I have the day off, remember?" He began stacking the kid-size chairs.

"Then you should be doing day off things. Laundry, grocery shopping…snowboarding, even." She tried to joke to defuse the new awareness that seemed to hum between them. The old attraction but overlaid with something else. "There's sure enough snow for winter sports."

"True." He laughed as he continued to move furniture where she indicated. "My snowboarding days are behind me, though. After falling on the wet deck of a ship and wrecking my left knee, the one I already hurt playing football, the doctor said I should stay off the slopes. That's another reason for leaving the navy. I'd been transferred to a desk job, which wasn't for me."

He shrugged like it didn't matter but it must. Cal had always been active and great at all sports, summer and winter.

"I'm sorry." Alana knotted the ends of the garbage and recycling bags and found her canvas tote to gather up books to return to the library's collection.

He shrugged again. "It is what it is. I'm luckier than a lot of others." A shadow flitted across his face, gone almost before Alana registered it. "The kids are great."

"They are, but so were you." She popped several books into the tote and then joined Cal in the middle of the room. "A real pro."

He gave Alana a mock bow and tugged on the pom-pom of her Santa hat. "You look like a cute candy cane."

He was teasing, of course, but it still sent a quiver through her. To play with kids, she'd paired black leggings with a casual red, green and white striped sweater. "I think we're done here and with time to spare." She took off the hat and smoothed her hair. Why did Cal have to make her feel so off balance? Clutching the book tote, she began to turn away.

"Wait." Cal's eyes sparkled and he pointed above their heads, where Alana had hung an artificial mistletoe decoration several days before. "I guess we have to, right?"

She hesitated. “It’s the season.” It was a joke. Neither of them were serious. Yet as she moved closer and tilted her face to his, her legs trembled and she caught her breath. Then he kissed her…or she kissed him—a brief touch of lips.

Voices came from the stairs, and Alana jumped backward. “I should—” She gave a vague wave. “There’s another group using this room.”

“Yeah.” Cal’s face was pink and he laughed.

“Good. That was fun. The party, I mean.” Her face must be pink, too, if not bright red. She put a hand to her mouth where, despite the fleeting contact, her lips still seemed to hold an imprint of his. She forced a laugh. Kissing under the mistletoe was a Christmas tradition. It meant nothing and would’ve been odd if she’d said no.

So why did it all of a sudden feel like that kiss was everything?

“YOU’RE AWFULLY QUIET.” Mrs. Barrett glanced at Cal where they stood near a display of hockey equipment in Kaminski’s Sporting Goods on Strawberry Pond’s Main Street. A store that had been here and in the same location when Cal had lived in town before. “Everything okay?”

“Fine.” He managed a smile. Even a few hours later and shopping with his foster mom, he couldn’t get that impulsive kiss with Alana out of his mind. The softness of her lips as they'd met his. The sweet, floral scent of her face and hair. That moment when time had seemed to stop. "Your grandson's eight, right?"

"Yes, and hockey's a big part of his life." She picked up a package of white skate laces. "Maybe I should give him a gift certificate. What do you think? He could use it when he and his mom and dad visit after Christmas. My son's gotten tickets to a game in Boston. Make the most of his leave. We'll have a second Christmas then."

By that time, Cal would've left Strawberry Pond again. "Sounds fun." Although he kept his voice light, his stomach rolled.

If he wasn't in Strawberry Pond, where would he be? Certainly not with Jesse. Cal hadn't even told his brother he'd left the military. He'd wanted to be settled somewhere before texting.

Also, as the elder brother, he was the one who'd been responsible for Jesse, not the other way around. But now, from the little Cal had heard, mostly through mutual acquaintances or online, Jesse had his life in order while Cal was floundering. It'd be embarrassing enough to reconnect with Jesse after all this time, let alone for his brother to think that Cal needed help.

Which he didn't, Cal reminded himself. He'd already looked into certifying as an auto mechanic, and there was a community college nearby where he could take the program. However, he'd also need an apprenticeship. And how could he stay here knowing he was likely to bump into Alana even when he wasn't working at Rustic Hearts?

Besides, Cal had left Strawberry Pond the first time *for* Jesse. Then, he'd longed to confide in Alana, but in the end he couldn't take that step. Alana was compassionate. Her folks were, too. But since he'd never mentioned Jesse, how could he all of a sudden tell Alana the truth about his brother? Or that he'd promised his mom, a deathbed promise no less, that he'd look out for his younger sibling?

If he'd been honest about Jesse's mistakes and run-ins with the law, Alana and her family might've thought less of Cal, too. No matter how kind and compassionate folks were, it was the way of the world. He'd seen it often enough before coming to Strawberry Pond. Teachers, foster parents, community leaders and even social workers. Jesse's choices and behavior had impacted Cal and people had judged him negatively by association. He couldn't take that risk with the Hansens.

While he'd missed his brother, joining the Barrett family had also been a relief. He'd had a fresh start, unencumbered by his brother's misdeeds, so it'd been easier to pretend Jesse had never existed. Cal Paquette was finally his own person, and nobody had to know about Jesse or share in Cal's shame about having a brother in juvenile detention programs. Or know of his guilt from breaking that promise to his mom that he would look out for Jesse.

It was better to have Alana think Cal had changed his mind about the timing of when they'd get engaged and married. Better for her to think he wanted to join the military first rather than have her pity or censure. Alana's brothers, and the rest of her family, were model citizens. Respectable, law-abiding and principled. How could he expect her to understand Jesse, or how he and Cal had lived?

"Cal?" Mrs. Barrett nudged his elbow. "I asked what you thought about a present for my grandson? A gift certificate or— "

"Why don't you get him something small that you can mail, like those skate laces or stick tape, and then take him to choose a main gift when he's here?"

He'd offered to help Mrs. Barrett with her holiday shopping because it seemed like she wanted the company. So far, though, he'd likely been more a hindrance, trailing after her from store to store but not really seeing what she pointed out to him.

"That's a good idea but..." Mrs. Barrett hesitated and then she patted Cal's arm. "Something's wrong. I know it is, but I can't help if you won't talk to me." Her pale blue eyes were soft.

Even after all these years, his foster mom still knew Cal well. "I don't know what to say." It was partly the truth, but he also feared that if he started to talk he might not be able to stop.

"You did a good thing being Santa for that library party." Keeping hold of the laces, she chose a roll of stick tape and added a small quick-dry sports towel with a hockey-player figure silhouetted in black. "The town's buzzing with how you stepped up for the kids and Alana."

Once again, Cal was reminded of how fast news traveled here. "Anybody would've done the same." As he followed Mrs. Barrett to the main counter to pay for her purchases, his gaze skittered over equipment for sports he could no longer play. Why had he told Alana about his knee? Like with Jesse, he didn't want her to feel sorry for him, and he hadn't missed that flash of sadness in her eyes.

"Hey, Santa. I'm Steve Kaminski." The gray-haired man behind the counter introduced himself and grinned at Cal as Mrs. Barrett chose a gift certificate from several designs. "My granddaughter, Harper, thinks you're the best. She's had a tough time this year after being diagnosed with a nut allergy, and you made her feel better about it. What was it you said? One of your elves has allergies, too? That meant a lot."

"Harper's a sweet girl." Cal gave Steve, whom he vaguely remembered, a self-deprecating smile.

"Staff discount for a friend of Santa." As the man processed Mrs. Barrett's credit-card payment, his smile broadened. "You ever need anything for yourself, let me know. Truly, Harper won't forget you, and we're all grateful."

"Thanks." The navy was an interconnected community, too, but Strawberry Pond felt different somehow. Was it because Cal was different? He hadn't appreciated it before, but the uniform had given him a certain degree of anonymity, especially when out in public. Now, he felt exposed, as if a protective shield had been torn off to leave him vulnerable in a way he hadn't been since he was a kid.

"It's my pleasure." The man handed Mrs. Barrett her purchases, and Cal helped her put them into a large shopping bag, which was now full. "It's good to have you back. We need people like you here. Real civic-minded."

Although Cal had never thought of himself that way, maybe if he put down roots somewhere he *could* be "civic-minded." Make a regular commitment to working at a food pantry, or pitch in to drive an elderly or disabled person to medical appointments. Do something that would truly honor his mom's memory and give back, like she'd always tried to do.

As they left the store, Mrs. Barrett tucked her arm through Cal's. "Even if you don't know what to say, I know how to listen. So when you're ready, I'm here for you. My official commitment as your foster mom stopped when you turned eighteen, but the love sure didn't. I love you like a bonus son, Cal and that'll never change."

His throat clogged with emotion, and he swallowed hard. "I don't know what to do with my life or anything else." *Alana.* Her, especially. This morning, before he'd kissed her under the mistletoe, something intangible had shifted between them. The past would always be there, but this feeling was new. And now, he'd kissed her, and even though it had been a joke, he wanted to kiss her again. For real.

"Even if it seems like it, nobody, me included, has their life all figured out." Mrs. Barrett's expression was wry.

As they walked along Main Street, crisp snow crunched beneath Cal's boots and in the dusk, the colored holiday lights strung from one side of the street to the other cast a cheerful glow. All the local businesses had also decorated for the season. From a miniature Christmas village in the window of Stella's Jewelers, to snowflakes and woodland scene decals at the diner, the small town was filled with holiday spirit.

"You're also in the middle of a big change." As Cal stayed silent, Mrs. Barrett continued. "It's different, but in a way it's similar to when you first came to live with us. Remember?"

"I don't know how you guys put up with me." Separated from Jesse for the first time, and lost, angry and consumed with guilt over not being able to look out for his brother like he'd promised, Cal had spent his first few months with the Barrett family only speaking when he had to and spending most of his time outside of school in his bedroom. Looking back, he now grasped that he'd also feared letting himself be happy, afraid that new sense of safety, security and acceptance would vanish almost like a dream. However, Mr. and Mrs. Barrett hadn't given up on him, and their two sons had followed their example.

"I knew there was a good boy underneath everything. One who had the makings of a good man, and I was proven right." She squeezed his arm. "You needed to feel safe before letting us see the real you, and that no matter what, we wouldn't let you down. Unconditional love and feeling special. That's the same as anybody needs."

"Well, you and your family sure gave me that and more." Had they seen the "real" Cal? Back then, he hadn't known who he was. Still didn't, if he was honest with himself, but it was something he was trying to figure out.

Cal turned over what she'd said in his mind. He wasn't a baby when he'd come to live with the Barretts. He'd had lots of history, most of it sad, but they'd accepted all of him. A big part of the man he'd become was down to their influence. And Alana. He'd wanted to be a good person for her. To be good enough to deserve her.

"Now you're widowed, it must be a big change for you as well." One he'd understood in theory, but the true realization hit him.

"It sure is, but since I've never been the kind to mope around, there's nothing for it but to get on with things." Despite holding sadness, her voice was also determined.

"That's always been your way." Donna Barrett was one of the strongest people Cal knew. Before retiring, she'd worked as an ER nurse at the local hospital, and while her family was her priority, she was also one of the first to step up to help anyone in need…including him. Although at the time she and her husband had planned to foster a younger child rather than a teen, they'd still welcomed him into their home.

"Getting on with things is your way, too, so it'll help you find your path. Give it time, and who knows? You might be surprised how things turn out. Even with Alana. You were over eighteen and no longer in my care, so what happened between you two at the end was none of my business. Same with why you really left town. I had to be content with you coming to say goodbye and wanting to keep in touch. It's the nature of being a foster parent, I'm afraid." As they passed the corner with a sign for the library, she gave Cal a sharp but still loving look. "Keep the good memories, sure, but you have to let go of the past to make a new future for yourself. We've all done and said things we regret, but it's no good thinking about how we can change them because we can't. You can only own up to them and do the best you can in the present."

Which wasn't easy, but maybe that was the point.

CHAPTER EIGHT

"GOOD CHOICE. THIS ONE'LL look great on your balcony." At Rustic Hearts several days after the library party, Alana picked up the small tree the customer had chosen and carried it by the trunk as her dad had taught her. "Do you need anything else? Lights, ornaments or a wreath? We've got fresh-made wreaths as well as artificial." With both hands holding the tree, she inclined her chin toward the store, where Maddie was on her own. Cal had taken a few hours off, which, given all the extra time he worked, was fine, but it meant Alana and Maddie were covering the tree lot and store between them.

"I think I'm set." The woman smiled. "I don't have as much space in my apartment as I did in the house, but I still have more than forty years' worth of decorations. I've downsized everything else but somehow...well, those Christmas ornaments are special."

"I understand." Alana was thirty-odd years younger than the silver-haired woman, but she couldn't imagine letting go of any of her cherished holiday ornaments. As she followed the woman to her car, Cal's truck pulled into the lot. "Here?" she asked and then eased the tree into the back of the woman's vehicle where she indicated.

She needed to focus on the customer, not Cal. However, in the past few days, she could hardly think of anything but him and that mistletoe kiss. As he parked and got out of his truck, Alana's heartbeat sped up. He'd arranged his time off through Ted and when she'd seen it on the schedule, she'd hoped it was nothing serious. However, when she'd arrived here earlier, the place felt empty without him.

Which was ridiculous. He'd only been at Rustic Hearts two weeks. How had he become a part of things so fast? And why did Alana miss him when he wasn't here? It wasn't as if they spent all their working hours together. He was usually out in the tree lot while she was in the store, but along with those sparks of attraction she kept trying to suppress, there was something about having him around that made her feel safe, comfortable and protected. Which was also ridiculous because she was an independent, self-sufficient adult woman. She didn't need Cal or any other man to be complete.

"Happy holidays." She waved as the woman drove off.

"Sorry I'm late." Cal came over to Alana as she walked back across the parking lot.

"It's not a problem." She glanced up at him. She was petite—"short" as her brothers said—and Cal was close to six feet, but it never felt like he towered over her. Instead, he'd always been caring while also giving her space, most of all to be herself. Together, they'd made a good team. "I hope everything's okay." She wouldn't pry. She was only asking as a concerned employer.

"It's fine. I had an appointment. It took longer than I expected." He paused as they entered the tree-lot yard, which, unusually, was empty of customers.

"'Bye, guys. No more customers in here." Maddie poked her head out the door of the store. "My mom let me borrow the car to drive home by myself today."

"Be safe." Alana cared about all the staff, but Maddie, whom she'd once babysat, was extra special.

"I will." The teen grinned and rolled her eyes.

"What?" Alana turned back to Cal.

"You sounded like a mom." He rubbed his gloved hands together.

Alana fiddled with the fringed end of her scarf. She wasn't a mom, but it was possible to care about a child or teen without being their parent. Just like how she was with her nieces and nephews. "I've known Maddie since she was born. Her family lives on my street."

"I shouldn't have teased." Cal's expression sobered. "I always liked how you cared about people. Animals, too."

Alana didn't have a pet, but it wasn't because she didn't want one. Between her work at the library and Hansen Farms, her life was busy and she was hardly at home. However, maybe that was an excuse. A cat wouldn't be high-maintenance, and there were lots of older cats who needed a loving owner. She shivered as a gust of wind seemed to go right through her.

"Hey, you're freezing." Cal's eyes darkened with concern. "When did you last go inside?"

"A while ago." Alana shrugged. "Until now it's been busy." Despite her down-filled parka, snow pants and heavy sweater, she *was* cold but hadn't recognized it.

"Let's go indoors." He put out his arm as if to draw her close, then dropped it and took a step back. "A hot drink will warm you up." All of a sudden, his voice was overly hearty.

"Good idea." She followed Cal as he went ahead and held open the store's side door for her. Warm air hit Alana's face, and she unwound her scarf, and took off and hung up her outer gear.

Male and female work colleagues, even if they were friendly, didn't hug each other. Cal had done the right thing so why did she feel such an unexpected sense of loss?

"Take a seat." Cal waved her toward the stool behind the cash counter. "I'll make cocoa. You've likely been on your feet for ages. I know what working in that lot's like. It's not only the cold, but wind. You get chilled to your bones and need to take regular breaks." Brushing away her attempt to protest, he went into the staff-room kitchen.

Listening to the sound of cupboards and the fridge door opening and closing, followed by a clatter of crockery, Alana relaxed into the stool's cushioned backrest. She'd gotten colder than she realized, and after rushing around all day and since she'd arrived at Rustic Hearts, it was nice to sit and take a break. She couldn't let herself relax too much, though. Since she was with Cal, she had to keep her guard up.

In only a few minutes, he returned carrying a tray, two mugs patterned with Christmas trees and a can of whipped cream.

"I couldn't find marshmallows." He took the lid off the whipped cream. "Like before?"

Alana nodded. "Maddie texted me we'd run out of marshmallows, but I forgot to buy more." She watched as he sprayed the sweet treat atop one of the steaming mugs of cocoa. It was a small thing, but he remembered she liked hot chocolate with marshmallows *and* cream. Did he remember other things, too? Thinking about that kiss, Maddie's text had slipped her mind so she'd neglected to stop at the grocery store on her way here. "Thanks." She cradled her cold hands around the warmth of the mug.

He touched his mug against hers. "Cheers."

She echoed his toast. There was a new lightness, almost playfulness between them, which was welcome.

"So…that appointment I had." He leaned on the counter across from her. "Before your dad mentioned it when I was at your folks' place during the blizzard, I'd already looked in to certifying as an auto mechanic but I'd only checked out a few websites. Nothing serious. Today I went to see a career adviser at that trade school over the mountain. He's an older guy. Really knows his stuff and he's also worked with lots of people transitioning out of the military." Cal was usually a man of few words but now his words tumbled out in a rapid stream. "He seemed to think I had a real shot at having a good career. It wouldn't take a lot of time to get qualified, either."

"That sounds great." Alana's heart swelled.

"People always need to have their vehicles fixed. You liked working at the garage here."

"Yeah, I did." He looked down and then drank cocoa. "It feels weird to be starting over in my mid-thirties, though."

"Lots of folks change direction." Alana made her voice encouraging. "The library's career workshops are always full and it's not only teenagers. Earlier this year, there was a woman who wasn't happy as a lawyer who's now retraining as a chef. You wouldn't be making that big a leap."

"I guess not." Cal shook his head. "I don't mean to burden you with my worries. They're my problems."

"It's fine." Alana's breath stuttered. What other problems did he have beyond work? "You weren't burdening me at all." She'd had the same kind of conversation with Maddie and several of the other high-school students who worked here, but questions about what someone wanted to be when they grew up didn't stop when they were an adult. "Instead of starting over, maybe you're restarting, shifting gears." Where was a customer when she needed one? They'd all arrived at once, and now, nothing. She couldn't even blame the weather as it was cold but clear. "Everyone deserves a second chance."

"Do they?" He drained his mug and set it aside.

"Well, with work, sure." Her heart thudded and her face was hotter than the cocoa merited. She needed to redirect this conversation fast.

"When I kissed you, it wasn't like I thought it would be. I mean it was great but I—"

"It was a joke." That's what she kept telling herself, unwilling to consider any other possibility. "We were under the mistletoe." A decoration she'd taken down and put in the bottom drawer of her filing cabinet as soon as she'd gotten to work this morning.

"That's how it started out, sure. A joke." Cal gave a short laugh. "So if I kissed you again, it would still be one?"

"You're not making sense." How had they gotten here? Alana felt as if she'd fallen into a fast-flowing river, or was skiing down a black run after only ever being on the gentle bunny hill.

"Aren't I?" He leaned across the counter, closer to her. "There's still something between us, Lanie."

"There isn't. We're working together, briefly, nothing more." Yet she didn't move away or tell him not to call her by the nickname. Instead, she moved closer still, and with barely a second's hesitation, her soft lips met his firm ones.

Heart-melting and intimate, it was everything a kiss should be. And this time it was for real.

It would only end in heartbreak. Another one. Yet, Cal couldn't resist kissing Alana. Sweet kisses that, while making him remember their past, also made him think about the future. With her.

"We can't." Alana was the first to pull away. "It's wrong. You, me." She stumbled to her feet and put a hand to her mouth as if brushing away those kisses, which had rocked and reset Cal's world.

"Even if it feels right?" Cal blinked, briefly dazzled by the twinkling lights from a nearby miniature tree. He was here in the store and no more than a minute had passed, but everything, at least for him, had changed.

"It doesn't matter." Alana gathered up their empty cocoa mugs, the tray and whipped cream. "Even if there *is* still something between us, which is doubtful, it's nothing more than casual attraction. It can't go anywhere. *We* can't go anywhere." Was that the sheen of tears in the depths of her brown eyes?

"Because you're afraid?" Cal tried to steady his breathing.

"Even if I am, don't you think I have good reason to be?" She held the loaded tray in front of her, the barrier between them going up again, this time maybe higher than ever.

"I didn't mean to hurt you, but I had to leave town." He paused. "I'd like it if we could try to be friends. I miss your friendship." Alana hadn't just been his love, she'd also been his best friend, the one who'd gotten the parts of himself he'd chosen to share. His hopes, fears and dreams.

But was it part of the problem that he'd never thought he could share all of himself with her? Had holding parts of himself back held the two of them back, and ultimately led to the end of their relationship? Although he'd dated occasionally over the years, he'd never been fully himself with any other woman, either.

Closed off. Guarded. What are you hiding?

Cal had always tried to laugh off what past girlfriends had said about him, but were they right? Along with awareness, there was the sting of discomfort.

"Friends." Her voice wobbled. "I don't know." Vehicle headlights cut across the store's front windows, accompanied by engine noise. "It'd be hard."

"So? Us working so closely together is already hard." He tried to crack a teasing smile but even to himself it fell short.

"It is." The engine noise stopped and a car

door slammed. "It's also confusing, but we'll only be working together for a few more weeks."

Was she trying to convince Cal or herself? His stomach dropped. A few more weeks. It wasn't enough, but it was all he had.

"Hi, Alana." A ruddy-faced man with a fringe of white hair beneath a dark knit hat came into the store, stamping his feet on the mat. "Cal Paquette. I heard you were back in town." He came toward them with a genial smile. "Fred Sinclair, editor of *The Strawberry Pond Gazette*."

Cal returned the man's greeting. He remembered Mr. Sinclair, since as a roving reporter he'd often covered high-school football games and other events. Apart from a few freelancers, Fred *was* the local paper and involved in everything that went on in the town.

"I'm here to pick up the wreath my wife ordered and take some pictures for next week's edition." He glanced around the store. "Candid shots. Rustic Hearts is almost as much a part of the holiday season as Santa." His gaze swiveled back to Cal. "Sorry I missed you at the library's party. I heard you were a big hit. Say, I could interview you—folks would be interested in your life in the military. Local-boy-makes-good feature and—"

"No." The word came out more sharply than

Cal intended. "Thanks, but I'm not that interesting." He tried to smile.

"Well, you only have to say the word." Fred smiled again as Alana disappeared with the tray and presumably to get the wreath he'd mentioned. "How's the farm's entry for the tractor holiday parade of lights coming along?"

"We're working on it." Ted and a few of the other guys had talked about the parade and the lights they planned to use were stacked in a separate area of one of the barns. Like so many other things here, the annual event was a fixture in town life, and Cal had gone to it with the Barrett family.

"You could reprise your role as Santa Claus. That'd be a thrill for the kids." Fred had always been a talker and he was in full flow, warming to his theme.

"Me being Santa was a one-off." Although playing the jolly old man and seeing the awe and wonder on the children's faces had been more fun than Cal expected. When he'd been Santa for military parties, it wasn't the same. *Because Alana wasn't there.* And he hadn't been helping her. "Saving the day" as Anne Sullivan called it.

"Here's the wreath." Alana was back, almost hidden by a large circle of pine boughs covered in red tartan ribbon bows, bells, red, white and silver balls and, in the center, a small wooden nutcracker soldier ornament. "I hope your wife feels better soon. There's lots of viruses going around."

"There sure are, but your mom's chicken soup was better for Linda than any medicine. Really perked her up and eased her coughing. Tell your mom so for me, won't you?" After taking out a camera from the bag slung over one shoulder, Fred snapped a few photos of the wreath. "Let's see you, Alana. Don't be shy. Get in there, too, Cal." He waved them into place.

Cal didn't like having his picture taken. It reminded him too much of having those photos taken of him and Jesse when they'd been available for adoption. It had turned out to be a waste of time because most families wanted younger kids. And while an older couple had considered adopting Cal, they only wanted one boy, not two. Especially when the second one was Jesse.

A kid who'd already been caught shoplifting twice and, only the week before, breaking a window in the school gym. On purpose rather than an accident. Instead of being contrite, Jesse had seemed almost proud of himself, and Cal hadn't known how to help. And the day the two of them had had their photos taken, Jesse had acted out, and Cal had wanted to be somewhere, anywhere, else. How could he smile like the social worker wanted when he was trying to keep his brother in line?

Unless it was with Alana, back then, whenever someone wanted to get Cal in a picture, either by himself or as part of a group, he remembered that earlier time and tried to make himself scarce. However, there was something about Fred's good-natured cajoling that was impossible to resist.

"There you are." Fred nodded approval and took a few more pictures. "Now, set down the wreath so I can get one of the two of you behind the counter. You've got a nice background there with the tree and hanging snowflake decorations. Smile. That's great."

As Fred packed up his camera, and Alana wrapped the wreath, the two of them chatting about the tractor parade and other holiday plans, Cal went out to the tree lot. Hopefully, the cold, fresh air and moving trees from a nearby field to the yard would clear his head.

If Alana hadn't moved away, he'd have wanted to keep kissing her. If Fred Sinclair hadn't arrived, Cal would've also wanted to keep talking to her. Try to break down that barrier she'd put up again. No matter how uncomfortable and awkward things were between them, they also somehow still felt unexpectedly right.

And he had no idea what to do about it.

CHAPTER NINE

As Alana rearranged the library's book display that celebrated December holidays, she admitted that she'd lied to Cal yesterday and herself as well. There *was* still something between them. That wasn't in doubt at all. It was also something important, not casual, no matter how much she might try to pretend otherwise. Second chances weren't only for work. Stories were full of second chances, romances especially.

Her hands trembled as she tucked books into place, the cheerful covers with their snowy vistas, trees decked in holiday lights, twinkling stars and cozy small-town scenes looking a lot like Strawberry Pond. However, fiction was an escape, not real life. Although she couldn't stop thinking about those kisses with Cal, she'd be foolish to get so caught up in the magic of her favorite season that she let herself think about having a second chance with *him*.

She'd also be foolish to think that any attraction between them was more than the dying embers of what they'd once shared. He'd left town so suddenly that she hadn't had any real closure. Whatever was happening between them now would give her that finality. Simple. Except, it wasn't.

"Morning. It's a cold one, isn't it?" she greeted Anne Sullivan, who'd come into the library, the first of the Strawberry Pond Knitters to arrive for the group's regular weekly meeting. "Go right upstairs. The room's set up for you."

"Thank you, dear." Anne's merry smile brightened the gray, overcast day. "There's snow in those clouds, don't you think?"

"I expect so." Alana looked out one of the library's windows. The gloomy weather matched her mood. While the rest of her shift with Cal yesterday evening had been uneventful, and he'd spent most of it out in the tree lot, the conversation Fred Sinclair had interrupted wasn't over. How could she be friends with Cal? The idea didn't make sense, but that didn't mean she didn't miss his friendship. There was still a giant, Cal-shaped hole in her life where their once-close friendship had been and maybe always would be.

"Alana?" Anne set her purse, knitting bag and a tin decorated with a horse and sleigh on a nearby table. "Are you all right?" Her eyebrows drew together and when she took off her winter hat, her silver-gray hair settled around her face in soft waves.

"Yes, of course." Alana produced a professional smile. "I had a few minutes to spare so I got the coffee brewing for you and water jugs filled."

"You always look after us so well. I brought the cookies this week." Anne indicated the tin. "I'll set some aside for you. I made gingerbread puffs from my grandmother's recipe. They always are a treat."

"I remember." Like so many other things in Strawberry Pond, Anne Sullivan's gingerbread puffs were a local tradition. The recipe was a closely guarded secret, only shared with family, which made them even more special. "I look forward to having one with my lunch."

"You do that." Anne nodded. "But you look tired. Those aren't only bags, but veritable suitcases under your eyes. Are you working too hard?"

"It's a busy time of year." People making personal comments was another part of small-town life, but with Anne it came from a place of concern, not criticism.

"As I tell Laura, it's not good to be too busy. Josie as well. You girls need to slow down. The holiday season's to be enjoyed, not gotten through."

Josie and Laura were in their forties, and along with Alana they weren't "girls," but Anne had watched the three of them grow up. For that reason, Alana supposed it was natural the older woman would think they were still youthful.

"Yes, ma'am." This time she gave Anne a real smile.

"Oh, go on with you." Anne chuckled. "You're as good as family. I worry over you."

"I know and I appreciate it." Anne was family to Alana as well, although unlike Laura, her niece, Alana wasn't close enough to be given the recipe for those melt-in-the-mouth gingerbread puffs.

A thud reverberated from the outside book-return slot, followed by a piercing meow.

"What on earth was that?" Anne glanced around.

"Usually books being returned but it sounds like a cat." Alana went toward the slot, which opened into a crate in the rear office, Anne following. "It was a cat. *In here.*" Two green eyes in a small, black-and-brown-striped face peered up at her from the crate of books that had been dropped off when the library was closed and Alana hadn't checked back in yet. "Hey, little fellow."

Anne gasped. "Of all the… Why wouldn't whoever left this animal here take it to a shelter? Since there aren't any windows or doors on this side of the building, I'll go around the front and—"

"Whoever left it didn't want to be seen." Thanks to a quirk of the building's Victorian architecture, the book-return area was tucked in a sheltered alcove that wasn't visible from either the nearby parking lot, or walkway leading to Main Street. "It'd be easy for someone to slip a cat into this slot undetected and leave."

"That's true enough." Anne huffed. "I suppose we must be grateful they didn't choose to drop it at night. If it had gotten trapped, the darling could've frozen to death."

Alana held out one hand for the cat to sniff, and its delicate whiskers quivered. "You aren't a baby, but you aren't very old, either." Hansen Farms had barn and house cats so she knew about felines. "Come here. I won't hurt you." She lifted up the cat and cradled it.

"Somebody must have cared for this animal. See here?" Anne rummaged in the crate piled with books, and took out a red fleece blanket, several tins of cat food and a worn, green plush fish toy from a brown paper grocery bag.

Still cuddling the cat, who, upon closer inspection, was female, Alana sighed. Even though Strawberry Pond was relatively prosperous, her recent shift at the food pantry was a reminder that their small town also had a lot of people experiencing hard times. “Perhaps the owner can no longer afford a pet after losing their job, or care for one after getting sick. Maybe they’re too embarrassed to admit to anyone that they’re struggling. It could even be someone from out of town who wanted a safe place to drop their pet.”

Anne shook her head, and her face softened with sympathy. “The poor soul.”

Alana fondled the cat’s ears, and the animal rubbed its face against her hand. She couldn’t stay back here. Although the library wasn’t busy, with only a few patrons browsing the shelves and others using computers, she still needed to be available if anyone needed help. “Let’s take a closer look at you out by the circulation desk.” Carrying the cat, she continued to soothe it. “You’re a beauty. Yes, you are, sweetheart.”

“A cat in the library?” Josie’s grams, Martha Ryan, had arrived alongside several other members of the knitting group. All of them, and most of the other patrons, made a beeline for Alana.

“Only temporarily. None of you are allergic, I hope?” She drew the cat closer and explained what had happened.

“Not a bit.” Martha answered for the group as everyone cooed over Alana’s unexpected find. “Isn’t there a history of cats living in libraries?”

“Going back to the Middle Ages, but not so

much nowadays because of health-and-safety regulations." Alana's regular health-and-safety training was thorough, but it hadn't covered what to do when finding a cat in the book return.

"What a love." Martha Ryan tickled the cat under her chin and was rewarded with a throaty purr. "I guess it wouldn't do any good to advertise? Not having been left the way she was."

"Not likely, but I'll make some posters and put them up here in the library, at the town hall and elsewhere, just in case," Alana said. "I'll also call Fred Sinclair. It'll make an interesting story for him in the paper."

Hopefully, a cute cat and such a heartwarming, but also heartbreaking, story would also divert attention from that picture Fred had taken of her and Cal at Rustic Hearts. It made sense he'd want pictures of store staff, but if only he'd either stuck with Alana alone or arrived when Maddie and the others were there, too. Still, it was lucky he hadn't turned up a few minutes earlier or he'd have caught Alana and Cal kissing. That would have been a much bigger and even more unwelcome story to broadcast to the town.

"Sorry, what did you say?" She turned back to Anne.

"I'll take this sweet girl straight to the animal rescue and get her settled. You can't keep her here." Anne studied Alana and then held out her arms for the cat.

"No, don't." Alana's voice wobbled as she held the now drowsy cat tighter. "I mean, of course, I can't keep a cat here, but don't take her to the rescue."

"No?" Anne quirked an eyebrow.

"No." Alana's voice was firm, decisive. "If this cat's owner doesn't have a change of heart and turn up, I'll adopt her myself. In the meantime, if the vet says she's okay, I'll foster her. I'd already been thinking about getting a cat, so why not this one?"

"Why not, indeed?" As Anne smiled, a shaft of sunshine filtered into the library, bathing the cat in warm, golden light.

"Yes, my mind's made up." What better time than Christmas for Alana to open her heart to an animal in need? She couldn't think about Cal right now, but she could think about a pet. And when he left town again, she'd still have this sweet girl.

Advertising for the owner was a formality. So was taking the cat to the vet for a health check. In Alana's heart, she and this cat already belonged with each other.

IN THE MIDDLE OF the afternoon, Cal parked a Hansen Farms pickup truck in front of the town green on Strawberry Pond's Main Street, got out and pulled a tree wrapped in netting from the bed. Rustic Hearts didn't usually make deliveries, but when the mayor's office had called in a last-minute order for an extra spruce for the town's outdoor carol service, Ted had made an exception.

"Over here." A burly, middle-aged man in a black parka hurried toward Cal. "The guys are all ready for you." He gestured to several younger men in yellow safety vests who followed him and took the tree from Cal. "The Hansens always come through for us. The mayor said to tell you she's grateful."

"Not a problem." Cal returned the man's friendly smile. "We're here to help, but Ted was surprised you needed another tree. He thought the first order would be enough."

"It would've been except for a snowplow driver accelerating forward when he should have gone backward." The man shook his head. "Least he only flattened one tree and not the whole row. Still, you have to expect the unexpected, don't you?"

Cal's life had been one unexpected thing after another. Even joining the military hadn't been planned, but what else could he have done? Navy discipline and routine had been the making of

Jesse, so at least in that sense, Cal's sacrifice had been worthwhile.

"Give us a call if you need anything else." He made himself focus on the man from the mayor's office. Thinking about what might have been was pointless. "Happy holidays."

Turning back to the truck, he stopped at the sight of Alana coming out of the pet store several doors down the street. Her arms were laden with shopping bags and what looked like a small, soft-sided animal carrier. "Hey." He darted over to meet her. "Let me give you a hand."

"Thanks." She handed over the bags but kept hold of the carrier.

"Where are you headed?" He fell into step beside her.

"To my house. I took a spur-of-the-moment half day off from the library." Her pink cheeks, and how her eyes sparkled beneath the fuzzy white hat she'd worn the night of the tree lighting, made Cal feel whole somehow. "Don't worry, I'll be at Rustic Hearts later."

"If it's a problem, I can manage without you." Along with that feeling of wholeness, which radiated from the tips of his toes to the top of his head, the irony of what he'd said struck him. He could manage without Alana at Rustic Hearts by messaging Ted, who'd ask one of the other staff to help. He'd also managed without Alana for the past fifteen years. But did he *want* to manage without her? He shook his head, mentally rebuking himself for his foolishness. Even if he and Alana could be friends, she couldn't be part of his life in any other meaningful way. He'd hurt her too much, and a few kisses wouldn't change that. "I meant that maybe Maddie could stay late or we could get someone else. If you want to go to the carol service?" He nodded to the guys putting the tree in place alongside the others.

"My folks are going, but I already said I'd work so I will." Her tone didn't brook any argument. "I took the afternoon off because…" She hesitated and then raised the carrier with a flourish. "I'm adopting a cat."

"A cat?" A pair of brilliant green eyes stared at Cal warily through a narrow mesh panel in one of the carrier's sides.

"It's unexpected. Kind of a long story."

There was that word again. For Cal, the unexpected was rarely good, but from Alana's face, this cat sure was. As they stopped by the truck, Cal opened the passenger door. "Come on. I'll drive you home. You said you usually walk to work?"

"Yes, but don't you have to be somewhere?" She hesitated.

"Ted or any of your family or friends would insist on driving you home, wouldn't they?"

Cal tried not to show how much he wanted to do something nice for her. "Besides, it's cold and your place can't be far out of my way." Except for a few outlying subdivisions with newer homes, Strawberry Pond was compact.

"Okay, I don't want this sweetie to get a chill. Isn't she precious?" Alana made a kissing noise, and Cal's heart almost turned over. "I've just been to the vet clinic and Trevor, that's Laura's husband, remember? He checked her over and said she's healthy. No microchip or other identification, though. Since it's the holiday season, I'm calling her Holly. Don't you think it suits her?"

As Alana scrambled into the truck, the cat continued to stare at Cal, its intense green gaze unnerving. Was Holly checking him out, making sure he was good enough for her new owner? No, she couldn't be. She was only a cat.

"Where to?" Moments later, Cal settled in the driver's seat and started the truck. He was taking Alana home like anyone would do. It was friendly, nothing more. He nodded as she gave him directions to one of the streets in the older part of town. "So you said adopting this cat was 'kind of a long story.' Fill me in." If they talked about the cat, they wouldn't risk veering toward more personal topics.

After Alana had recounted finding Holly in

the book-return box, Cal darted another sideways glance at her. With the two of them and the cat carrier, the truck's cab seemed smaller than usual and especially close quarters. And as they drove along the snow-covered streets, Cal turning where Alana indicated, it was as if they were in a cozy bubble separate from the rest of the world. "You did a good thing. If Fred writes a story, and Holly's previous owner sees it, they'll know you're giving their pet the best life you can."

"I hope so. I made some *found-cat* posters and put them up in a few places, but I don't expect any response." Alana's voice caught. "I can't imagine someone being that desperate."

Cal pressed his lips together. He hadn't had a pet as a kid, so it wasn't one of the things they'd had to give up, but his mom had been desperate in other ways. Only now as an adult did he truly understand how hard it must have been for her not to be able to feed her kids. To rely on the kindness of others for everyday essentials most everyone else took for granted. To know that she'd have to leave those kids for someone else to care for.

The image of how she'd clasped his hand tight that last day, her dark eyes pleading, and then what she'd said.

Promise me, Cal? You'll look out for Jesse? I'm counting on you.

He'd promised, but at what cost?

As he pulled into Alana's street, a tree-lined avenue Cal remembered, she pointed to her property, a two-story wooden house with an upstairs gable. Painted off-white with green trim and a small porch out front, it was a typical New England home. Unpretentious and, from the evergreen wreath, a Rustic Hearts design, on the door, to the three ornamental light-up reindeer on the lawn, it was also welcoming. A house that invited a person to come in and stay a while.

"Here we are." For the short journey, Alana had kept her arms wrapped around the cat carrier.

Cal shifted and looked at her. "That cat, Holly..." He swallowed the lump of emotion that threatened. "She's lucky you didn't send her to a rescue."

"I couldn't." In the midst of unbuckling her seat belt, Alana gave him a quick smile. "I know the local rescue's great, but it's also sad. All those animals looking for their forever home and family."

He nodded. "It's a lot like being in foster care. You're always hoping to find a place where you belong and feel wanted. That someone'll maybe even adopt you so you have a real family and don't have to keep moving." Cal stopped himself. He never talked about that time in his life, but the words had come out almost unbidden. "Sorry. I didn't mean—"

"It's okay." Alana's voice was soft. "I mean, it's not okay how your life was. How could it be? I never knew."

"I never told you because…well, I didn't want to make a big thing of it. I got lucky with Mr. and Mrs. Barrett. Foster parents do their best, but it's hard for everyone, you know?" His gaze drifted to Holly, who rested her chin on her paws, and then to the three reindeer on the lawn. A mom, dad and calf. *A family.* His stomach knotted.

"I can't know because I've never experienced what you have but if you ever need to talk or—"

"It's fine. I'm fine." If he kept telling himself that it would be true. Those emotions he'd buried deep had only come up because it was the holiday season. Working at Rustic Hearts, he was smack in the middle of holiday celebrations and couldn't ignore them like he usually did. Many people had mixed feelings about Christmas. Lots felt lonely at this time of year as well. Like Mrs. Barrett, and she was the reason he'd returned to Strawberry Pond in the first place.

"All right." Alana studied him with the same intensity Holly had. As if she could see beneath Cal's brittle outer shell, one he'd constructed to keep himself safe, through to his soul and the essence of who he was. "See you later at work?"

"Sure thing." After gathering the shopping bags, he helped her and Holly out of the truck, and walked them to the front door of the cozy house, keeping his eyes fixed on his steel-toe winter work boots.

It wasn't his home, and Alana wasn't his family. She'd rescued him once, a stray foster kid desperate to be loved, but he wasn't that person anymore. He didn't need rescuing by anyone, especially her.

CHAPTER TEN

"Do you want the one with gingerbread, Mrs. Claus or red and green tartan?" A few days later, in her snug kitchen with its white café curtains and functional wood center island, Alana held out holiday aprons for Josie and Laura to choose from. They took it in turns to host their annual Christmas cookie baking evening, and the last time Alana had done so she'd lived in a rented apartment. Now, she was making memories in her own home.

"Laura's still a newlywed. She should have Mrs. Claus." Josie gave them a dimpled smile while choosing the gingerbread-patterned one for herself. "I'm an old, married woman."

"Hardly. What are you and Heath doing to celebrate your first anniversary? This year's sure gone fast." As Alana covered her black leggings and snowman-themed sweater with the tartan apron, she made herself smile in return. It was wonderful both her friends were happily married, but although the three of them still spent time together, sometimes Alana couldn't help feeling like the odd one out.

"Since our anniversary's so close to Christmas, we're going out for dinner on the day and then away for a weekend in January. Grams and Gramps are always happy to stay with the girls."

"Your grandparents must miss living with you." Laura propped her phone against a utensil holder decorated with reindeer. Unlike Alana and Josie, who used family holiday recipe books, Laura kept her recipes online. While a digital collection was undoubtedly neater and more efficient, Alana couldn't give up her battered notebook, which didn't only hold instructions for making Christmas treats, but also contained multigenerational seasonal memories.

"Maybe, but Grams and Gramps are only next door. They drop in all the time. If anything it's hard for me to get used to the idea that the farmhouse kitchen is now 'mine' rather than Grams's domain." After choosing a holiday music playlist, Josie glanced around. "Where's Holly?"

"I left her asleep in my bedroom. You can meet her later. She's shy." Alana held out her own phone to show Josie and Laura pictures. In only a few days, she'd taken plenty of photos of her new cat and had become one of the pet store's best customers.

"That article Fred wrote about you adopting Holly was really heartwarming." Swaying in time to "Rockin' Around the Christmas Tree," a seasonal favorite that Josie called their "cookie-baking anthem," Laura mixed dry ingredients for sugar cookies. "I bumped into him at the diner at lunchtime, and he said the story's boosted donations at both the animal rescue and food pantry."

"That's great, but I hope that whoever dropped off Holly is able to get the help they must need. Nobody responded to any of my lost-cat posters or the messages I posted in the town's social-media groups." The backs of Alana's eyes stung. Holly hadn't been part of her life for long but having to give up the cat would break her heart. How much worse it must be for Holly's previous owner, who hadn't seen any other option but to leave their pet in the book return and hope someone would care for her.

Josie patted Alana's hand. "Like I tell my girls, even though we can't help everyone, we can still make a difference. Lottie's organizing a holiday food drive with friends from her figure-skating class, and Bella's doing extra chores to earn money for the animal rescue."

Laura nodded approval. "Good for them. Even small, individual actions can make a big impact. I'm working with the town business association to see how we can better support our local charities. You finding Holly where you did was a wake-up call for all of us. If folks are struggling, they need to know where and how they can reach out without being embarrassed or feeling judged."

As a kid, had Cal felt embarrassed and judged? Alana couldn't stop thinking about what he'd said about being in foster care and having somebody want him. Why hadn't he ever talked to her about those feelings? She'd thought she'd known him but maybe she hadn't. Or not some of the most important parts. As a girl, she'd been open with her emotions but she'd grown up in a close and loving family where they talked to each other.

Cal hadn't. *And that made all the difference.*

As she measured flour to make the dough for candy-cane cookies, a recipe she'd first learned as a small girl standing on a stool beside her mom in the farm kitchen, awareness rolled over her. On the surface, Cal had been fun and easygoing, but that was only the outside. What hurts and fears had he hidden behind that external image?

"On a lighter topic, while Holly was on the front page of *The Strawberry Pond Gazette*, we also spotted another interesting picture several pages in." Beside her at the kitchen island, Laura nudged Alana's elbow.

"The one of you and Cal at Rustic Hearts," Josie added.

"You know what Fred's like." Alana made her tone casual. She hadn't needed Josie to describe the picture Laura meant. Ted had cut the piece out of the paper and pinned it to the staff notice board at the tree farm, so Alana saw it almost daily. "He's always looking for something he calls newsworthy. Cal and me were at work, and Fred came to pick up a wreath his wife ordered. No big deal."

"Really?" Her sugar cookies forgotten, Laura lolled against the counter and gave Alana a teasing grin. "The fact you said it wasn't a 'big deal' makes me think it might be."

"We know you well." Josie gestured with one of Alana's snowflake-patterned spatulas. "Fred likes to take pictures, and he also has a knack for catching people in awkward situations. He sure caught Heath and me like that one time." Her light chuckle was like the tinkle of a bell. "But you and Cal looked…not only cozy but somehow right together."

"You did," Laura said. "Is Cal the reason you've never settled down with anyone else?"

"Of course not." Alana shrugged. "I've never met the right man, that's all." Discomfort needled her. Could she have had feelings for Cal all these years, and was that why no other man had ever measured up? And was that why she'd cut the article and picture of the two of them out of her own copy of *The Strawberry Pond Gazette* and tucked it into her memory box at the back of her bottom dresser drawer?

Alana had packed that box away after she and Cal had broken up and hadn't looked at it in years. To be truthful, she hadn't looked inside the box now, either, only shoved the clipping in on top, but it had nevertheless sparked other memories.

"What if Cal wasn't the right guy then but he could be now?" Josie cracked one of the eggs she'd brought with her, laid by one of her own hens. "You're both adults, and fifteen years is a long time."

It was a very long time so why was Alana still so churned up? Anxious about seeing Cal and then awkward when she did. Hyperaware of everything about him from the small white scar in the center of his chin, an old football injury, to his crisp, clean scent when he came into the store after spending a few hours in the tree lot. His crooked, almost hesitant smile and those changeable gray eyes. The tenderness with which he'd looked at Alana before they kissed. As if she was still special to him.

"Cal's also supercute. Boyish but manly." Laura's slow smile was impish. "He may have left the military, but he still has that man-in-uniform vibe. He's strong, too. You should've seen how he lifted the big Christmas tree I chose. As if it weighed nothing at all."

"Oh, my." Josie batted her eyelashes and joined in the teasing.

Alana saw Cal lifting Christmas trees most days of the week, and, yes, she'd noticed how effortless he made it look. But he was a member of her family's staff. Anyone would do the same. It wasn't like she was being obvious or inappropriate.

"Stop it." Alana felt her face get warm. "You two are married, remember?"

"We are, but *you* aren't," Laura said. "Cal's so kind to Mrs. Barrett. She's friends with Trevor's mom, and my mother-in-law says Mrs. Barrett's always singing Cal's praises."

"We care about you, Alana," Josie added. "We also want you to be happy, and Cal seems like a good man. Back then, the two of you were kids. We've all done stuff when we were younger we regret. But like I also tell my girls—and myself—we have to learn from our mistakes."

"It's the only way." Laura put an arm around Alana. "Understanding I was wrong is why I *am* happily married."

"Me, too," Josie said, joining the hug. "Maybe

it sounds trite, but the past's gone. Oh, keep the good memories, but the rest? Let it go."

"What if I can't?" Alana swallowed. Her friends wanted to help, and she loved them for it, but there were some problems even her closest friends couldn't fix. Those problems were on her.

"Well, that's a choice, too." Laura's expression was serious. "Cal hasn't been in your life for years and you've done fine. When he leaves town again, everything will go back to the way it was before." She paused. "If you want it to."

Things couldn't go back to how they were before because Cal's return to Strawberry Pond, and the two of them spending time together and kissing each other meant Alana wasn't the same. In the sudden silence, John Legend's rich, silky voice singing "This Christmas" wrapped around the kitchen and Alana's heart.

It would be a bad idea to let herself fall in love with Cal again. He was only in town for the holidays, and after traveling the world in the navy, could he really settle in small-town Strawberry Pond for good? She'd also vowed that because he'd let her down once, she had to guard her heart from further hurt.

But as Alana returned to her candy-cane cookies, turning over the dough and smoothing it, she also turned over new ideas. Yes, she and

Cal had broken up in a horrible way, but what if that situation wasn't as straightforward as she'd always thought.

Understanding I was wrong is why I'm happily married.

Laura's words reverberated in Alana's ears. When it came to Cal, she'd always considered herself the one he'd wronged rather than *in* the wrong. While that was still true, maybe it wasn't the whole truth. She still had feelings for Cal, and she owed it to herself—and him—to figure out if they were transitory or real, a temporary attraction or deeper and longer-lasting. So no matter what, she still had a choice to make.

"If Ted's okay with me leaving work for a few hours, I can take your dad to his physical-therapy appointment. No problem. It's been slow this afternoon." In the empty tree lot, Cal pressed his phone to his ear. It was a picture-perfect December day, with a clear blue sky, and the surrounding mountains were topped with fresh, white snow like whipped cream atop a dessert. But even the bright sunshine didn't warm him as much as Alana's voice or the fact she'd called him when she needed help. "You already talked to Ted?" He listened as she explained she'd cleared it with Cal's boss and then gave him the details of Mr. Hansen's appointment.

"It'd be fine if Dad was seeing his physical therapist here in town, but this one's at the hospital." Alana's voice was threaded with anxiety. "Dad's insisting he can drive himself, but neither Mom nor me want him to. He's independent, which is good, but there are times when it's also good to be willing to accept help."

"I'll go pick up your dad now." Cal drew in a breath of crisp, clean winter air. It was only a half-hour drive to the hospital, and it'd be easy to avoid contentious conversational topics. Besides, he'd always liked Mark Hansen. Cal could hardly remember his own dad, who'd passed when Cal was four, but as a teen, along with Mr. Barrett, Alana's father was the kind of man he'd wanted to emulate. One who was devoted to his family, honest, upstanding and respected in the community. "Take the time you need and don't worry about rushing back. Drive safe, especially in that bookmobile."

He'd almost said he was worried about her. While Alana was a good driver, the bookmobile, which she'd mentioned taking to several outlying communities every few weeks, was a large vehicle. He didn't like to think of her driving it alone, in winter especially. *Because he cared about her.*

His breakup with Alana was the biggest regret of Cal's life. Since he'd been back in Strawberry Pond, his previous feelings for her had resurfaced. If he was honest with himself, they'd never really gone away.

He wanted her friendship because once she'd been not only his girlfriend, but also his best friend. Yet, he also wanted more than friendship. Kissing her under the mistletoe, and then for real, had shown him he wanted to build a life with her for keeps. Although he'd wanted that before, they'd been so young. He'd convinced himself he'd somehow, with time, get over her. Now in his thirties, he knew his feelings for Alana were real and wouldn't change.

"Thanks again." Cal heard the relief in Alana's voice. "The only day I'm running late, my mom's come down with a cold, and my brothers and everyone else we'd ordinarily ask to drive dad to his appointment can't get away from work. You're being great, and I appreciate it."

It was a casual turn of phrase and didn't mean anything significant, but it nevertheless gave Cal hope. Maybe she'd been able to move on from their breakup even a little and had begun to think of him as a friend. Or not her enemy.

After waving goodbye to the other staff members, Cal ended the call with Alana, went out to his truck and was soon pulling up to the Hansens' farmhouse, where her dad waited outside the back door. He stopped the vehicle, then went around to the passenger side and had the door open, ready to help the older man in.

"I can manage." Mr. Hansen grunted and levered himself into the vehicle. "But thank you." He shook his head. "Even though I'm only letting you drive me to keep my wife and daughter happy."

"I understand." Smothering a smile, Cal closed the door and returned to the driver's seat. He understood more than Alana's dad would realize. After the accident that had wrecked his knee, Cal hadn't been happy to have to depend on others for help and transportation, either. Even when he'd gotten more mobile, he'd still found it uncomfortable to need assistance and resented well-meaning folks offering. All of which made no sense, but when a person was used to being independent, it was hard to accept not being invincible. "Alana told me where your appointment is and we should get there in no time. The roads are clear and dry. Do you want to listen to music, or a news-and-talk station on the radio?"

"No." After Mr. Hansen wedged his cane between the door and his seat, he raised a hand to stop Cal. "What I want is to have a talk with you, son."

While a part of Cal wanted to stop the truck even before they'd left the farm lane and get someone else—anyone—to take Alana's dad to his appointment, he couldn't. As the saying went, he had to "man up" and listen to whatever Mr. Hansen wanted to say. "Okay." He swallowed, his mouth all of a sudden dry.

"You left town real sudden, didn't you?" After Cal had turned left onto the county road, Mr. Hansen stared out the window at the snow-covered fields.

"Yes, sir." There wasn't anything else Cal could say. No excuse he could offer to try to make what he'd done any better.

"I expect you had your reasons, but you didn't only hurt Alana. You hurt all of us." His breath hitched, suggesting he was as uncomfortable as Cal, but was determined to say what he thought he must. "You were like a member of our family. As well as everything else, we were bewildered. Leaving without even time for a goodbye party isn't the Strawberry Pond way. I didn't think it was your way, either."

This conversation had been a long time coming, but Cal wasn't ready for it. Perhaps he never would be. However, maybe it was a chance to clear up something that had bothered him for years and would finally give him closure before leaving town again. "I'm sorry I left so quick, but at the time I thought I had to." While he'd just turned twenty, in a lot of ways, and despite his superficial maturity, he'd still been an impulsive teen. Quick to react instead of thinking through situations calmly and carefully. Besides, he'd been so accustomed to looking out for Jesse and needing to protect his brother, in the heat of the moment that's all he'd been able to focus on.

"Looking back, I know I didn't handle things the right way, with Alana especially, but leaving was to do with a promise I made to my mom when she was dying." It was the truth, but would Mr. Hansen believe him?

"I understand the importance of a promise to anyone, family especially. And a deathbed promise, well, that's on another level entirely." Mr. Hansen darted a sideways glance at Cal. "But why didn't you say so at the time?"

"I wasn't thinking straight. But I also thought I wasn't good enough for Alana. You said so yourself." That sense of not being good enough had taken root in all those foster homes and shaped how Cal saw himself for years. It was only in the military that he'd gained the confidence to take a fresh look at his past decisions and choices.

"What are you talking about?" Mr. Hansen's voice was disbelieving. "I never said any such thing."

"You did. It was when you brought your car into the garage for a service a week or so before I left. I heard you tell my boss you wanted what you called ‘the best’ for Alana. I wasn’t good enough for her or you. How could I be? I thought you’d be glad when I left.”

That’s how he’d convinced himself things wouldn’t have worked out between him and Alana, anyway. But it was a convenient excuse. Before that random, overheard comment, Mr. Hansen had never given him any reason to think he disapproved of Cal dating Alana. However, without the maturity to make responsible decisions, Cal had seized on the idea of Mr. Hansen’s disapproval to justify himself. To justify not telling Alana and her family about Jesse when his brother had turned up so unexpectedly.

Old guilt mixed with new settled in the pit of Cal’s stomach. It’d been a spontaneous, poorly thought out choice he’d fallen into that’d had life-changing consequences. He’d had all that responsibility for Jesse—too much, too young—and perhaps it had confused him and he’d gotten it wrong. Mr. and Mrs. Barrett had done their best, but Cal had only lived with them for four years and those early patterns were ingrained. While he’d been an adult, it felt like he hadn’t truly made decisions like one, until his mid-twenties or even a few years later.

As Cal stopped the truck at an intersection and waited to turn from the county road onto a highway, Mr. Hansen stared at him wide-eyed.

"You thought I… I wasn't talking about you at all. For a start, unlike some in this town I'm not in the habit of gabbing about my family's business in public. Obviously, I want the best for my daughter, any dad would, but when you heard me, you misunderstood. All I meant was giving Alana the opportunity to reach her potential. Still sending her to college later on if that's what she decided she wanted. Not making her feel she had to stick with the farm."

"Oh." Cal pulled onto the highway. Anger at himself and the situation flowed through him. So soon after aging out of foster care, he'd been insecure and sure everyone would be against him that he'd often imagined slights where none existed. And he'd seized on a few overheard words, taken out of context, as an excuse to tell Alana he was joining the navy because he wanted to be worthy of her.

Then she'd gotten angry and broke up with him. In all the upset—and the two of them talking over each other and Alana crying—Cal hadn't known what to do. Another case where more maturity and clearheaded thinking would've been useful. He *did* want to be worthy of her. That'd never been in doubt, and it was why he'd worked so hard at the garage. But he'd gone about everything else the wrong way.

"I also want my daughter to be happy," Mr.

Hansen continued. "Back then, you made her happy. You also treated her and our family with respect and kindness. You had a steady job at the garage and were well on the way to making something of yourself. We were all proud of you. That's why you leaving like you did hit us so hard. It was as if joining the military came out of nowhere."

"It did and I'm sorry." This time, Cal's words were honest, heartfelt and open. As a kid desperate for approval and afraid of being rejected, Cal had apologized all the time, even for things that weren't his fault. While he'd managed to break that habit, he still had trouble letting himself be truly open with anyone. Was that what had held him back with Alana and so many others?

"It's Alana, not me, you need to apologize to." Mr. Hansen made a harrumphing noise.

"I will." Cal had been wrestling with that apology ever since coming back to Strawberry Pond. However, as they drove the rest of the way to the hospital in silence, Cal knew that to start over with Alana, even if it was only as friends, he had to be honest with her about why he'd left so suddenly.

The part of the truth that was his to share.

CHAPTER ELEVEN

"IT'S SUCH A gorgeous night." As Alana and Cal stepped out of the library, where he'd delivered a tree for a special program, she looked up at the inky sky spangled with stars. "Cold but clear and with the snow sparkling in the lights, it's magical, isn't it?"

"It sure is." Like her, Cal was bundled up in a parka, scarf and hat. Walking side by side, their booted feet crunched in the hard-packed snow.

"You chose a good tree for us. Not that the first one isn't great. You saw yourself how nice it looks in the library's entrance." She gave him a quick smile. "But this smaller one is the perfect size for the ornaments the kids will make at the library's workshop tomorrow. The first and second graders are visiting with their teachers."

The session would be fun for Alana. She loved spending time with children of all ages, but the six- and seven-year-olds were a special delight. Old enough to understand and savor the holiday excitement, they weren't so grown up to have lost some of their belief in the enchantment of the season.

"Oh, look. The Christmas market's still going on. I worried it'd close before I finished work." She gestured to the town green, where a cluster of white tents had been set up and people thronged between them. While Alana didn't usually do evening shifts, two of her part-time staff were sick so she'd filled in. "Cal? What is it? What's wrong?" He'd always been quiet, but since they'd left the library, she could count the number of words he'd said on the fingers of one hand.

"Nothing." His smile was weary. "Only that it's been a long day."

"I hope you aren't working too much. Talk to Ted if you need a schedule change." With several staff at the tree farm off sick, too, they were all working overtime, but Alana's folks took pride in caring for their staff as if they were family. "If we have to close early or open later at Rustic Hearts for a few days, it'd be fine. You should head back to Mrs. Barrett's. I can walk home from here." However, it was almost like old times with Cal at her side and enjoying each other's company. She could tour the market on her own, but in the midst of all the couples and family groups, it was nice to be with someone. *To be with him.*

When she let herself live in the here and now, not thinking about the past or future, she could enjoy Cal's companionship. When they'd set up the tree in the stand Cal had also brought, they'd hadn't talked about anything important, but it was still easier and less awkward between them. As if they were truly finding their way to some kind of friendship.

"I'm okay, and I'll make sure you get home safely." Cal's expression brightened. "It'd be nice to take a look at the market. Maybe you can help me find a Christmas present for Mrs. Barrett. She says she doesn't need anything, but I'd still like to get her something special. I've seen you with customers at Rustic Hearts. You have a real knack for choosing a gift that'll suit a person."

"Sure. I'd like to help." Cal was asking for Alana's input as a friend and colleague. The request didn't mean anything significant.

As they came onto the green, where the snow had been cleared to make a network of narrow paths, she waved at Laura, Trevor and Trevor's teenage nephew, Danny. After Danny's mom passed a year ago, Trevor had become Danny's guardian. Now with Laura, the three of them talking and laughing as they went into a tent selling pretzels, they looked like a family.

Emotion pinched Alana's heart. She no longer let herself dream about having a family of her own. Instead, she focused on other things, finding fulfilment in her job, her friends, crafts and being a fun aunt to her nieces and nephews. And now, she had Holly. The cat was as good as family. All that was enough. It had to be.

"I smell chestnuts roasting, don't you?" She made her voice bright, pushing away uncomfortable thoughts. "Since I only had a cheese sandwich and an apple for supper, I'm starving."

"I'm hungry, too, although unlike you, I had a proper meal." Cal's mouth tilted up in a self-deprecating grin. "Mrs. Barrett spoils me. No ordinary packed lunches for her. Since I had to work late, she dropped by Rustic Hearts with oatmeal cookies and a plate of meat loaf, mashed potatoes and green beans. All I had to do was heat the meal up in the microwave."

"I hope that wasn't too hard for you," Alana teased. "It's lucky you're cute seeing as you were never great at cooking. Remember that time you made popcorn and the kernels ended up all over my mom's kitchen? Even stuck to the walls." She stopped and her face heated. "I'm sorry… I didn't mean…"

Cal had missed so much of the ordinary family life Alana took for granted. When he'd visited the farm, her mom had treated him the same as Alana and her brothers, expecting Cal to pitch in with kitchen and other chores as the three of them did. He'd tried to learn, but there were inevitable mishaps. Lots of them. She'd spoken without thinking, not only drawing attention to what he hadn't grown up with, but also calling him cute. It was mortifying on both counts.

"That's why being in the navy was great for me." Hardly missing a beat, Cal picked up the conversation where she'd dropped it without drawing attention to her blunder. "Most of the time I ate at the base or on a ship and rarely had to cook for myself. I can now make a pretty good lasagna and a few other dishes, though, so I'm not quite a hopeless case." Cal pointed to a nearby stall. "Those *are* roasted chestnuts. My treat."

As Cal left, Alana's heart pounded. She couldn't change what she'd said, but hopefully he'd forget it. If she said anything more—offered a further apology or explanation—it would only make things worse.

"Here you go. Careful, they're hot." A minute later, Cal rejoined her, and when Alana held out her mittened hands, he put the small paper sack of chestnuts into them.

"Mmm." She savored the rich scent of the roasted nuts. Like so many other things, including this market itself, eating chestnuts outside was a cherished holiday tradition. But maybe while cherishing the old, she also needed to make new memories. Things between her and Cal couldn't be like they once were, and she didn't want them to be. But perhaps they could find something new. For the first time, she didn't dismiss the thought out of hand. "Did you have any ideas about a present for Mrs. Barrett?" She took off a mitten to nibble on a chestnut.

"Not really." Eating from his own bag, Cal made a dejected face. "Apart from a gift certificate, or one of those subscription box things with books, since she likes reading, or for pampering, a spa-and-relaxation gift, but those seem kind of impersonal."

"They don't have to be." They wandered over to a stall selling Christmas ornaments, and Alana still considered what she'd said. From now on, she needed to keep things light and easy and think before speaking. Cal was still cute, although in truth he'd grown into a fine-looking man, but she couldn't let herself think of him that way. "You could get Mrs. Barrett a gift certificate or subscription box along with something else. A meaningful ornament, for example." She glanced around the brightly lit kiosk, where white lights glowed above and around tables displaying small artificial trees laden with holiday decorations. "What about one of these?" After tucking the bag of chestnuts into a pocket to save the rest for later, she eased a small silver colored heart-shaped disc off a tree. "Family isn't only the people you're related to by blood. It's about love." She gestured to the ornament, one of several commemorating the theme of chosen rather than biological family.

If she could get the maker's name, these ornaments would be popular at Rustic Hearts. Her folks liked featuring the work of local artisans and were always on the lookout for more.

"That's beautiful." Cal's voice caught, and as he took the ornament from Alana, his fingers brushed against hers. "I bet Mrs. Barrett would treasure it forever."

Alana's fingers quivered and for an instant, she stood motionless, everything else forgotten. Mrs. Barrett *would* treasure the special decoration, but Alana would also treasure this moment, no matter what had come before or might come after. She and Cal together, connected as if by an invisible thread or sprinkling of Christmas magic.

The stallholder, a woman around Alana's age wearing a sprig of holly in her curly brown hair, bustled over to them with a welcoming smile. "Do you need help with anything?"

"No, I think we're set but thanks." As Cal purchased the ornament, Alana sensed him looking at her.

A quick look that held admiration, affection

and something more. Something that made her stomach flutter and her breath get short. A lot like how he'd once looked at her. As if for him she was the only girl in the world.

ALANA HAD CALLED him cute. Cal hadn't wanted to embarrass her further so he'd let the comment pass, but maybe she wasn't as immune to him as she tried to pretend to be. He certainly wasn't immune to her, and it was getting harder and harder to hide those sparks of attraction.

Despite his tiredness from the long day of work, it wasn't the reason he'd been quiet after they'd left the library. However, it was the only thing he could think to say when Alana asked if anything was wrong. He certainly couldn't tell her he wanted to hold her hand or slip an arm around her shoulders. Tell her he wanted them to look like a real couple.

Driving her home after the Christmas market, he kept glancing at her in the passenger seat of the farm truck. It'd been fun to spend time together, almost like it used to be. Easier than he'd expected, too, as if by mutual but unspoken agreement they'd decided the past didn't exist and so for a little while they could truly "be" in the present.

While they hadn't talked much since getting into the truck, this silence was comfortable, not awkward. It was too much to hope this feeling of ease would last, but even if it was only for this evening, Cal was grateful. It'd be a holiday memory to cherish.

The ring of Alana's phone broke the quiet, and she dug in her purse to find and answer it. "Hey, Josie. What's up?" She made an apologetic face at Cal. After a brief pause, she responded to whatever Josie had said. "No, I understand. Don't worry. I'll ask someone else. Of course, you can't be in two places at once. You need to be there for Lottie. Tell her I say to have fun. I hope she has a great skate." As she put her phone away again, her brow creased in a familiar worried expression.

"Something wrong?" Now, he was the one attuned to Alana like she'd been to him. After turning the truck onto Alana's street, Cal found a parking spot in front of her house. The ornamental deer family he'd spotted when he'd driven her here the day she'd adopted Holly was lit up and beamed white light across the snowy lawn. Red and green lights, along with more white ones, edged the home's roofline and several evergreen shrubs by the porch.

"Not 'wrong' as such but there's been a mix-up with dates. Josie was supposed to come with me tomorrow afternoon to distribute holiday hampers and toys to families and children in need. However, her daughter has a figure-skating practice for a show after Christmas and the arena's almost an hour away. I booked time off work especially, and it's too short notice to change the library's staffing schedule."

"Could Laura help?" Cal was off work tomorrow afternoon so he could go with Alana, but would she want him to?

He'd already asked about volunteering to make hamper deliveries, but none of the free slots had aligned with when he was available. He'd taken part in similar activities when he was in the navy. The year before his mom passed, they'd been given a community hamper and it had made their last Christmas together special. Now, he wanted to give back by helping share seasonal joy with other families who could use the help.

"No, I asked Laura first, back in October, but she'll be out of town for a real-estate-association training workshop." Alana huffed out a breath, her frustration palpable. "It's not Josie's fault. It's such a busy time of year and it's easy to get confused and double-booked. Ordinarily, my dad would go with me but it'd still be too much walking for him. I'm also afraid of him slipping and falling on the snow and ice. I'll put out a call on one of the town's social-media groups. We really need two people because those hampers are bulky to carry and—"

"I'll give you a hand." Cal looked down. "I'd like to. I mean…it's for a great cause and since I'm used to moving trees around, a few hampers should be easy. If that's… If it wouldn't be too weird for you." She'd talked about her dad and asking for help on social media, but she hadn't turned to Cal, who was sitting right next to her. It hurt more than he expected. Once, he'd have been her first choice. Yet another example of how he'd broken her trust.

"Weird? It's already weird seeing you almost daily at Rustic Hearts. You driving me home like this." She waved a hand around. "You being back in Strawberry Pond and…everything… It's all weird. Delivering hampers together wouldn't be any different."

"No, I guess not." The brief feeling of ease and familiarity between them disappeared as if Cal had imagined it. Gone in a puff of smoke, like Alana snuffed out the scented candle on the cash desk the nights they closed Rustic Hearts together.

"I'm sorry." Her voice softened. "You offered to help, and I appreciate it. I shouldn't have been so dismissive. It'd be great if you could lend a hand. Families depend on these hampers. One of the board members from the Pond Pantry was in the library earlier and told me the need's greater than ever this year."

Alana didn't have to tell Cal about the hampers being needed. He'd lived that need and while it was hard at any time of year, the holiday season was the worst. He cleared his throat. "Let me know where I have to be and when. I don't want to let those families down." Although it was too late, he also didn't want to let Alana down.

"Sure." She found her phone again, tapped at the screen and sent him the details. "I guess I'll see you then?" She opened the truck door and looked back at him over one shoulder.

He nodded. "Hang on, I'll walk you to your door."

"No need." She gave him a tight smile, already partway out of the vehicle. "It's not like when I had Holly and all that shopping. Besides, I'm used to managing on my own."

"That's not what I meant." Certainly, she could manage. Even as a girl, Alana had been strong and independent. Now, as a woman, those qualities were still integral to who she was. "I only wanted to—"

The door shut behind Alana, and its dull thud made Cal's stomach knot. First his mom and then Mrs. Barrett had stressed the importance of gentlemanly behavior. While some might consider it old-fashioned, they'd taught him that good manners were a mark of respect, kindness and care for others.

That's what he wanted to give Alana.

He watched her march up the front walk, unlock the door of her house and disappear inside—all without looking back—and his stomach knotted.

His motive for walking her to the door wasn't just being a gentleman.

He'd also wanted to spend a few more minutes with her. Try to regain that connection they'd had at the Christmas market and before Josie's call.

Something else, like trust and the love they'd once shared, he guessed was gone forever.

CHAPTER TWELVE

"ONE MORE HAMPER LEFT." Alana checked the list of deliveries on her phone and found the address. "It's on Hutchinson Road, only a quarter of a mile outside town, so it won't take long." She mentioned the property number as much to remind herself as him. Although she and Cal had worked well together, focusing on the task at hand, the past two hours delivering hampers had also felt endless and uncomfortable.

"Sure." He shut the hatch of her car and slid back into the passenger seat.

Cal had been polite, almost excessively so, but it was as if the time they'd spent at the Christmas market had never happened.

And it was Alana's fault. Regret mixed with frustration, annoyance and too many other emotions she'd thought she was over years ago.

If she hadn't been stressed about Josie not being able to make these deliveries with her, she'd never have been flippant. However, when Cal had asked whether it would be "weird" for him to help, it had triggered something inside her. Old resentment, certainly, but pain as well. Spending time together at the market had been fun, but it had also been a reminder of what she'd lost. Love and friendship, but trust and commitment as well. Or the illusion of them.

Getting into the driver's seat, she gritted her teeth. She had to concentrate on the families who needed these hampers, not Cal. She was mad at him, but she was also attracted to him, which made no sense. She didn't want to be attracted to him. And while one part of her wanted the holidays to be over so he'd leave Strawberry Pond and she could get back to her ordinary life, another part of her dreaded the thought of his departure.

She started the car, then navigated the familiar streets lined with tidy homes, most of them, like hers, decorated for the holidays.

"Looks like you need to turn right up ahead." Cal broke into her reverie and pointed to a road sign.

"Thanks." She'd been on autopilot so almost without her noticing, they'd left town. Still, in and around Strawberry Pond she was familiar with each road, mountain and hiking trail. While she carried a map of the local area in her head, it was also in her heart.

She turned off the county road, then drove

along a narrow lane that led uphill, twisting and turning beside a frozen creek that meandered deeper into woodland.

"There's the address we want. With the mailbox shaped like a fish." Cal pointed to it.

"I remember coming up here with my dad a few times." Alana slowed to make the turn. "He used to help a farmer who lived on Hutchinson Road with spring planting. Mr. Walsh had thick white hair and a curly beard. When I was really small, I thought he was Santa Claus. He and his wife moved into town a few years back. Whenever I see him, he teases me about it."

Alana navigated an even narrower lane, lined with tall trees, which opened into a clearing. A small blue-clapboard house with white shutters nestled in a stand of trees, and smoke curled up from a single chimney. From the outside, it looked like a house in one of the illustrated fairy tales she read to young children at the library, with a curving, snow-covered path leading to an arched front door. However, unlike other homes they'd visited today, here, there were no signs of the holiday season. No strands of lights. Not even a simple evergreen bough on the door.

She parked in a cleared space and cut the engine. In the silence, Cal's breathing sounded louder than usual, almost labored.

"You okay?" She glanced at him as she unbuckled her seat belt.

"Why wouldn't I be?" Avoiding her gaze, he unbuckled his own belt and was out of the vehicle and opening the hatch to retrieve the hamper.

She caught up with him halfway along the curved path. For families with children like this one, she added a few extra things beyond the usual hamper contents. The reindeer-patterned gift bag she carried held a book for each of the kids, a game and some basic art supplies—all donated by generous library patrons and local business owners. "Cal, wait." She touched his arm, and he yanked it away. It had taken her a few seconds to recognize it, but that hadn't been anger in his expression. Instead, it was raw, soul-deep pain.

"I'm fine." He rapped on the door, using a shiny brass knocker with a pine-cone motif.

The door opened, stopping Alana from saying anything more, and a dark-haired boy of about ten stood in the entryway. "Hi." She gave him a warm smile. "I'm Alana and this is Cal. We're from the Pond Pantry. Is your mom or dad home?"

The boy nodded and eyed the gift bag and hamper box as a younger boy hovered behind him. "Dad's out chopping wood, but Mom's in the living room. Come in." He gestured to them.

After they took off their boots, he led them through a dark hall and into a small living room, where a pale-faced woman sat in a recliner wrapped in a throw.

"Hi. I'm Cal. We brought a few things to brighten the holidays for you and your family."

"Heather." She held out a thin hand. "And my boys. Mason and Noah. My husband doesn't want us to accept charity but…" Her voice trailed away and she darted a quick glance at her sons.

"I get it, but tell him it's a helping hand from folks who care." Cal's voice was gruff and he also glanced at the boys. "Would you two like to help me unpack this box? Alana's got some things for you as well."

As Noah jumped forward, Mason, the older boy, hung back.

"It's okay." Heather gave them a faint smile. "We're grateful, truly, but…" Once again she stopped. "My husband lost his job, you see, and I haven't been doing so good and can't work."

"Like Cal said, think of these gifts as a helping hand when you need it." Alana tried to make her smile and tone reassuring. Heather seemed small, as if fading into nothingness. If these boys lost their mom, what would happen to this family?

"You're the Hansens' daughter, aren't you?" Heather's face brightened as she watched the boys and Cal unpack the hamper. "I remember your folks from going to the farm stand as a kid."

"That's right." Although Alana didn't recall meeting Heather before today, the library and her family's history in Strawberry Pond meant she was used to being recognized around town. "I also work at the library." She gestured to the gift bag and lowered her voice. "You might save this bag and give it to your boys on Christmas morning."

"That's real kind." Heather's voice caught.

"There's candy, Mom." Noah ran over to his mom. "Chocolate bars and a bunch of food and other stuff. Even gifts and decorations."

"Which we'll save for Christmas, except the decorations." Heather stroked her son's tousled hair. "Those you can put up now. Why don't you show me?"

As Noah chattered, and Mason returned from what must be the kitchen, where he'd helped Cal put the food away, Alana knew they had to leave. Yet as always, she wanted to do more for this family and all the others who'd fallen on hard times.

"If you need anything, call me." On impulse, she tore a piece of paper from a small notebook she carried in her purse and scribbled her cell number on it. "I can drop by with library books or whatever. It's not too much trouble." She waved away Heather's protest. There was something about this woman and her boys that tugged at Alana's heart. "If your husband's interested, tell him we can always use good workers at Hansen Farms. I'd be happy to talk to him."

"I'll let him know. Thank you." Heather gripped the edge of the throw and her eyes shone with unshed tears.

"You take care now." Cal crouched at Heather's side, and as the boys clustered around, he hugged all three of them with the same warmth and compassion he'd have shown as if they were his own family.

The same warmth and compassion Alana remembered he'd once shown her. She swallowed a lump of emotion as Mason took them back to the door, talking to Cal about the navy.

Did he see himself in this family and others they'd met today? Was that one of the reasons he'd kept his distance?

They returned to her car in silence, and Alana studied his once-again stiff demeanor. While she'd helped deliver hampers for years, even her senior year of high school, she'd never connected that need with Cal. There'd been no reason to because by then he'd been part of the Barrett family.

Today, though, she'd glimpsed a different part

of him. One he'd been careful to keep hidden. Now, she was the one who wanted to hug him—to comfort the child he was and the man he'd become.

The true meaning of Christmas wasn't what was received, but rather what was given to others. That's what Cal's mom told her boys, and while Jesse had been too young to understand, unlike his brother, Cal had taken it to heart. As he got back into Alana's vehicle, he knew there was no better time than the present to finally talk to her. Attempt that apology he owed her.

"I hope Heather's husband calls me." Alana settled in the driver's seat and started the car. "While we do need good workers at the farm, we also want to give folks help when they need it. Do you want me to drop you off at Mrs. Barrett's place or…?"

"Mrs. Barrett's, but I need to tell you something." Inside his winter gloves, Cal's palms were damp and his breathing was unsteady. "Something important."

"Okay." Alana kept her gaze fixed on the lane. "Go on."

As a kid and even now, while Cal had never found it easy to talk about his feelings, it'd always been better in a vehicle. Somehow, it felt less threatening, and knowing the journey had an end point helped him focus and get his point across.

He took several deep breaths as they turned back onto the road. "I never told you much about my family on purpose. You and your folks, you're close. Your brothers as well. I didn't want you to feel sorry for me or think… Well, I was a mixed-up kid who wasn't thinking clearly."

"All teens are mixed up, but I knew your family was different than mine." There was no judgment in Alana's voice, only kindness and caring.

"Like I told you before, my dad, I barely remember him. He died when I was really little, hadn't even started school. A car accident. It wasn't his fault." Somehow, it seemed important to reiterate that fact. From everything Cal's mom said, his dad had been a good man. "My mom did her best to raise me and my younger brother on her own, but then she got sick." Cal clenched his hands together to stop them shaking. "We were on our own because she hadn't had anything to do with her family in years. They cut her off. Something about marrying a man they didn't approve of."

"You never told me you had a brother." In the light snow, Alana turned on the wipers to clean the windshield. The soft, regular swishing sound calmed Cal and helped him continue.

"No, I didn't. I should have but…" He took

a deep breath. Cal wasn't proud of what he'd done, but avoiding and ignoring it wouldn't make his shame and guilt go away. "My mom passed when I was ten and Jesse, my brother, was eight, almost nine. She'd been sick for a year or so." That endless year when Cal finally understood what was happening. And that he couldn't save his mom, no matter how hard he tried or wished for it to happen. Was that part of why he'd sacrificed everything to save Jesse? To somehow make up for failing their mom? Kid logic, but in a way it also made sense. "With no family to take care of us, that's when we went into foster care."

"I can't imagine how rough that must have been for you." Alana briefly took one hand away from the wheel to touch Cal's arm.

"It was hard, yeah." So hard Cal didn't like to dwell on that time. Outside the car, the winter landscape was muted, snowy fields meeting snow-covered mountains bumping against a gray sky. In the quiet, Cal got caught up in memories. "I tried to make the best of it, be the perfect foster kid and fit in, but Jesse didn't. Every home we were placed in, and most were real nice, Jesse ran away. We had like six or seven foster families in only a few years."

He'd promised his mom he'd look out for Jesse, but he'd been a kid, too. He couldn't stop Jesse from running away or getting in with what his last foster mom before Mrs. Barrett had called "a bad crowd."

"Why didn't Jesse come to Strawberry Pond with you?" Alana's voice was soft as if she expected the worst.

Although it wasn't the worst—Jesse hadn't died—it was still bad. "Jesse ran away once too often and got caught up in some bad stuff. Shoplifting and so on. The police and state's juvenile justice services got involved." Cal paused. Alana was kind and open-minded. Unlike a lot of others, she hadn't judged him for being a foster kid, but he'd been scared she'd judge him for Jesse. Ashamed, as well.

That kid's out of control. We can't have either of the Paquette boys here. There's the safety of the others to consider. Bad blood will come out, you know.

When he'd heard a dad at soccer practice say that about him and Jesse Cal hadn't known what it meant. However, after Jesse had lost his temper and started a fistfight with two other kids, they'd both been asked to leave the team. Only a few days later, they'd been moved from their foster home, too.

And when Cal had asked a teacher what "bad blood will come out" meant—and she explained—he'd refused to tell her why he wanted to know. Instead, he'd convinced himself it was only a matter of time until he became like Jesse. Because of his brother, he was doomed.

He wasn't. The intervening years had proved him wrong, but as a kid and teen that belief had seemed like a prophecy he couldn't escape. So by not telling Alana he had a brother, he'd tricked himself into thinking he'd escaped Jesse's shadow. At least, for a little while.

"You mentioned the state's juvenile justice services and the police?"

Cal nodded. "Once they got involved, Jesse ended up going to a kids' detention center and then on to various community-based programs. I came here to stay with the Barrett family." And Cal had never forgiven himself for not being able to help his brother and keep the two of them together. For letting down their mom. "For the first time since my mom had gotten sick, I could be an ordinary kid. I started high school, met you and...life was good." Better than it had been before or since. "But see, I was ashamed of Jesse. Embarrassed. Guilty. And I..." He gulped. "I was afraid if I told you about him, you'd think I'd be like him."

"But I knew you. Or, I thought I did." Alana's voice was low.

"I know and as an adult it sounds...well, it doesn't make sense. But all those foster homes and schools… I was Jesse's brother and a lot of folks assumed we were alike because of what he did. They saw him acting out, and we got lumped together as being the same."

"That's unfair."

"It is, but that doesn't mean that kind of judgment doesn't happen." Cal had lived it. "The day you and I broke up, Jesse unexpectedly came here. He was waiting for me after work at the garage one night. I had a late shift." When Cal had spotted his brother lurking in the shadows behind the dumpster, he could hardly believe his eyes. "At first, I almost didn't recognize him, but when I did… He swore to me he'd changed. He'd just turned eighteen, and he had the idea of joining the navy to turn his life around. We were adults on paper but in reality…" Cal shrugged, remembering his younger self. "It was only later I learned how much longer it takes to finally start to act and think like the age you are."

Alana let out a heavy breath. "So you decided to join the navy with Jesse."

"I did. I wanted to watch over him because I promised our mom I would. I'd already let her down by not making sure he stayed out of trouble. I also thought I'd let her down by not being able to keep the two of us together. But what I said to you then, that I wanted to make something of myself, it was also the truth. I never thought I was good enough for you. And I overheard something your dad said and misunderstood… So I used it as a reason, an excuse, really. I talked to your dad that day I took him to his physical-therapy appointment." As Cal forestalled Alana's question, he felt almost as shaky now as he did then. "I'm sorry. I told your dad I'd apologize to you and I meant it. I'm sorrier than I can ever say. Losing you and what we had together is the biggest regret of my life."

He hadn't intended to tell her about that regret but maybe it was good. She knew where he stood.

When they stopped at a traffic light on the outskirts of town, Alana turned to look at Cal. "It's a lot for me to take in. Even though I get it, that you were ashamed and embarrassed and guilty, I still wish you'd told me all this before. I like to think I'd have tried to understand, but I don't know. As soon as I heard you say 'joining the navy,' I flipped out." She gave him a wry smile. "I guess I wasn't acting my age, either."

"If I could go back and change things, I would." But he couldn't. He had to make the best of what had happened and try to move forward.

"Me, too, but we can't change the past." Alana's wistful tone told Cal that like him, she wished everything had been different. "But, where's Jesse now? Do you two keep in touch?"

"He lives in Boston. He's married and he and his wife had a baby earlier this year. A boy." The traffic light turned green, and Alana continued driving. "Thanks to the navy, Jesse *did* turn his life around and he works as a firefighter." All of which was true and the rest didn't matter. Or so Cal had convinced himself. "Over the years, we drifted apart. No big argument or anything like that, but one time, just before he left the military, Jesse told me he was okay and didn't need me offering advice. I took what he said literally. Backed right off. We still text and email occasionally, and a few months ago, Jesse invited me to come visit and meet my nephew and sister-in-law, but I haven't gone yet." Or even replied to his brother's text.

Cal had been avoiding not only his brother and the memories seeing him brought, but it was also that Jesse, the guy whose life had always been a mess, now had everything Cal didn't. A wife, family and settled home, as well as a steady job. He also did a lot of volunteer work, even winning a neighborhood award a few months ago for helping organize a club for at-risk youth. Would Cal look like a failure in the face of his brother's success?

"You shouldn't blame yourself for what happened with Jesse, although I understand about the promise to your mom. Maybe you should think about reconnecting. Family's important." Alana paused. "As for being 'worthy of me,' I can't believe you thought that way, but maybe neither of us was thinking clearly. I was so mad back then, I likely wouldn't have listened to anything you'd said. It's not all on you. I was the one who told you to go if you wanted the navy more than me. We'd talked about getting engaged that Christmas and then married a year or so later. All of a sudden, everything I'd thought and planned got messed up. In that moment, I could only think about myself. I was also the one who said we were over as a couple." Her cheeks turned red. "With you joining the navy, it sort of felt like you were breaking up with me, so I jumped to do it first, I guess, figuring it'd hurt less. I was wrong, but like you, I was embarrassed. I didn't want to look bad in front of my friends and family. Everyone was expecting an engagement. I'd even bought a stack of wedding magazines and had bridesmaids dresses picked out. I felt so foolish. Again, it wasn't logical but it's what it was."

They turned onto Mrs. Barrett's street, and Cal's stomach rolled. "You're a lot more understanding than I expected." And while he was grateful, guilt also burned his insides.

He hadn't told Alana the whole story, but even if he did, what purpose would it serve so many years later? That night, meeting at the dumpster, Jesse had told Cal he'd changed, but only an hour later he'd been in trouble again. It was worse than before because at eighteen Jesse was an adult and would have gotten a permanent criminal record. It was also the kind of trouble that, then or now, Cal couldn't expect Alana to forgive. One that had impacted her family and their livelihood.

But the fact remained that he wouldn't be in Strawberry Pond much longer. For the short time left in his stay here, it was best to keep the peace. Especially because they still had to work together at Rustic Hearts.

She parked her car in Mrs. Barrett's driveway and turned off the engine. "I'm a lot older than I was then. No longer a teenager." Alana's smile was bittersweet. "I also, despite everything, regret losing you. Us."

"You do?" His breath caught in his throat.

She nodded. "I'd be lying if I said I didn't. Those kisses were really something, and they reminded me…" She paused and then shrugged. "I don't know what I'm feeling. You were my first love so maybe seeing you again is only a fleeting echo of that time. I also don't know if I can trust you, but it's Christmas. Before, when we talked about being friends, I said it'd be hard but if I don't try, I won't know whether there could be anything more between us. Or maybe I need closure. You left so fast and we had such a huge argument, I never got that closure and I… What I'm trying to say is I was at fault as well, and I'm sorry." She stopped. "Today, delivering those hampers to families like yours must have been really tough. Come here." She held out her arms.

Cal unbuckled his seat belt, then leaned across the seat and into her embrace. Alana had always been intuitive, sensing what he was thinking and feeling, sometimes before he did himself. And as he wrapped his arms around her, the hug seemed to go on forever.

Friends for real but with a hint, a possibility, of something more. Because, like she said, those kisses *were* really something. Something that although he hadn't truly realized it, he'd spent the past fifteen years longing for.

CHAPTER THIRTEEN

"MERRY CHRISTMAS AND happy holidays." At the Strawberry Pond Diner, decorated with evergreen garlands, twinkling lights and several Christmas trees draped in ribbon and red, green and silver ornaments, Josie raised her coffee mug in a toast.

"Cheers." Laura clinked with her glass of orange juice and Alana followed suit.

Although she and her friends usually met for breakfast on a Saturday morning, it was such a busy time of year that they'd squeezed in a Thursday get-together instead. With only a week until Christmas day, Alana had never felt so ill-prepared for the holiday season. She hadn't even bought or decorated a tree or wrapped her gifts. She'd planned to tackle the gift wrapping last night after delivering the hampers with Cal.

Instead, after she'd gone into her house after that long hug—one she wished didn't have to end—she'd sat on the sofa with Holly. And with the cat cuddled in her lap, she'd dug out old high-school yearbooks and that memory box. It was finally time to go through the contents again. Several dried corsages Cal had given her at dances, tickets to school concerts and football games, notes he'd left in her locker and photos of the two of them together. So many pictures of that smiling girl who'd thought their future was bright. The box was a time capsule of their relationship, but after yesterday, Alana now knew for certain she'd only seen part of Cal.

She hadn't recognized it as a teen, but as an adult looking at those faded snapshots there was a sadness in Cal's eyes and face, a darkness even, that belied his youth. A wariness, too, as if he couldn't let himself fully relax and live in the moment. But how could he have? Not worrying about his brother and believing he'd let their mom down.

Now that she'd had time to think, his guilt and hurt, as well as the harsh reaction he half expected also made sense. There were families right here in Strawberry Pond where what older folks called "one bad apple in the barrel" impacted negatively on the entire group and influenced how others saw them. She'd been lucky, but she also hadn't had the maturity to see other perspectives like she could now.

"Alana?" Laura's voice broke into her rambling thoughts.

"Sorry. I've got a lot on my mind."

"Anything you want to talk to us about?" Josie paused with a forkful of home fries halfway to her mouth. "You haven't mentioned how delivering those hampers with Cal went yesterday. I'm really sorry I left you in the lurch."

"It was fine, but how did you know Cal took your place?" To forestall questions, Alana hadn't said anything to anyone, not just Josie and Laura.

"It's the Strawberry Pond way, don't you know?" Laura exchanged a grin with Josie. "The two of you had hardly left the Pond Pantry before the news went around town."

"My grams saw you when she was coming out of the bakery with Anne Sullivan." Josie returned to her breakfast.

"And Aunt Anne mentioned it to me when she called last night." Laura cradled her mug between her hands. "I already knew, though, because someone told Trevor at the vet clinic."

"I thought the Strawberry Pond way was about helping others, not talking about them behind their back." Alana huffed out a breath. She supposed she shouldn't have expected otherwise. If folks weren't looking *out* for their neighbors, they were looking *at* them.

"Any talk wasn't meant unkindly," Laura reassured Alana. "Most everyone here knows you and Cal broke up before. They care about you. Like we do."

"I know." Alana's brief flash of irritation subsided. "Sorry." She gave her friends an apologetic smile. "I guess I'm touchy. The usual holiday-season stress." She tried to make her shrug casual. People knew they'd parted ways because Cal had left to join the navy, but the situation was so much more complex, and Alana was still trying to make sense of it all.

"You love Christmas," Josie said, "even if it sometimes gets a bit stressful with everything going on."

"Josie's right." Laura nodded. "You're the only person I know who even gets excited for Christmas in July. I had my doubts at first, but even though it was almost ninety degrees, that Christmas-in-July party you hosted was fun."

"Things are…different now." Although only five months prior, July and that party seemed like a lifetime ago. Alana ate the last of her oatmeal drizzled with local maple syrup. "Maybe I've lost my mojo. With my dad not back at work, I'm doing more hours at Rustic Hearts and on the farm. It all adds up."

"I can help." Josie's voice softened. "Tell me what you need."

"Me, too," Laura said.

"I appreciate you offering but I don't know

what I need, not really." Tears pricked at the backs of Alana's eyes and she blinked them away. She'd managed extra work no problem before, but now it all seemed overwhelming. No, if she was honest with herself, it was Cal who made everything too much. "I'm worried, that's all. Dad's doing great but he and my mom are getting older and it feels like all of a sudden, everything's changing." And she was stuck. Not only as the perennial singleton, but also, with Cal back in town, reminders of what she'd lost—the husband, family and home she'd counted on—were ever-present and sharp.

"I thought you had a plan for your brothers to take over Hansen Farms," Josie said, putting her cutlery on her empty plate.

"We do and they are. I'll still be involved in the farm and Rustic Hearts, like I am now, but Dad being off due to his surgery has made me think more about the future." And Alana wasn't sure she liked it, especially the thought of growing older herself and still being alone. Before Josie and Laura had married, the three of them used to joke about one day living together and looking out for each other. But when first Josie and then Laura had settled into married life, the joking had stopped and Alana knew she'd be on her own.

"Does Cal have something to do with how

you're feeling?" Josie reached across the table and patted Alana's hand. "He'll be gone soon so you won't have to see him much longer. Working together at Rustic Hearts can't be easy, and in such a small town, it must seem like you're always bumping into each other."

"That's part of the problem." If she couldn't talk to her closest friends, who could she talk to? Not her mom, who, in between taking Alana's dad to medical appointments, was also working extra hours. In a typical holiday season, life got so busy they didn't see much of each other but this year that was even more the case. "I still…kind of like Cal." Her face burned and she gulped a mouthful of ice water. "I know I shouldn't like him, not after how we broke up, but we've been talking and, well, it's complicated."

"Sure it is and why wouldn't you like him?" Josie sighed. "Believe me, I know all about complicated."

"Same here," Laura said. "Your head says one thing but your heart has other ideas." Her smile was wry.

"Exactly." Alana lowered her voice further. "What if there could be another chance for Cal and me? He apologized. I did, too, and he… We—we both have regrets. Before everything, we were good together. We're also mature adults, not kids, and there's still something between us. I can't pretend there isn't."

"So what are you going to do?" Laura's brown eyes filled with compassion. "Take a risk or forever wonder?"

Always a logical thinker, Laura had gone right to the heart of the issue Alana was grappling with. "That's what I don't know." She knew how she felt when Cal kissed her. It was everything else she was confused about.

"I had to take a risk for love," Josie said. "I'd never say it was easy but it was worth it. Along with a bunch of other things, I had to let myself be vulnerable, no matter how scared I was."

"Same here," Laura agreed. "Falling in love is one of life's biggest risks, but it's also one you can't avoid. Not if you want the joy that finding your person and loving them, truly loving them, brings." Laura's cell phone vibrated and she glanced at it. "Sorry, that's Danny texting me. He needs a ride to a friend's house. Trevor has a shift at the vet clinic today."

"I promised my grams the girls and I would decorate sugar cookies with her." Josie glanced at her phone, too. "I should get going but if—"

"It's okay." Alana mustered a smile. As well as being a busy time of year, they all had busy lives. She herself had to get to work at Rustic Hearts.

Where she'd see Cal, and the two of them

would put the finishing touches to the farm's entry for Strawberry Pond's annual holiday tractor parade of lights.

He'd shared an important part of his life with her. He'd also been honest about what had happened back then. The scared foster kid with the troubled younger brother. A boy who'd loved her, but who also loved Jesse and had been determined to look out for him because he'd promised their mom he would.

But had Cal told her everything? For a brief instant, there'd been something in his expression that had made her wonder… No, she was second-guessing herself and him. Besides, the two of them would have a lot more time to talk. Their conversation had been intense, and they both needed to settle and decompress. And for Cal, delivering those hampers had brought so many emotions to the fore. Alana needed to give him time and not press for more details.

As Laura and Josie gathered up their coats, chatting about the parade and a seasonal tour of local historic homes, Alana only half paid attention.

Risk. She'd always disliked uncertainty, preferring her predictable routine. But she'd already acknowledged she was stuck so maybe it *was* time to shake things up.

Starting with kissing Cal again. It couldn't be as good as she remembered, could it?

"WHAT DO YOU THINK?" In a small barn several hundred yards from the store at Rustic Hearts, Cal stepped back and surveyed the green tractor they'd covered in red, green and white lights. "Too much?"

"No, exactly right." Across from him, Alana held a bundle of fake snow. "When it comes to this parade, less isn't more. We go all out, remember?" She chuckled, the sound low and throaty.

Cal's heartbeat sped up. Between that chuckle, which made attraction spiral along his nerve endings, and her rosy cheeks and tousled hair, he remembered more than was wise. Not only about the tractor parade, but also her. Alana. The girl he'd once loved with every part of himself, and been sure they'd be together forever. "The trailer looks good, too." *Focus on the tractor holiday parade of lights, not her.* "That tree's sure a beauty." He gestured to the trailer hitched to the tractor, where Alana had set up a winter woodland scene with one of their own trees as the centerpiece. "And with all the animals, the kids are going to love it." A fox, deer, rabbit, squirrel, raccoon and bear gathered around the tree surrounded by wrapped presents.

"Those animals are older than I am." She moved to the trailer and added extra snow around the deer. "My dad remembers them from when he was a child. They're part of our family tradition. Now, my nieces and nephews look forward to seeing them come out each year. Isla, she's my youngest niece, has been excited about this parade since the summer. It's her turn to ride in the tractor cab, and she doesn't let any of us forget it." Alana chuckled again but this time her laugh was bittersweet. "She's five, and soon, well, they'll all be too old to get excited about the parade and Christmas."

Cal's heart squeezed. The years went by so fast. His nephew was still a baby, less than a year old, but he'd grow up whether or not Cal was part of his life. Alana said that Cal should think about reconnecting with his brother. She was right, and Christmas would be a natural time to renew that familial bond. Finally answer his brother's text. Boston wasn't far away, only three hours or so of driving. Cal could go there for a day trip, and maybe the baby would help break the ice between him and Jesse. Ice that had built up without maybe either of them intending it to, but which was still there because life had taken them in different directions.

Yet, by inviting Cal to come and visit, Jesse had opened a door. Perhaps it was time for Cal to conquer his embarrassment and pride and walk through it.

"I guess with working at the library there's always more little ones coming along to be excited about Santa and the holidays." It was all he could think of to say, but as soon as the words came out of his mouth, he knew by Alana's stiff posture and the way she pressed her lips tight together that he'd made a mistake. "I mean, it's not the same as your own family, but you still have children in your life." *Unlike him.*

"Here. Let's test the lights." Ignoring his comment, Alana heaved the large portable battery pack onto an inconspicuous spot on the trailer before Cal could offer to help. Seconds later, the tractor was illuminated, its lights dazzling.

"Magical." Cal cleared his throat. A steady stream of tree-farm staff came in and out of the barn because the Hansens stored tools and extra store stock here. However, right now, he and Alana were alone. "I bet this will win your farm a prize in the parade for sure."

"Although that's not the goal, it'd be a nice bonus for my folks." The lights bathed Alana in a soft glow and turned her hair a rich golden brown. "There'll be people walking alongside the tractors on the parade route collecting food and cash for the Pond Pantry, but as you might remember we include a donation box as well."

She moved a wooden crate, like apples were once stored in, with *Hansen Farms* in painted black letters on the sides, into position between the raccoon and rabbit.

Cal's breath caught. He still wasn't worthy of Alana, but she was even more perfect than the winter-wonderland scene she'd created with such care. She always had been perfect, a girl he'd maybe idealized but who'd lived up to everything he thought she was. Not only beautiful, but also kind, compassionate and never judgmental. As a kid in foster care, he'd gotten used to being judged. Trying to be his brother's "keeper" meant he'd often shared the blame for things Jesse had done, sometimes by choice and others not. Even then, it still hadn't been enough. He'd sacrificed himself and his relationship with Alana for his brother, but in the end, it was Jesse who'd moved on with his life and left Cam behind. Had Jesse appreciated Cal's sacrifices? He'd never said so. In fact, he'd pushed Cal away and that had hurt.

But had Cal been too interfering? Maybe, but the two of them were older now. Real rather than pretend adults. And Jesse was a dad. Somehow, Cal had to try to make things if not right, at least better between them.

"Have you given any more thought to certifying as an auto mechanic?" Alana switched off the tractor's lights, and the magical moment between them evaporated.

He shook his head as if to clear it. Now, only the ordinary overhead lights brightened the barn, and outside, snow once again fell from a pewter sky. "I'm working on my application for that college course I told you about. I'll have to start looking for an apprenticeship as well."

Although Mrs. Barrett had said Cal could stay with her for as long as he wanted, he was a grown man and should have his own place. Along with the military covering the cost of Cal's tuition and other expenses while he was a student, any apprenticeship would also be a paid one, enabling him to support himself.

"So does that mean you're thinking of sticking around?" Alana's voice hitched, and her expression mixed hope and wariness.

"If you'll have me." He tried to joke and then stopped. "I mean, not you personally, of course, but Strawberry Pond still feels a lot like home." Since returning, he knew it always would. He'd put down roots here, and there were people he cared about. Mrs. Barrett. Alana. How could he leave her again?

"I'm proud of you for going back to school." Alana fussed with arranging more artificial snow, avoiding Cal's gaze. "Not that you haven't made something of yourself already, you have, but I know you'll do great in that program."

Although returning to a classroom in his thirties felt uncomfortable—would he be the oldest one there?—it also felt right.

"I mean it." As if she'd read his thoughts, Alana came around the trailer to face him. "You've got life experience, motivation, maturity and a natural aptitude for mechanics. You'll leave the younger ones in the shade. You only have to believe in yourself."

As a guy who'd always been prone to self-doubt, self-belief wasn't easy. After finally fitting into military life, and being used to its rules and hierarchy, now, Cal was back in the civilian world and on his own. "I'll give it my best shot."

"Good." She gave a purposeful nod. "Like my mom says, your best is always good enough. If you fall short of what you set for yourself, well, it's part of learning and growing, isn't it?"

"I guess." Cal turned her words over in his mind. He'd liked Alana's mom, who'd opened her home and heart to him when he and Alana were dating. And from the little he'd seen of her recently, she hadn't changed much. Kind, wise and also forthright—a lot like her daughter. "Do you think that learning and growing... Is it the same for all parts of life?" He let out a shaky breath. Things were changing between him and Alana. Changing for the better. If he stuck around Strawberry Pond maybe—

"Sure it is. Life's all about learning and growing." She patted the rabbit's ears with a fond smile.

"I've done a lot of learning and growing since we broke up. I also meant what I said that losing you, us, was the biggest regret of my life." He glanced around the old barn with its weathered beams and shadowy, mysterious corners. It seemed like it was hushed, waiting, time folding in on itself so past and present intertwined. "Do you think…? Is there any way you might give me, our relationship another chance?"

"I've been thinking about it." One side of her mouth quirked in a half smile. "And if you're planning on staying in Strawberry Pond, maybe making a life here…" Alana studied Cal as if she could see inside him down to his soul. "I suppose I could try. Hang on—" As Cal moved toward her, she stopped him. "I'm not making any promises, but you've told me what happened back then. Family's important to me, too, and in the heat of the moment, I get why you thought you needed to leave town. I was angry and everything escalated. We thought we were adults, but in many ways we were still impulsive kids not thinking rationally." Her smile widened. "I only see that in retrospect, of course."

"Me, too." While a part of Cal wanted to clamber onto the tractor and shout with excitement, he wasn't a kid but a more measured adult. The past was gone and there was no sense digging it all up again. Now, all he wanted was to kiss her.

Did he move first or did Alana? He didn't know and it didn't matter. All that was important was that they were in each other's arms and their lips met. Hers were soft, sweet and inviting, and in the kiss he tasted forgiveness, hope and maybe even that second chance he longed for.

CHAPTER FOURTEEN

"WE'LL HAVE YOUR car checked and serviced by lunchtime." From behind the counter at Strawberry Pond Automotive, Brad Johnson, the business owner, took the key fob Alana handed over. "I'll also have one of the guys give you a ride to work and come get you when you're ready to pick up your vehicle."

"That'd be great. Usually, I'd walk, it's not far, but..." She gestured out one of the auto shop's windows, where overnight a mixture of snow and ice had made the town look like the inside of a holiday snow globe. It was pretty but treacherous, for pedestrians especially.

"I wouldn't hear of it. Nobody wants Strawberry Pond's favorite librarian taking a tumble and being laid up for the holidays." Above Brad's head, large red-and-green holiday baubles strung on artificial evergreen strands swung gently in the breeze coming from the half-open door to the garage itself.

"I'm the Pond's only librarian. A full-time

one, anyway." She grinned at Brad, whose kids, although now in high school, had come to the library's toddler rhyme-time activities.

"And we're all grateful for it. That library's a public service we depend on and not only for borrowing books. According to my great-grandma, those how-to-use-your-new-cell-phone classes for seniors you've been running are fantastic. I also see the proof. She's texting almost as fast as my kids."

"I'm glad she enjoyed the sessions." Alana glanced around the service center. At seven thirty in the morning, the place bustled with activity as customers dropped off their vehicles. While some people headed straight to work, others enjoyed coffee and pastries in the small waiting area, reading magazines, watching a news show on the overhead TV or chatting with neighbors. Cal had worked here before, and Brad's business, which he'd taken over from his dad, was as busy as ever. Maybe even busier. "If you're ever looking for an apprentice mechanic, I know someone who might be interested. Cal Paquette. You might remember him or your dad will."

"The name rings a bell." Brad's eyebrows creased and he stroked his clean-shaven chin. "Would he have been in town when I was away at college?"

"Probably." Brad was older than Alana and had studied business at college before certifying as a mechanic himself. "Cal left Strawberry Pond years ago to join the military, but now, he's back and helping us out at Hansen Farms temporarily for the holidays. He worked for your dad here for eighteen months or so." Since Brad evidently wasn't aware, Alana didn't have to field any questions about Cal's departure or her relationship with him. She breathed a silent sigh of relief. "Cal only did basic maintenance and cleaning jobs because he wasn't licensed for anything more complex, but he's always been good with cars and able to fix almost anything. He trained as a mechanic in the navy to work on ships and aircraft, but now, back in civilian life, he's looking to certify as an automotive mechanic." Alana also mentioned the trade-school program Cal was applying to.

Brad nodded. "Sure, tell him to drop by and see me. If it seems like he'd be a good fit, I'd be happy to give him a chance. I always like helping one of Strawberry Pond's own, and since my grandpa was in the army, I have a soft spot for ex-military personnel. Dad and I have hired a few of them over the years. They've all been hard-working, dependable and bring lots of other good skills as well."

"Great. I'll let Cal know. Thanks." Alana

smiled as Brad waved to one of his staff to arrange her ride to the library. Like Brad, she wanted to help Cal, and as soon as she got to her office, she'd call him to share the good news. While Cal had often worried about being an outsider here, Brad's comment about him being "one of the town's own" would surely make him feel he truly belonged.

"It's my pleasure. Oh..." Brad reached under the reception desk. "My mom's on the organizing committee for this year's Holiday Candlelight evening at the Old Beech Home. She gave my wife and me two tickets for tonight, but since we now can't go, I'd like to pass them on. Are you interested? You could take a friend."

"I'd love to go." Alana took the tickets Brad held out. "I intended to buy tickets myself but by the time I got around to it, they were sold out." The annual Holiday Candlelight evening was popular, and usually Alana went with Laura. She enjoyed seeing one of the town's old houses, now a museum, decorated for Christmas, as well as music by local choirs and seasonal refreshments served by high-school students in historic costumes. This year, though, Laura had plans with Trevor. While Alana had thought about inviting her mom to go with her, she'd been so caught up with Cal's sudden reappearance that buying tickets had slipped her mind and then it was too late.

"Hang on." She dug in her purse for her wallet. "I'll pay you for these tickets."

"Don't worry about it." Brad shook his head. "Consider it a thank-you for being so kind to Grammy. She's been sort of lost since my great-grandpa passed, but going to the library and those cell-phone classes and your book recommendations have made her feel part of life again. She calls the library her 'home away from home' and we're all grateful."

"Mrs. Johnson's a wonderful lady." And the petite, white-haired woman was one of Alana's favorite library patrons, greeting her with a sweet smile and often bringing homemade cookies, brownies or other treats for the staff to enjoy. "I'm happy to help her." Strawberry Pond's library was at the heart of the community, and for older people especially, it was as much a place that fostered social connections and reduced isolation as a source of books and other information. As the town's librarian, Alana took that part of her role seriously, and it was one of the many reasons she loved her job.

After saying goodbye to Brad, she tucked the tickets in her purse and went to the waiting-room door, where her ride to work, a four-wheel drive SUV, waited outside.

Take a friend. Neither Alana nor Cal were scheduled to work at Rustic Hearts tonight, and when she'd talked to her earlier, her mom had mentioned that it was her quilting group's holiday dinner. As Alana went outside and got into the SUV, exchanging pleasantries with the driver, a new thought hit her. Would Cal like to join her for the Holiday Candlelight evening at the Old Beech Home?

It wouldn't be an official date. She'd make that clear when she invited him. But it could be the start of trying to give their relationship another chance and letting herself think about putting the past behind them and maybe having a real future together.

WAITING FOR ALANA under the covered porch at the Old Beech Home, Cal loosened his scarf and took off his hat to tuck it in his parka pocket. It was warmer than it had been all day, and after a stormy start, the early evening stars shone overhead, soft points of light in the velvety darkness. The porch was decked with holiday lights, and from the curving path lined with evergreen trees to the antique sleigh on the snow-covered lawn, the scene could've come from Mrs. Barrett's miniature Christmas-village set.

From a school field trip, Cal remembered that the house had been preserved as it would have been when the wealthy Beech family built it after moving to Strawberry Pond from England in the mid-nineteenth century. While he'd never been too interested in history, he *was* interested in spending time with Alana. If only he'd been able to talk to her today, but it'd been busy at both Hansen Farms and the library so they'd exchanged texts. She'd said she had something important to tell him, and all day he'd wondered what it might be. Although she'd seemed at pains to point out that tonight wasn't a date, mentioning she'd been given the tickets to take a friend with her and she'd meet him here, her insistence had made Cal chuckle.

They weren't calling it a date, but he'd still dressed for one in black trousers and a blue collared shirt. He'd also taken extra care shaving and asked Mrs. Barrett to give him a once-over before leaving. She hadn't asked Cal why it was important he looked good, but after his foster mom had told him he was "spick-and-span," she'd hugged him tight, like a real mom would have, and wished him well.

He peered into the darkness beyond the lighted porch as several figures approached from the parking lot. Worried about being late, he'd arrived much too early. While the museum's staff had invited him to wait inside, he'd preferred to be out here in the quiet. At the time it was built, the Old Beech Home would've been on the edge of town. Despite more than a century of subsequent growth, since it sat on a large piece of land, it nevertheless felt somewhat rural. Several Beech descendants lived in Strawberry Pond today. What would it be like to have that kind of long history in a place? Maybe Cal wasn't interested in history because, unlike Alana, he didn't have any of his own. "Alana?"

"Cal." She reached the porch steps, and even though she walked near another couple, he only had eyes for her. "You're here."

"Where else would I be?" he teased her gently and when he held out his hand, she took it. "I'd have picked you up at your home." He knew where she lived, but he'd never seen inside her house, because so far she'd kept him at a distance. He understood why, but it still stung and was yet another reminder of how badly he'd let her down. Never again, he told himself, as much a promise as it was a reminder.

As the couple brushed passed them and went into the house, Alana held back. "Between work and having to pick up my car from Strawberry Pond Automotive, it was easier to meet you here. Oh, it was only for a regular service." He evidently looked concerned because she'd rushed to explain. "I went home to check on Holly earlier so I came straight here from the library."

"How's Holly doing?" They entered the home, then left their coats and boots with an attendant near the door and changed into shoes, and Cal's breath caught. In a black velvet skirt and white sparkly sweater, except for at their long-ago prom, Alana was more dressed up than he'd ever seen her. But even wearing heels, she still didn't even reach his shoulder, and the old protectiveness he'd once felt for her surged back. He took her hand again to guide her into the living room so she wouldn't get bumped in what had quickly turned into a big crowd.

"Holly's great." A sweet smile curved Alana's rosy lips, reminding Cal of the kisses they'd shared. "She's smart, curious and more playful every day. She's filling out more, too, and her fur's glossier."

"That's because you've given her a wonderful home and loving care." In the living room, which smelled of cloves and other strong spices, candles flickered. A big white spruce in one corner, which the museum had bought from Rustic Hearts, was decorated with lights, delicate antique glass ornaments, paper chains and strings of popcorn. "Holly's a lucky cat."

"She is, but I'm lucky as well having her in my life." Alana beamed at him. "I'm a bit concerned about putting up a Christmas tree, but I figured out how to anchor it to a wall with fishing wire. I also won't bring out my most breakable ornaments until I see how she reacts." Alana gestured to the tree they now stood beside. "Those lights are battery-operated, but a long time ago, people used to have lighted candles on Christmas trees. Can you imagine?" She laughed and shook her head. "Fire risk or what? Especially with children running around. The first Beech family who lived here had seven kids."

"So what did you want to tell me?" He'd dropped Alana's hand when they stopped near the tree, but she stayed close to him.

"It's the best news." Her eyes sparkled before she took a star-shaped shortbread cookie from a teenage girl dressed in a long skirt, apron and white cap, like servants in historical movies and TV shows wore. "You know I said my car was in the garage today?"

He nodded, took a piece of shortbread himself and bit into its buttery goodness.

"Eggnog?" A boy wearing a white shirt, striped trousers and old-fashioned waistcoat offered them two glasses as a children's choir came into the living room, their high voices singing "Deck the Halls."

Cal declined the drink, still focused on Alana.

She leaned nearer and spoke into his ear. "I talked to Brad Johnson, he's the son of the Mr. Johnson you worked for and took over Strawberry Pond Automotive from his dad. Well, I told him you'd likely be looking for an apprenticeship for certifying as a mechanic, and he said you should drop by and talk to him. If it's a good fit, he'd take you on. He called you one of the town's own. He's hired several ex-military people like you and said lots of good things about their work ethic and skills. Isn't that fantastic news?"

"It is fantastic, but..." Why did he find it so hard to accept help? He liked to give that help to others, and it warmed his heart to hear that Mr. Johnson's son had called Cal "one of the town's own," so what was the problem?

"Cal?" Alana tugged on his arm. "We can talk more later, but want to see the rest of the house?" She gestured to a gray-haired man in breeches and a tailcoat with shiny buttons. "Mr. Bouchard, remember him? He taught art at the high school but retired a few years ago. Tonight, he's playing the first Mr. Beech and taking small groups on tours of 'Christmas Past.' It's fun, and with a ghost story a bit spooky."

Cal nodded. On a tour, he wouldn't be expected to talk, which was good, because he didn't know what to say. Alana meant well by mentioning Cal needing an apprenticeship. There was nothing for him to be upset about. She drew him toward Mr. Bouchard, whom Cal recognized, although he'd never taken art in high school.

As Mr. Bouchard marshalled a group together and talked about the home's history and Christmas in Victorian times, Cal's thoughts whirled.

Alana. He couldn't let her guess anything was wrong, especially because it was nothing to do with her, not really. People wanting to help him was good. Like he'd said when they delivered that hamper to Heather and her family, it wasn't charity. It was a boost when folks needed it. Freely given.

Except when it wasn't.

Charity kids. Paid to look after you. They're only doing it for the money. All foster kids are bad.

Long-buried schoolyard taunts resurfaced in Cal's mind. The foster parents who'd looked after him and Jesse weren't in it for financial gain. They'd been good people who wanted to make a positive difference in a kid's life, the Barretts especially. But there were also lots of stereotypes about foster parents and the young people they took in, and in every school there were bullies. Jesse *had* been a "bad" kid, and some foster parents couldn't cope with him, but he'd acted out because he was hurting. He also needed special care most of their foster families weren't trained in or equipped to give.

However, until now, Cal hadn't realized how

much those stereotypes—and taunts—had persisted and shaped his way of thinking.

"Cal?" Alana's soft voice was concerned and compassionate. "What's wrong?"

"Nothing." The word stuck in his throat.

"It's me, remember? I know you so I know when something's not right."

Mr. Bouchard's voice faded as he took the group into a room off the dining room, what he called a butler's pantry.

Alana did know him. Cal felt as if layers of himself were being peeled away, leaving him as vulnerable as he'd been as a boy. Except now, with her, he couldn't keep pretending.

CHAPTER FIFTEEN

For a minute, Cal had gone as white as a sheet and looked like he was going to pass out. After muttering an apology to Mr. Bouchard, Alana had grabbed her coat and Cal's and then taken him out through the kitchen door to the Old Beech Home's back porch. She sat on a cushioned wooden bench, grabbed a cozy throw from one of the arms and patted the space at her side. "Take a seat. What's up?"

As she arranged the throw over her knees, she also studied him in the silvery moonlight. His closed-off expression didn't give her any clues, but something was obviously wrong. Cal hadn't seemed himself since she'd told him about the possibility of an apprenticeship at Strawberry Pond Automotive. Was that the issue? If so, what was the problem? He'd agreed with her that it was fantastic news.

"Mr. Bouchard hadn't even got to the ghost-story part of the tour, but you've never been one to get scared by ghosts," she said, trying to joke.

"Real life's scary enough." Cal's voice was as strained as his expression. "There's no need to pretend or tell silly stories." He paused, and although the bench was small, ensuring they sat close together, he still seemed far away. Unapproachable and shutting her out.

"I thought you'd enjoy coming here. These Holiday Candlelight evenings are a local tradition. The house is also really interesting." Or maybe that was only to her. She liked learning about how people lived long ago. How her own family had lived since her mom's ancestors had been in and near Strawberry Pond going back almost two hundred years.

"It's not the house." Cal's head was now bent so Alana couldn't see his face.

"Well, if I said or did something to upset you, I didn't mean to." Except on the football field, Cal never showed frustration or anger. Instead, he went inside himself, where Alana couldn't reach him. Even when they'd broken up, unlike her he'd kept his cool. But in a way that icy calm had been worse and more final than if he'd raised his voice.

When Cal lifted his head, the moonlight sharpened the planes of his face and made him look older. A stranger almost. "It's not you, it's me. You did a really nice thing speaking to Mr.

Johnson's son about me maybe needing an apprenticeship."

"I'd have done it for anyone, not only you." But Cal was special and more important to her. "It's being part of a community and what we do here. We look out for each other." That's why Alana had never wanted to live anywhere else.

"It's great and..." Cal's voice was gruff and when he finally turned to look at Alana, his eyes were wide, almost disbelieving. "Sometimes I have a hard time believing that good things are happening for me. It's like I'm conditioned to always expect the worst. Before I came to Strawberry Pond, as a foster kid and Jesse's brother, I was a target. A guy I thought was my friend..." Cal shrugged. "He said he only tried to be my friend because his mom made him. Like I was a charity project or service activity."

"That's awful."

"It was but then we moved schools and foster homes so... I made myself forget what happened. When you told me about the apprenticeship possibility, a bunch of stuff came rushing back. I also hadn't talked to anyone but you and Mrs. Barrett about qualifying as a mechanic so it threw me. I'm not mad, but since I've only just applied for the course, I kind of panicked."

"That's understandable. I didn't mean to stick my nose in your business but it might've seemed that way." She patted her nose, an instinctive gesture, and Cal's face softened as he grinned.

"No, you cared and wanted to help. Besides, it's a cute nose. Like a button on your face." His smile widened, and his gray eyes held a teasing twinkle. "Adorable, actually." He wrapped one arm around Alana's shoulders in a half hug. "I overreacted."

"And I got ahead of myself. I should've talked to you before mentioning anything to Brad. It's only that I was excited for you. Proud as well. I spoke before thinking." Which Alana tended to do because she was naturally exuberant and had always been more outgoing than Cal. In that sense, they'd been opposites but still, they'd complemented each other—except when they didn't.

New awareness dawned. She'd spoken without thinking in breaking up with Cal, too. And made assumptions. To truly give their relationship a second chance, they had to talk about their expectations and learn how to communicate. Shame and embarrassment curdled in the pit of her stomach.

"We both messed up." Cal hugged Alana tighter. "I wish I could trust as easily as you do, just see things for what they are and not look for agendas. I'll do that for you and me, okay, we're not in a relationship, not really, but I mean, if we ever were again."

Alana nodded, pausing to organize her thoughts instead of rushing to fill the silence. With growing up as he did and not being able to count on a stable family unit, it made sense that Cal was vulnerable when it came to relationships. All kinds.

"Even though I said tonight wasn't a date, there's still something between us. Something important." She looked at the stars, the vastness of the sky and surrounding mountains making her feel small but also somehow grounded. "But it's different now than before. We're in our thirties, not teenagers, and we have more life experience, good and bad." She took Cal's free hand and squeezed it. "I've been thinking a lot about how we broke up. Some of it was because we didn't know how to communicate with each other and made assumptions. I assumed you joining the navy was the end of us being together but maybe it didn't have to be. What do you think?" This time she was determined to listen as much, if not more than she spoke.

"I don't know. Maybe in the end we'd have broken up anyway. Military life's hard on even the most committed relationships. One person in the couple can be deployed for months at a time, and the other's left at home waiting. As

I saw with some of my shipmates, it's tough." Cal's hand rested in hers, motionless. "You're right, though, about needing to talk to each other and not making assumptions." His voice hitched. "If we were to try again, we'd need to figure out what we both expected from a relationship. Make sure we're on the same page. I'd want to get it, us, right."

"Me, too." She hesitated. What had Laura said at their last breakfast get-together? Would Alana "take a risk or forever wonder." At the time, she'd said she didn't know, but now, she did. Once, she'd loved Cal with her whole heart, and in the intervening years she hadn't come close to feeling that way about anyone else.

If there was a chance for them to find that love again, as responsible adults rather than immature teenagers, she had to take a risk no matter how much it scared her. Cal had been vulnerable with her. Could she be as vulnerable with him? "I'd like to try again. If you would."

"I would. More than anything." His voice was low and threaded with emotion.

"Good." One word but it was a big one. Maybe even life changing. She wasn't stuck. She was moving forward.

His half smile was wry. "I liked Mr. Johnson, and while I never met Brad, the guys in the shop spoke well of him. I'll go talk to him. It can't hurt."

"No, it can't. Who knows, you might even get some other ideas. Like what's called an informational interview." At Cal's puzzled expression, Alana continued. "It's when you talk to someone about their career to help you figure out your own path. Most people enjoy talking about their work, and you get advice, insights and professional connections. It's a win-win."

"The career counselor I talked to before leaving the military suggested something similar, but…well, I'm not sure if I can handle it on my own." Cal's breath made a soft gray cloud in the winter air.

"You can count on me." Alana squeezed his hand again, and this time Cal squeezed back. "I believe in you." When it came to his career, she'd do everything possible to support and encourage Cal. As for the rest? It would take time, but she also wanted to take that chance.

She pushed away a flicker of doubt. Cal had been honest with her. He'd been embarrassed about his brother. That's why he'd never mentioned Jesse to her before. It made sense.

"I won't take your belief in me for granted again." Cal's voice was low and resolute. "I never thought you'd give me a fresh start and now, well, by talking to each other, we'll figure everything out."

"We will. Small steps." Her heart constricted. The past couldn't be swept aside so easily or fully, but they were making a start and that's what counted. "But first, it's almost Christmas and I haven't chosen or decorated my tree yet. I could use a hand. Anchoring a tree to a wall is easier with two people."

"I'd be happy to help." Cal's eyes softened. "Pick out a tree at Rustic Hearts tomorrow and, if you're free, let's decorate it after our shift. We're closing early, aren't we, because of the holiday tractor parade of lights?"

"We are and that'd be fun. We could go to the parade afterward. It's a good time, remember? Most of the town goes." Josie, Laura and their families would be there, and Alana would be with Cal. They'd be making new memories. Together.

"Sure do. Let me know what size of tree you're looking for and I'll set aside some good ones." Cal's voice pulled her back to practicalities.

"That wouldn't be fair. I appreciate the offer, but the best trees have to be for customers." Alana leaned into his side like she once had. Comfortable, familiar and right.

"Okay, you're the boss," Cal teased her. "Do you want to go back inside?" Somewhere a door or window opened, and the choir's voices rose in "Silent Night," clear, crisp and hopeful. "Join another tour to see the rest of the house? Have some eggnog?" He wrinkled his nose and made a face.

"I've never been a big eggnog fan, but, yes, let's see the rest of the house. The decorations are gorgeous and always put me in the festive spirit." Since Cal had appeared at her parents' farm on Thanksgiving, she'd struggled to find seasonal cheer, but after talking with him, Alana felt more settled in herself. Maybe it wasn't too optimistic to think that this might still be a good Christmas. "However, I'm also starving since I didn't have supper, only a few snacks. That piece of shortbread wasn't enough."

"Then what do you say we take a quick house tour and go to the diner for some real food?" Cal tugged Alana to her feet. "Burgers, milkshakes and pie."

"I say that sounds great." After folding the throw and putting it back on the arm of the bench, she put her hand into Cal's again. As they made their way back into the house, there was a new understanding and ease between them.

Alana wouldn't delude herself or see this situation through rose-colored glasses. She and Cal had a lot to work through, but they were on the right path. One day, if they kept on being honest with each other, that path might lead to a true and forever love. One even better than they'd had before.

"THAT BREAKFAST COOKING sure smells good." The next morning, Cal joined Mrs. Barrett in her kitchen and rubbed a hand through his sleep-tousled hair to smooth it. His hair was longer than it had been in years, but he wasn't in the military, where he'd gotten a cut every few weeks. Now, he didn't look much different than Alana's brothers, Ted or the other men who worked at the Christmas tree farm.

Yet although he might blend in better than he once did, he still felt different. Even without a military haircut, because of the way he'd grown up, he'd never felt the same as his peers. He guessed it was something he had to live with, but today he'd woken up with a new sense of lightness.

He'd turned a corner with Alana, and while neither of them had talked about "dating" as such, chatting and laughing over plates of food at the diner was like old times. In fact, they'd talked so long they'd closed the place. While it hadn't been about anything deep, talking about Cal's life in the military, and Alana's work at the library and for Hansen Farms, had helped them get to know each other again. He smiled to himself as he took a mug from a cupboard and went to the coffeemaker to pour himself some of the fragrant brew.

"You had a late night." From the stove where she was frying eggs, Mrs. Barrett greeted him with a smile.

Ten thirty was hardly late, but since Mrs. Barrett usually turned in by nine, and Cal had been in bed by ten since he'd stayed with her, he supposed it did seem like a departure from his usual schedule. "I hope I didn't disturb you coming in." He'd tried to be quiet, but the house was so still that even the squeak of the front door sounded louder than usual.

"Not at all." Her smile widened. "I was awake reading, but even if I hadn't been, I'd have heard you. I'm a mom. Whenever one of my kids is here, if they're out I always wake up when they come in. That mom alert system is pretty powerful." She flipped a fried egg onto a plate, then added a piece of toast and several strips of bacon. "Take a seat." She gestured to Cal's usual place at the table, where a glass of orange juice and bowl of cut-up fruit was already waiting.

"You're spoiling me." He pulled out the chair and sat as she set the food in front of him. "I can make my own breakfast, you know? Especially when you've likely been up for a few hours and have already eaten." He didn't have to be at work until nine thirty and last night Cal had slept better than he had in weeks, before or since coming to Strawberry Pond.

"Sure, you can make breakfast. I taught you, didn't I?" After pouring herself a cup of coffee, Mrs. Barrett sat across from him.

"You did, and I appreciate it." Despite Mrs. Barrett's efforts, Cal rarely made himself a cooked breakfast. Being on his own, it never seemed worth the effort.

"So did you have a nice time last night?"

Cal stopped with a forkful of egg partway to his mouth. Mrs. Barrett had always respected his privacy and never pried, but knowing Strawberry Pond, somebody would likely have already told her that he'd been out with Alana. Both the Old Beech Home and diner had been busy and lots of folks had spotted them together. "It was good. I went out with Alana and we're…kind of giving our relationship another chance."

"Kind of?" Mrs. Barrett raised an eyebrow. "You either are or you aren't."

"We are but…it's not as simple as it might sound." Cal swallowed a mouthful of egg.

"Relationships never are, whether it's the first, second or however many times going at them. Marriage isn't easy, either, but if you find your soul mate it's worth it." She studied him from behind her coffee cup. "I was lucky with my Gary, but even then it wasn't all plain sailing."

"It wasn't?" From everything Cal had seen, Mr. and Mrs. Barrett had had the perfect marriage. Loving, respectful and mutually supportive. A true partnership. Or had he idealized their relationship because it was the only one he'd experienced up close and for the long-term?

"No." A small smile played around Mrs. Barrett's mouth. "We were high-school sweethearts, you know, but we broke up for a while when we moved on to different colleges. Our lives went in separate directions for a few years."

"But you got back together." Of course, they had, because they'd been married for forty-some years at the time Gary Barrett had passed.

"Yes, but we had to work at it. Figure out what went wrong the first time around, commit to doing better and let go of the past. Fully let go, not only pay lip service to it." She drank some coffee and looked out the window into her small backyard, where a pale blue sky reflected off snowdrifts.

"I told Alana about Jesse and how the two of us grew up." Cal crumbled an edge of toast. "How I promised our mom I'd look out for him."

"And why you came to our family on your own and never told anyone about your brother?"

Her steady, blue gaze, almost the same color as the sky, never wavered from his.

"I did and Alana said she understood." She'd probably have understood all those years ago, too, but Cal had been a different person then. So afraid of those schoolyard taunts following him to Strawberry Pond, he'd convinced himself he needed an entirely fresh start. One where Jesse, apart from Cal's few scheduled visits to him with a social worker, was firmly in the past.

"That's good." Mrs. Barrett nodded. "You can't move forward without facing the past and telling the truth. As for Jesse, you also can't keep feeling guilty and thinking you let your mom down by not being able to keep your brother out of trouble. Like you, Jesse made his own choices."

Cal's stomach knotted, and he pushed away his half-eaten plate of food. He hadn't told Alana the whole truth. "How'd you guess I keep thinking I let Mom down?" That guilt had eaten him up for years.

Mrs. Barrett reached across the table and covered one of his hands with hers. "Another part of that mom alert. I didn't give birth to you, and I'd never think of trying to take your mother's place, but I've spent my life around kids. My own and those Gary and I fostered. Before you came to live with us, we read your file and talked to your social worker. Knew you had a brother and why the two of you were split up. The fact you never talked about Jesse, shut down whenever I asked about him, told me something else was going on. And when you and Alana broke up, and you left town so suddenly, well, there was more to that than met the eye, too, but you were an adult." Her eyebrows furrowed in a familiar worried frown. "If you'd had a notion to join the military, I only hoped it was what *you* wanted and not because of something *Jesse* had done."

Cal tried to work moisture into his dry mouth. Mrs. Barrett was both smart and wise. As well as Alana, he had to tell Mrs. Barrett the truth. *All of it.*

"Oh, yes," she continued. "I always wondered if you had something to do with the Hansens' barn burning down, but after talking it over with Gary, we decided we couldn't ask. It would've been overstepping. You were no longer in our care or living under our roof."

"It wasn't me, but I was there. With Jesse." Even now, fifteen years later, that guilt hadn't left Cal, either.

"I suspected as much." Mrs. Barrett's concerned voice drew him back to the present—and the enormity of what he had to do. "I'm not judging. You covered for your brother, and I understand why. However, you can't base your relationship with Alana on half truths. The whole truth always comes out somehow, and when it does she'll think you lied to her, betrayed her even."

Mrs. Barrett was right, but that didn't make things any easier. Although he hadn't wanted to admit it, Cal had already recognized most of what she'd said himself. "Thanks for breakfast. If I don't get a move on, I'll be late for work." He manufactured a smile. "I'll be late back again tonight. I promised Alana that after we finish our shifts at Rustic Hearts, I'd help her set up and decorate her Christmas tree. Then it's the holiday tractor parade of lights."

"That'll be nice for you both." Still Mrs. Barrett studied him, and as Cal got up to clear his place, he could feel her eyes following him to the compost bin and dishwasher.

This conversation wasn't over, only on hold. She knew it, and so did Cal.

CHAPTER SIXTEEN

"Hey, Mom." On the last Saturday morning before Christmas, Alana came into the store at Rustic Hearts in a swirl of snow. "I wasn't expecting to see you here today." She brushed snowflakes off her coat and hat. "It's sure windy out there. And cold." After taking off her mittens, she rubbed her hands together to warm them.

"I'm only here for an hour or so." Her mom sat behind the counter with her laptop open. "You know how Ted's had that sore tooth? He got a short-notice dental appointment, a cancellation, and needed someone to cover until you got here. It's been quiet, so I've been catching up on paperwork. Cal's out in the tree lot." She gestured to the side door.

Cal. The man Alana could hardly stop thinking about. Spending time with him last night at the Old Beech Home and then the diner had been good. As teenagers, he'd only ever let her see part of himself. The outside layers. Now that he'd begun to open up, she was getting to know the real Cal and the hurts he carried.

"You look tired, Mom. Is everything okay?" Once she took off her winter gear and put it in the staff area at the back, Alana returned to the store and glanced from the spreadsheet open on the laptop screen to the dark circles under her mom's eyes.

"I *am* tired." Her mom let out a long sigh. "Your dad's chomping at the bit to get back to work, but he's not ready yet. His doctor cleared him to take on light tasks but that's all. It could be up to a year before your dad's back to full strength again."

Or he might never be as strong as before.

The thought that Alana had tried to suppress could no longer be ignored. Usually, she faced reality head-on, but when it came to her parents and their family farm, it was easier to go on as they were, rather than asking questions that might lead to an uncomfortable conversation. "You and dad still have the farm-succession plan, right?" Her friend Josie had talked about such a plan for their own family farm, and how her gramps was slowly transferring all aspects of the operation into Josie's capable hands.

"We do. Your brothers are set to take over when the time comes, but that doesn't mean it isn't hard." Her mom sighed again. "I worry that we'll still need more help before then."

"Can Ted stay on longer?" Their temporary farm manager was good at the job and had skills Alana's dad didn't.

"He can but it will only ever be a stopgap. Ted likes being retired, and he and his wife want to travel more. They have an RV and, well, Ted only came to work here because with your dad's surgery, we were desperate."

"I see." Alana likely saw more than her mom intended. Her parents probably wanted to retire as well, or only work part-time, but would Hansen Farms sustain her brothers and their families? Times had changed, and while Alana's mom had only ever worked on the farm, like Alana both Jordy's and Ben's wives had off-farm jobs. Alana had never wanted to work full-time on the farm, even if it'd been feasible financially, and she wouldn't want to stop working at the library. She loved her job and many of the library patrons were like family.

"Don't worry. I'm sure everything will work out." Her mom gave Alana a bright smile that didn't reach her eyes. "So, you and Cal, are you… Well, I heard that the two of you were at the Old Beech Home event last night and then the diner."

Was that hurt in her mom's expression? Alana

and her mom were close and talked almost daily. So why hadn't Alana told her mom about going out with Cal? "I would've told you but it was last-minute. Brad Johnson at Strawberry Pond Automotive gave me the tickets for the house tour because he and his wife couldn't use them. I knew you were busy and, well… I didn't want to make it seem more important than it was. As for the diner, we only went there because I didn't have time for supper." Alana's face felt hot, and she busied herself topping up the treat bowl with more candy canes. "I've also had a hectic few days at work. That's why I haven't called."

"You're a grown woman, dear. I don't expect you to tell me everything going on in your life." Her mom gave Alana an understanding smile. "I also hope you've never seen me as the nosy or interfering type."

"No, you've always been great."

However, Alana knew what Strawberry Pond was like. If only she'd taken the time to call her mom and give her a heads-up.

"I didn't mean for you to hear about me sort of going out with Cal from anyone else. We're not officially dating, but we agreed to try to give our relationship another chance." Alana hadn't worked out how that differed from dating but in her own mind it somehow did.

"I see." Now, Alana's mom was the one who probably saw more than Alana intended.

"We talked and we're both different now. Older and more mature. Cal really opened up to me, Mom." What he'd told her about Jesse was private, not to be shared with her mom or anyone else. Cal had trusted her, and it felt like the first step in the two of them starting fresh.

"That's great." Her mom closed the laptop. "As long as you're happy, I'm happy."

"I *am* happy." Despite that niggling sense of unease she couldn't seem to shake. Cal joining the military with his brother was a big deal, sure, but was there another reason he hadn't mentioned Jesse or that promise he'd made to their mom? And what was the rush to enlist? Surely, Cal could've waited a few weeks instead of racing out of town like he'd done something wrong. As for Cal thinking she wasn't good enough for him, that was ridiculous. He'd loved her and it had always been enough.

Her mom hesitated in packing up the laptop. "While I'm glad you're happy, even though you're older that doesn't mean you still can't be hurt. Cal, what happened before, your dad and I worried over you so much. Cal broke your heart and—"

"My heart's a lot more resilient now than it was back then." Alana had made certain of it, which was why she'd never dated anyone seriously since Cal. "You have enough to worry about with Dad. Don't fuss over me."

"I can't help it." Her mom's expression was tender. "Moms and their children are connected. Every night before I go to sleep, I think about each of my kids and what's going on with you. I know you're adults, but it settles me to think of you all living your independent lives. Like boats bobbing along on the ocean. I'm lucky you're all nearby and I see you often."

"We're lucky, too." What her mom had said was sweet, but it still left Alana with a bitter taste in her mouth.

Would she ever have that connection with a child of her own? Until Cal returned, she'd hadn't let herself think about everything which might have been. She'd convinced herself she was happy and settled. However, now she knew the truth. She'd accepted that her life was fine as it was, but true happiness was different. She still wanted a husband and children, maybe even more than she had before. Yet she was still almost as far away from having them. If Cal took that college course and completed an apprenticeship at Strawberry Pond Automative or somewhere else, would he want to settle down? He was starting over in his life, not just in their relationship, and would likely be focused on career goals. Where did starting a family fit into that? Once, they'd talked about having kids, when the time was right, but did Cal still want children? There was so much they had to talk about, but even if he stayed in Strawberry Pond beyond Christmas, unlike hers, his life was in flux.

"Alana." The side door of the store opened, and Cal came in. "I picked out a few trees for you to look at. There's a gorgeous balsam fir that a couple of folks have been eyeing." His face was red with cold and frost edged his Hansen Farms stocking hat, but his eyes sparkled. "If you have a few minutes, can you come see? The parking lot's empty and we'll spot anybody driving in."

"Sure, that sounds fine." As her mom greeted Cal and prepared to leave the store, warmth slid through Alana. She was worrying unnecessarily. One thing at a time. Along with truly getting to know and understand each other again, and figuring out what they both wanted in a relationship, they had to rebuild trust.

The door closed behind her mom, and Alana's gaze locked with Cal's.

Without trust, they couldn't have a relationship at all.

"OKAY?" CAL FLIPPED a switch and the multicolored lights he'd strung on the balsam fir Alana had chosen illuminated both the tree and her living room. All day, he'd thought about that conversation he'd had with Mrs. Barrett at breakfast. He'd tell Alana the truth and soon, but he had to find the right time.

"Great job. You got the strands on really even." Alana studied the tree from behind the coffee table, where she was unpacking ornaments. "You can't really see the chicken wire, either."

"Oh, no, you don't." He grabbed Holly by her pink, jewel-studded collar and gently moved her away from a low branch. "This tree's fixed to the wall, but you still can't climb it."

The cat meowed and swished her tail.

"She's scrappy and got some attitude." Alana laughed as she tossed a squeaky rubber ball to Holly.

"Like her owner, maybe?" Cal got up from where he'd sprawled half under the tree and joined Alana.

"Are you comparing me to a cat?" She held out an ornament made from green beads in the shape of a bow.

"Meow." Cal made a cat sound, and Holly looked up at them, her green eyes curious. "Not at all. Cats are cute, this one especially. Like you." He dropped a kiss on Alana's cheek. "It's also good to be scrappy with attitude. Means you have a survival instinct." Without having his own instinct for survival, Cal wouldn't be where he was today.

He glanced around Alana's comfy living room. A dark blue sofa was piled with red-and-green toss pillows and a matching armchair held a book, a red throw and, on a side table, Alana's phone sat next to his. He could almost trick himself that they were a couple for real, decorating their Christmas tree together. A family. Not one that would replace the family he'd lost, but a new one he'd love and protect always.

"I made this beaded bow in the third grade." Alana fixed a small wire hook on the bow's top and hung it on the tree. "I made one for my parents, too. They still have it on their tree. For me, the best ornaments are ones collected over time. Either handmade or I got for a special occasion."

Family and tradition. There it was again. What Alana had and Cal missed.

"Remember this one?" She picked it up and handed it to him. "You gave it to me our senior-year class trip to Boston."

"I remember." He held the wooden cutout of the city skyline.

That Boston excursion had been the first and only overnight class trip Cal had ever gone on, which made it special in itself. Mr. and Mrs. Barrett had chipped in, and Cal had saved as much money as he could from shoveling snow and working part-time at the diner washing dishes. But it was seeing the city with Alana that had made the trip truly amazing. He knew how much she loved Christmas, so when he'd spotted a store that sold holiday decorations, he'd bought her this one and had it personalized with the year. And when he'd given her his carefully chosen gift on Christmas Eve, her eyes had lit up like a Christmas tree, and she'd promised to keep the ornament always.

"Here, let's put it on the tree together." Alana's hand covered his and then they hung the decoration by its red ribbon cord on a high branch. The fragrant scent of fir filled Cal's nostrils, reminding him of Christmases before his mom got sick and everything changed. "There." Taking her hand away, Alana nodded her approval. "Do you want me to put on some holiday music?" She gestured to her phone.

"Okay." Music or not, all that mattered was sharing this special time with the woman he'd loved. *The woman he still loved and always would.* Could Cal risk telling her that his feelings for her hadn't changed?

His breath caught as, oblivious, Alana crossed the room to pick up her phone, scrolled to a playlist and swayed in time to Carrie Underwood singing "Favorite Time of Year."

Cal remembered that song because he'd been

deployed near Hawaii around the time it came out. Spending Christmas in a tropical climate, the song's lyrics about snow and sitting by a fire had reminded him of New Hampshire…and Alana.

"Cal?" Alana hung several more decorations on the tree, Holly now eyeing them from the armchair. "All right?"

"Yes, fine." He forced himself to return to the present. "Where do you want this one?" He picked up a small fabric mouse wearing a pink tutu, ballet slippers and a red-and-white Santa hat.

"Anywhere is fine." She grinned. "My tree's more about memories than any special order or color scheme. My mom gave me that mouse after she took me to see *The Nutcracker* ballet when I was seven." Her smile slipped. "I'm worried about my folks. Today, before you came into the store, Mom was talking to me about Hansen Farms. My brothers will take it over, and I'll continue pitching in when I can, but it's a big operation. I got the impression Mom would like to retire or work part-time. Dad's hip-replacement surgery and recovery have gotten her thinking more about the future."

"The day I took him to his physical-therapy appointment, your dad seemed to be doing really well." Cal hung up a holiday stocking made of paper and colored in shades of green and red, evidently made by a child.

"He is, but…" Alana worried her lower lip. "Ted's only managing the farm temporarily, so when he leaves, Dad will have to take on most of the load again. From what Mom said, it might be a year or more before Dad's fully up to speed. If he ever is." Her voice quavered. "My parents are growing older and, well, it's hard. Hansen Farms is our family's legacy."

"Hey." Cal put an arm around Alana's tight shoulders. "Your family's close and you've always worked together to find solutions to problems." In that way, along with the Barretts, they'd shown Cal what it meant to be a family—something he'd hoped to model in his own life one day. "You, Jordy and Ben will figure things out."

"We will, but from what Mom said, we're also going to need more help sooner rather than later. I don't want to give up my job at the library, but—"

"I could help. I mean…if you'd have me." The words popped out before Cal thought but he meant them. He owed the Hansens a lot. More than he could ever repay. "Seasonally or something more, either at the Christmas-tree farm or your market garden and orchard. I'm a hard worker and I'm willing to learn." He made himself stop before he said too much.

"But if you're going to school and doing an apprenticeship, how would you fit it all in?" Alana stared at him wide-eyed.

"Like I did before with those part-time jobs I had in high school and that year I worked at the garage after graduating." He hesitated. "Or maybe you could hire other military veterans looking to upskill. College students. There's also Heather's husband. You heard anything from him yet?" Cal doubted it because without Heather saying much that day they'd delivered the hamper to her family, he'd gotten a sense of where the guy must be coming from. He'd be embarrassed to reach out and also ashamed he need a handout from the town to feed his family.

"No, not a word." Alana confirmed what Cal expected.

"I planned to drop by, anyway. I got a few gifts for the boys, so I could ask if you want? Find out more about what kind of job their dad did before he got laid off." Cal also felt compelled to check on Heather. She reminded him so much of his mom, and the two boys were like him and Jesse.

"That's really nice of you." Still in his half embrace, some of the tension in Alana's shoulders seemed to lessen.

"It's more a way of trying to give back." As Alana leaned into his arm, Cal let himself soak up the wonderful feeling of closeness and connection it gave him. "Strawberry Pond was always like a big family, so Heather and her kids, I want to look out for them." He cleared his throat. "Speaking of family, I took your advice."

"What do you mean?" When Alana looked at him, her expression was almost as loving as it'd been of old.

Did she still love him, too? And if she did... Cal's face warmed, and he curbed the errant thoughts. He had to fix his own family before he took things any further with her. "I texted Jesse. He... We... I'm going to Boston to see him on my day off tomorrow. Meet Jesse's wife and my nephew."

"That's great." When Alana smiled, Cal felt like he was ten feet tall and, with her at his side, he could do anything he set his mind to.

"It is. Really great." Although he'd been surprised to hear from Cal, and that Cal was back in Strawberry Pond, Jesse had seemed happy, too. Could the two of them make a fresh start like Cal was doing with Alana? This time be brothers for real? He wouldn't know unless he tried.

"Family's about love and what better time than Christmas, a season of love, for you guys to reconnect?"

As she rested her head against him, everything felt right in Cal's world. Decorating a Christmas tree together was the kind of thing a couple would do. Could he and Alana get married and decorate their own tree together, and add more ornaments to her cherished collection?

Like with Jesse, Cal wouldn't know unless he took the biggest risk of all, but it was one he was ready for. He couldn't move forward with Alana without it.

CHAPTER SEVENTEEN

ALANA CLAPPED HER mittened hands as the Hansen Farms tractor passed the corner between Strawberry Pond's post office and the town green. "There's Isla. See?" She pointed to her small niece in the tractor's cab, waving and smiling at the crowd, sparkly reindeer antlers on her head. "It's way past her bedtime, and she'll be tired tomorrow, but as I remember from my own turn in that tractor, it's worth it."

At Alana's side, Cal clapped, too, and behind them, cheers went up as they had for each parade entry. After decorating her tree and ordering pizza for a quick meal, she and Cal had walked over to what folks in Strawberry Pond called "downtown" to catch the tractor holiday parade of lights, meeting family and friends along the way. For Alana, this parade, a time to honor and celebrate the local agricultural community, was one of the most magical events in Strawberry Pond's holiday season calendar. Tonight, she and Cal were once again sharing it together.

"As always, your tractor and that winter-wonderland display on the trailer are fantastic." On Alana's other side, Josie gestured to the animals her girls were oohing and aahing over. She handed several cans to one of the fire-department volunteers collecting nonperishable food for the Pond Pantry. "I remember those woodland animals from when I was a kid."

"Like your grandparents, my folks aren't big on change." Alana glanced at the line of tractors, sixty of them or more, decked out for the holidays. With everything from inflatable Santas to cartoon characters, and the more minimal white lights and silver or gold tinsel stars, it was a colorful display. However, for her mom and dad, things had already begun to change. This year was the first time Alana's dad hadn't been out to the parade. Her dad still couldn't stand for such a long time, and although she'd suggested bringing a folding chair for him, her mom had vetoed that idea, saying it was also too cold. So her parents had stayed home, and it was Jordy driving the Hansen Farms tractor.

"Have you heard from Laura lately?" Josie asked into Alana's ear.

"No." Which, when Alana thought about it, was more than a little odd. "I thought she was supposed to be here tonight. That's what her message this morning said, anyway." Even when they didn't get together in person, the three friends stayed connected via an online group chat. Then again, Alana had been so caught up with Cal, except for keeping an eye out for any urgent messages from her folks, she hadn't paid much attention to her phone in the past few hours.

So caught up with Cal. She loved him, and in a part of her she'd never let herself admit, she'd never truly stopped loving him. That love had been dormant for a while, but now it was back, coming into flower like the Christmas cactus on the plant stand in her sunny den window.

After tonight, she wouldn't see Cal for more than twenty-four hours because he was going to Boston to visit Jesse, but perhaps they'd share their feelings for each other when he came back. He loved her, too, she was sure of it. It had been in the way he'd looked at her when they were decorating her tree. The tenderness and care in his face and eyes had made her heart skip a beat. However, her heart now sped up whenever she was around him or even heard his voice on the phone or in the tree lot. It was a lot to admit and in such a short time, too.

"Sorry, what did you say?" She turned her attention back to Josie.

"Laura's sick. I texted her a few minutes ago when I didn't see her here and that's what she said. But she was fine earlier. She dropped by our farm store around suppertime on her way back from a house showing." Josie tilted her head to one side and frowned. "I hope she hasn't caught a virus just before Christmas. It feels like something's been off with her for longer, though. Haven't you noticed? Usually, she's really chatty but for the past week or so, nothing. She was even kind of distant with me at the store. I mean, she was friendly enough, but it seemed like her mind was elsewhere."

Alana hadn't noticed Laura's silence. Another part of being caught up with Cal. She fidgeted with the fringe on her scarf and darted a glance at him. Since the main part of the parade had passed, he was chatting with Heath. Something about Boston traffic and navigating what for nonresidents could be the city's often confusing street layout. Not that Alana was eavesdropping. Rather, whenever she and Cal were together, it was as if she was connected to him by an invisible force, and hyperaware of what he was saying and doing.

"Like the rest of us, between work and the holiday season, Laura's busy. That's probably why she seemed distracted." But now that Alana considered it, when Laura had popped into the library yesterday to pick up Danny from the after-school robotics club for teens, she hadn't stopped to talk like she usually did. Instead, she'd waved at Alana from the doorway before rushing off.

Although she was dressed for the winter weather and wasn't cold, Alana hugged herself. Change was everywhere, and she couldn't stop it or slow time even if she might want to. For the first time, neither Josie nor her gramps were driving their vintage tractor, affectionately called Fifi, in this parade, instead leaving it to one of their farmhands to do the honors.

"I should round up my daughters and get home." Josie gave Alana's parka-clad arm a consoling pat. "I didn't drive Fifi because I thought we could watch the parade as a family, but at the last minute the girls wanted to be with their friends leaving me and Heath on our own." She inclined her head to a cluster of tween girls who were far enough away from their parents to consider themselves independent, but close enough for those same parents to keep an eye on them. "Bella and Lottie are growing up way too fast. It seems like yesterday I was bringing them to the library for toddler rhyme time, and now, look at them."

Alana nodded as she followed where Josie indicated. Her friend's daughters were like "bonus nieces" to Alana, and she loved being part of their lives. Yet like her brothers' children, as Bella and Lottie grew older they developed new interests and became involved in more activities. While Alana wasn't sidelined, she also wasn't as important to them as she'd once been. She bit back a sigh. What was wrong with her? It was right that children became busier and more independent as they grew, and she had plenty of little ones at the library to spend time with. That time was structured, though, and she didn't have a personal connection with those young children. Isla was five so Alana would have to make the most of the next year or so with her.

"Hey, kiddo." As Isla charged toward her followed by Jordy, Alana caught her niece in a hug. "Did you have fun?"

"It was the best ever." Isla bounced up and down, and her reindeer antlers flashed in the darkness, illuminating her wide-eyed, excited face. "Daddy said I can ride with him again next year. Since there's no other kids coming along in the family, I'm the youngest."

"That'll be fun for you." When Alana answered Isla she forced a smile. Over the years her family, friends and acquaintances had married and started families of their own, and she'd been part of too many weddings and baby showers to count. At each one, she'd joined in, happy for the couple or mom-to-be, ignoring any well-intentioned comments about it soon being her "turn."

"Come on, Isla-bee." Jordy tugged on his daughter's parka hood, the gesture and nickname loving. "We need to find your mom and brothers. If you don't get to bed soon, you'll be a grumpy girl tomorrow."

Isla gave him a mock pout and then with a final hug to Alana and a flurry of goodbyes, the two of them and Josie and Heath were gone, leaving Alana alone.

But not truly alone. Before she had time to wonder where he'd gotten to, Cal was at her side again. "Sorry I missed saying hi to your brother and niece. I was talking to Brad from the garage. He came to find me."

"And?" Alana suppressed her eagerness, but it must be good news since Cal's face was flushed and his gray eyes sparkled.

"Brad said he talked to his dad, who said good things about me, so if I'm interested in an apprenticeship as a mechanic, it's mine." He cleared his throat. "I'd made an appointment to talk to Brad after Christmas, but his dad was here and recognized me and, well… I'll be visiting Strawberry Pond Automotive to have a look around instead of a formal interview."

"That's wonderful." Alana could've bounced with excitement like Isla had but she didn't. "I mean, what do you think about it?" Unlike before, she wouldn't get ahead of herself.

"It *is* wonderful." He beamed and, despite being in public, wrapped both his arms around her in a hug. "When I told Brad I was worried about getting into that trade-school program, he also said I'm sure to be accepted. He knows a few people who teach in it and apparently they're always looking for students like me."

"Sure they are." Joy bubbled up inside Alana as she returned Cal's hug. "Like Strawberry Pond Automative, they'd be lucky to have you."

"Thanks for believing in me and for…everything." Cal held Alana ever closer.

"Happy to." Her breath caught. She knew and remembered that soft and loving look in his eyes and face. "You have an early start tomorrow morning, and it'll be a long day going to Boston and back. I can walk home on my own. It's not late and there's lots of people going my way." She gestured to the stream of pedestrians on the town green and nearby sidewalks.

"I'm not leaving you on your own, Lanie, no matter how many people are around. I'll see you home safely." Cal cupped her chin and drew her gaze back to his. "And when I come back from Boston, we need to talk."

"Okay." Alana trembled, the rest of the crowd seemed to melt away, and then, as they crossed the green, Cal drew her behind one of the lit holiday trees, briefly sheltered from curious onlookers.

His eyes darkened. "But for now, know that I love you and I always will, no matter what."

"Me, too. I love you." She murmured the words and then his mouth covered hers in a kiss that she'd never forget. Ever.

They still had a lot to figure out, but if they kept talking—and kissing—everything would be okay.

THE FOLLOWING AFTERNOON, Cal glanced around the small living room in the bungalow that Jesse, his wife, Maria, a nurse, and their eight-month-old son, Lucas, called home. Decorated in neutral tones with festive red pillows on the sofa and evergreen garlands around both windows, from the Christmas tree in a corner to the baby books and toys on the coffee table and in the wooden toy box, it was warm and welcoming.

And a world away from how Cal and Jesse had grown up.

"More coffee or a soda?" Jesse came back into the room from taking a phone call and stopped Cal's musings. While Cal took after their mother with light hair and gray eyes, Jesse's curly black hair and snapping dark eyes was how Cal remembered their dad.

"I'm good, thanks." Despite the friendliness,

this meeting was far from easy, and after exchanging a few pleasantries, Maria had taken Lucas to another part of the house, leaving the two brothers alone.

"Sorry," Jesse said. "That was a check-in with a friend from work. We traded shifts so I could be here. To meet you."

"Thanks. I know it was short notice." Cal paused, considering where best to start. "Maria seems great, and Lucas is wonderful." He spoke around an unexpected lump in his throat. He'd known Jesse was married with a child and settled in a job but "knowing" was different than seeing this "reality." As well as a respected firefighter, his wild and reckless brother had become a doting family man.

"They are." Jesse sat in a chair across from Cal on the sofa. "I'm a lucky guy, and when you texted to say you wanted to visit…well, it's good to see you, bro."

"You, too." Cal rested his hands on his knees. He'd always been a sounding board for Jesse when they were growing up, but all of a sudden it was as if their roles were reversed.

"It's also good to have a chance to thank you." Jesse drained his coffee mug. "I never made your life easy, but you were always there for me, even when it came to running off to join the military together. That's what helped me finally turn my life around and start heading in a better, more positive direction. If not for you, I'd have an adult criminal record, which is a lot harder to move beyond. I owe you more than I can ever say or repay. I know the last time we saw each other, I gave you a hard time about giving me advice, but I was out of line." He gave a self-deprecating smile. "I've missed you, and I'm sorry for everything."

"I'm your brother. I'd always be there for you. I've missed you, too." Until now, Cal hadn't realized quite how much. "There's nothing more to say or repay." Squirming on the plump sofa cushions, he heard the roughness in his voice and cleared his throat. He'd sacrificed everything for Jesse, including the love and family he'd expected to have with Alana. But seeing his brother so happy and settled, Cal had finally fulfilled his promise to their mom.

Jesse was okay. More than okay, and Cal was proud of how far he'd come. Any debt, if he'd ever looked at it that way, was paid.

"Not all brothers would be so supportive as well as forgiving. Not after everything I did." Jesse's cheeks flushed pink. "And when I came to see you in Strawberry Pond, snuck into town like a criminal and waited for you behind that dumpster and then everything went wrong, I—"

"What else could I do? We were both there

when that barn burned down." Cal didn't want to talk about what had happened that day, but he couldn't avoid it any longer. He guessed he'd been lucky nobody had taken any notice of Jesse when the trucker he'd hitched a ride with had dropped him off near the garage as dusk had fallen. Nobody had taken any notice of the two of them walking out of town, either, but Cal had been sure to take a back way across the fields. While he'd wanted to believe that Jesse was different—a reformed character—a part of him still had doubts.

"Yes, but I was the one who lit the match, waved it around and then dropped it in the dry grass. It was an accident, but still… Even now, I keep replaying that day over and over again in my head. I told you I'd changed but I was still angry and frustrated with my life. I was adrift, but like always you had everything figured out."

"Maybe it looked that way." Yet Cal had been on the right path back then, which, unlike Jesse's, had been a productive one. In the intervening years, he'd done a lot of good in his life and his military service had been honorable, but in some ways he'd also been marking time.

"Mistake, accident, whatever… What happened that day because of me goofing around is a big part of why I became a firefighter." For an instant, when Jesse dropped his chin into his hands, he looked a lot like the boy Cal remembered. Small, vulnerable and defeated. "I felt so bad about starting that fire, now I give talks to kids to try to show them there's a better way than causing trouble. Maria, who, along with you, is one of the most forgiving people I ever met, says it's me atoning for my bad decisions." His laugh was strained.

"You were eighteen and had just been released from the state's care." Cal repeated what he'd said to himself so many times over the years. "I'd had Mr. and Mrs. Barrett to guide me. You didn't, I mean, have people like them. You didn't know how to make good choices."

"True but not the whole truth." Jesse raised his head and stared at Cal straight on. Two men rather than the boys they'd been. "You and me, we had pretty much the same start in life, but I was the one who ended up in front of a judge and in juvenile detention and everywhere else. You didn't. You were a kid as well, not my parent. It wasn't your job to keep me out of trouble. You also weren't responsible for my dumb behavior. Looking back at everything I got up to, I'm amazed and grateful I'm still here and in one piece."

"But, you… I—I promised Mom I'd look out for you." And from the age of ten onward, that promise and what he'd considered his responsibility for his younger brother had shaped Cal's life. "I took that promise seriously." Why was he trying to explain himself?

"You did look out for me, but back then anybody would've struggled to keep me in line." Jesse's smile was wry. "I didn't care what you or anybody else said or tried to get me to do. I was mad at Mom for dying. Mad at Dad, too, even though I didn't really remember him. I was mad at the world, scared and lost, but I didn't know how to acknowledge my emotions let alone express them." He shrugged. "As Maria would tell you, I still struggle with recognizing or talking about what I'm feeling, but I'm making progress. Causing trouble was a way of getting attention. You were perfect. I couldn't measure up."

"I wasn't perfect." Most of the time, Cal had been so afraid of putting a foot wrong maybe it had looked like perfection, but underneath he'd been as angry, afraid and lost as Jesse. "But I—I don't know what to say."

"Me, neither." Jesse laughed, the sound awkward but also real. "Except I'd like to try to figure it out and for us to be brothers again. Maria's got four brothers, so Lucas already has a bunch of uncles, but my boy still needs you. *I* need you. That's one of the reasons why I texted you a few months back… And when you didn't answer, I thought you never wanted to see me again." His voice cracked.

"I need you, too." Cal always had but had never seen it quite so clearly before. "You're the only brother I have." He tried to mask the emotion with a joke. "As for not answering for a while, I had some stuff to figure out. I also… well, I guess I let my pride get in the way." A mistake he wouldn't repeat and which, one day soon, he hoped he and Jesse could talk about.

"Pride. Tell me about it. That's why I as good as told you to butt out of my life that time." Jesse shook his head.

Then Cal and his brother stood and embraced. It was a long time coming but it was nevertheless heartfelt.

If Cal settled in Strawberry Pond, Boston wasn't far away. He could be part of Jesse's life again. Lucas's and Maria's as well.

And if he and Alana had kids, they wouldn't just have the Hansens, they'd also have Jesse, Maria and Lucas. A new family. Not the one Cal had lost, that was gone forever, but a new family of his very own.

It was another fresh start and, without either of them saying a word, for Cal that hug marked another promise. One that was for the future and helped him let go of the past that had smothered him and kept him trapped. A future where he and Jesse were equals, their relationship based on love and mutual respect, not duty or obligation.

No matter what happened with Alana, Cal had his brother back. He hoped that somewhere, their folks knew and were proud of their sons. It hadn't been easy, but the two of them had made it through. And for the first time, Cal also felt that he was good enough. Not only for Alana, but, more importantly, also for himself.

CHAPTER EIGHTEEN

"Cal must have been tired when he got back to town last night. He had a long day." In the store at Rustic Hearts, Alana helped Mrs. Barrett pack the Christmas-tree topper and other items she'd bought into a reusable bag patterned with red poinsettias.

Cal had sent her several brief texts when he'd arrived in Boston and then left the city and was safely back in Strawberry Pond, but hadn't said how his meeting with Jesse had gone. Alana had expected as much. The brothers' relationship was between the two of them, and in time Cal would tell her what he was comfortable sharing. At least she hoped he would. He'd said they needed to talk when he returned from Boston so what else could it be about?

Cal had also said he loved her no matter what. That's what she wanted to focus on and over the past day, she'd hugged that love close like a precious jewel. Sharing how they felt about each other had given Alana a new spring in her step and a happiness that, although still fragile, was a foundation for the future. *Their future.* In the meantime, it was only a few days until Christmas and despite the last-minute holiday rush, she intended to make the most of this wonderful time of year.

"Cal was worn out when he got to my place." Mrs. Barrett tucked a jar of local strawberry jam into her shopping bag, having already told Alana she was stocking up for when her sons and their families visited. "I waited up to make sure I could give him a hot meal if he wanted one, but his brother's wife had packed Cal a nice lunch for the road."

That sounded promising, and as Alana nodded and smiled while Mrs. Barrett talked about holiday preparations, more hope bloomed in her heart. She'd been prepared to console Cal if things hadn't gone well with his brother, but now, they might be celebrating.

"Yes, I'm taking part in the Strawberry Pond Knitters' Christmas cookie exchange." Although it was the third one she'd been involved in, including the one with Josie and Laura, Alana couldn't say no when the club's president had invited her. "It's such a shame about Anne Sullivan coming down with that awful flu. I'm helping with the children's play for Christmas Eve church in her place. I couldn't leave them in the lurch."

Alana didn't want to hurry Mrs. Barrett on her way, but the line of customers behind her was growing and stretched around the store's main aisle. However, Maddie would be here soon. And Cal. Her heartbeat quickened. She'd caught a glimpse of him earlier when he and Ted had come by the tree lot to drop off some equipment, but he'd spent the rest of the day working elsewhere. She longed to see him and that brief glimpse hadn't been enough. Indeed, it had only hastened her impatience and yearning.

"Thank you, dear." Mrs. Barrett picked up her bag. "I'm so glad you still had some angel tree toppers in stock. I suppose it's not surprising mine broke. I've had it for forty years, same as my washing machine. Things back then were sure built to last." She laughed.

"We always try to help." Following her parents' example, Alana kept extras of a few of their essential items—like tree toppers—in the back so they'd be prepared for any last-minute crises. "Sorry to keep you waiting. It's really busy today." She turned to the next customer, a mom around her age with two small children. "Someone's dog will be happy." She scanned a package of the handcrafted, small-batch dog treats they carried and made other cheerful small talk. "Oh, hey Maddie." She greeted the teenager with a relieved smile. "I'm so glad you're here. Can you…?"

"Alana?" The door to the tree lot banged open, and Ted appeared. "Come quick. Your dad… He slipped on a patch of ice, carrying a tree…" Whatever else Ted said was lost in a collective gasp and then rising voices from the line of store customers.

"My dad?" With a panicked look at Maddie, who took over at the cash like the professional she was, Alana made her suddenly shaky legs move toward Ted, who was still half-inside the store.

What was her dad doing working in the tree lot or carrying trees? The last time she'd seen him, he was in Rustic Hearts' barn sitting behind a table organizing inventory. A job Alana had given him. Irritation mixed with alarm as she reached the door and grabbed one of the store-branded jackets left on a nearby hook for anyone who needed to go outside unexpectedly. "Dad?" Thankful she'd kept her boots on, she tugged on the jacket and, with Ted at her side, dashed across to where her father was lying on the ground in the tree lot near where it opened into the parking area. A knot of people were gathered around his prone body. "Oh, Dad." She kneeled at his head, cushioned by a folded blanket someone must have brought from a nearby car.

"I'm fine. Lost my footing, that's all." Her dad peered up at Alana with a sheepish expression.

"Why were you moving a tree at all?" Taking in the wrapped Christmas tree, which was also on the ground several feet away, Alana pressed a hand to her mouth to hold back a sob. "We need to get you to the hospital. Don't move. I'll call an ambulance."

"Now, now, no need to call an ambulance." Her dad patted Alana's hand seemingly to try to soothe her. "I'm only shaken up. I wanted to help you and your mom. The two of you've been carrying a heavy load since I've been out of commission."

"It doesn't matter. We love you and—"

"I'll see to your dad. Get him to the hospital if needed." At Alana's side, Ted spoke in an undertone. "I saw him go down, and he didn't hit his head. Several folks were with him and two of the guys caught him mid-fall and kind of eased him down." Ted's smile was both consoling and wry. "If I'd spotted him carrying that tree in the first place, I'd have headed him off, but…" He shrugged. "I guess he got a bee in his bonnet."

"I guess he did." Alana didn't know whether to laugh or cry. From a few things her mom had said and Alana herself had noted, her dad was far from an ideal patient. She understood his frustration at not being able to work like he usually did, but lugging Christmas trees, even if he hadn't slipped and fallen, wouldn't hasten his recovery.

"Here you go, Mark." With two other men, presumably the ones who'd also caught his fall, Ted got Alana's dad upright. "I'll drive you home, shall I? You don't want your wife worrying, do you?" Behind her dad's back, Ted winked at Alana.

"My wife's a worrier, that's for sure." Her dad brushed snow off his jacket.

"That's because she loves you. We all do." Alana shook her head. "Call me if you need to go to the doctor or anything else." Would it be overstepping if she called her mom? She'd likely be doing chores on the main farm, but she'd want to be at the house when Ted arrived with her husband. Her mom needed to know what had happened and—

"I can see those wheels cranking away in your head." Her dad gave Alana one of his teasing smiles. "I'll call your mother from the truck. No need for you to get involved."

Her parents knew her too well. They weren't old, only in their early sixties, but she wanted to be there for them. "I'll drop by later after I finish my shift. No more doing anything the doctor wouldn't want you to," Alana teased back, wagging her index finger at him like he often did to her. What a day. It'd been nonstop at the store and between a constant stream of customers, fielding questions about the children's play at the church and still needing to make six dozen cookies for that cookie exchange before she turned in tonight, her "day off" from the library had been anything but. "Behave!" She forced a laugh as she returned the makeshift pillow that had cushioned her dad's head to its owner with thanks.

With an answering finger wag, her dad moved away with Ted, his steps slower and more cautious than usual.

As the small crowd dispersed, Alana glanced back at the store. Now, the line of customers was even longer and stretched out the door, and cars continued to come into the lot. They had extra staff to handle trees, but Maddie would need her help in the store.

"Hey, Lanie." Cal approached and greeted her with a warm smile.

"You're back." She smiled in return and stepped into his hug enthusiastically.

"Didn't you expect me to return?" As Cal stepped away, his brow wrinkled in concern.

"Yes, I did. I knew you had a shift scheduled, but it's..." She waved in the direction of Rustic Hearts. "We're busy and—"

"I get it but..." He touched her arm. "I really have to talk to you. It's important."

"I know. I remember you mentioning it before but...later maybe?" Somewhere in between closing up, checking on her folks and those six dozen cookies. She wrapped the jacket tighter around herself as a gust of wind kicked up. This wasn't a good time for a break, not really.

"I guess." It was as if a shutter came down across Cal's face, the previous brightness wiped away.

"I'm sorry. What is it?" Alana stopped. The customers would still be there in a few minutes. If Cal needed her, he should be her priority. "Is everything all right?"

"Yes and no." He hesitated and glanced about. "Over here." He gestured around the side of the store, out of view and earshot of the customers waiting patiently in line. "Things went great with Jesse, but I have to tell you something. I should've told you a long time ago. I'm ashamed of myself but... When your family's barn burned down, it was Jesse who started the fire. And I—I was there, too, and I covered for him."

"What?" Alana's heart seemed to hammer in her ears. He hadn't said what she thought he had. It must be a mistake.

"The fire. Your barn." Cal's face was red. "It was Jesse. And me. I didn't light the match. Or drop it. But I'm still guilty. I didn't mean to lie to you, but Jesse, he'd turned eighteen a few days before. It was an accident, but if he'd been caught and convicted, he'd have been charged as an adult rather than a juvenile. I couldn't let that happen. Like I said, I promised our mom… So I had to look out for him." He stuttered to a stop.

Alana wished that she could fly away, disappear, be anywhere else in this moment. Although she couldn't believe what she was hearing, it would change everything. And there was no way Cal could explain his way out of it.

INSIDE THE STAFF ROOM, where he'd insisted she come in out of the cold, Cal stared at Alana, willing her to understand that he'd needed to protect Jesse. All the way back from Boston, he'd gone over what he needed to say to her. He'd also lain awake most of the night thinking of it…and her. Then, Ted had asked him to work late, after closing, so he wouldn't be able to talk to Alana tonight. And when he found her in the tree lot, he'd been so desperate to get the words out…he couldn't wait any longer.

"I'm really sorry. Honestly." He broke the heavy silence. "But I heard that the insurance payment covered rebuilding the barn and replacing damaged farm equipment. Luckily there were no animals or people inside at the time."

He held out a hand to her, but Alana took two slow deliberate steps back.

"Of course, nobody was inside. It was night. You knew we didn't keep our horses, Mom's chickens or the goats and rabbits I raised in that barn. As for the insurance payment?" She almost spat out the words. "That barn meant a whole lot more to me and my family than money. My great-grandfather built it. He carved his initials into one of the roof beams. Growing up, all us kids had our height measured on the big front door. Like my dad and his sisters before us did. My grandfather built the market garden stall my dad had just finished repainting earlier that day and moved it into the barn to dry. We stored a collection of heritage apple seeds in that barn. All those things were destroyed and they were irreplaceable" She drew in a shuddery breath. "Maybe you don't understand the importance of a family legacy, but I do."

Cal put a hand to his stomach as if she'd punched him. "I—I know it was bad, but—"

"Bad?" Her eyes were like flints and two red patches bloomed on her cheeks. The only other time Cal had seen Alana look that way was when they'd broken up. "You and your brother could've destroyed Hansen Farms. Only because my folks…well, all of us, we pitched in and with a lot of hard work we came back even stronger.

Jesse was an adult when he started that fire, so why was it more important to you to protect him than me? I was your girlfriend. The girlfriend you said you loved, wanted to marry and have a family with. If the fire was truly an accident, no matter what you promised your mom about looking out for your brother, why didn't you tell me the truth before now? Love doesn't mean anything without honesty." Beneath a white sweatshirt with a Christmas tree and Hansen Farms logo outlined in green, Alana's chest heaved. "You said you loved me no matter what. Before you went to Boston. I believed you."

"I do love you and that'll never change. I've always loved you, and you giving me a second chance, it means everything." How could Cal explain himself? He couldn't lose Alana again. "But you see, in promising my mom I'd be there for Jesse, it was because he was younger and… The night of the fire, I also panicked. Jesse had come to see me, he'd only been in town an hour or so. He assured me he'd wasn't the same person anymore, that he was determined to stay out of trouble and joining the navy would help. I wanted him to meet you. That's why we went up to the farm. But when we got there, the farmhouse was in darkness. It was too late so I said we'd have to come back the next day. Then Jesse started fooling around. He was a smoker back then, and he lit a couple of matches. Said I needed to smoke, too, if we were what he called 'blood brothers.' He pushed me, and I said no and shoved him away. He dropped one of the lit matches and the wind caught it… I swear that fire was an accident. I've felt guilty about it and everything else for years."

And in the shock of the moment, Cal had gone so far as to say he'd join the military, too, to make sure his brother would live up to that promise to follow a new, positive direction. While he'd expected Alana to be upset, he'd also thought she'd listen and that she'd understand why he'd done what he had.

The family legacy. Of course, he hadn't considered or, even if he had, truly recognized its importance. All his "family legacy" consisted of was a few pictures in that old album and his mom's engagement ring. Jesse had her wedding ring, and Maria now wore it. Which was right and meaningful, but it'd still given Cal a shock when he'd seen the plain strip of yellow-gold on his sister-in-law's finger. The pain in his stomach increased so bad he wanted to double over. Instead of making things better, finally being honest with Alana had made everything worse.

"It was a mistake for us to get back together." Alana wrapped her arms around herself.

"A mistake?" Cal longed to go to her and hold

her close. To tell her that from now on, there wouldn't be any more secrets between them. That she had his whole heart and always would. "How can what we feel for each other be a mistake?" His mind spun. He couldn't seem to control his thoughts or his emotions.

"Those feelings were based on a lie. Or, if not an outright lie, an omission of truth. I have to get back to work. Maddie's on her own, and I've been away too long as it is." She walked toward the door leading from the staff room to the store.

"But why won't you listen to me? Let me explain how I—"

"I've heard enough." Her voice sounded like shards of ice hitting a windowpane, like they had in that storm a few weeks ago. "There's nothing more to say."

"If that's truly how you feel, I'll finish my shift and leave town the day after Christmas." Along with hurt, Cal's own temper sparked and anger slid through him, as hot and quick as the fire that had once caught those old barn boards. He'd never been as swift to anger as Jesse, but that didn't mean the anger wasn't there. He only hid it better. "Ted said he's hired a few high-school students to work casual shifts tomorrow and Christmas Eve. He even said if I wanted, I could take some time off seeing as I've worked so much overtime."

"Fine." Alana turned away, her shoulders stiff. "We don't need you here. *I* don't need you." Then she was gone, and the door banged shut behind her.

But not before Cal caught the refrain of Mariah Carey singing "All I Want For Christmas Is You" from the Rustic Hearts playlist. He'd heard that song so many times over the past few weeks, he'd begun to think of it as *their* song, his and Alana's.

Which only went to show he was still as big a fool for love as when he'd lost Alana the first time. Except this second loss hurt even more, and he couldn't run away to join the military to try to escape or dull the pain.

CHAPTER NINETEEN

SITTING BOLT UPRIGHT in bed with Holly gently pawing at her arm, Alana fumbled for her phone. Since she'd taken a few days off from the library until after Christmas and didn't need to be at Rustic Hearts until the afternoon, she hadn't set her alarm last night. She glanced at the bright sunlight flooding under and through her bedroom curtains and then squinted at the phone screen.

Ten o'clock. With a groan, she shoved her tumbled hair away from her face and made herself get out of bed. She never slept this late, but considering she'd only fallen asleep around five thirty, maybe it wasn't surprising.

"You're hungry for your breakfast, aren't you?" She made an apologetic face at the cat. "Sorry."

Putting a hand to her throbbing head, she padded barefoot to the kitchen to fill Holly's food dish and top up her water bowl. Coffee. A jolt of caffeine would help her face the day. She set the kettle to boil and found a mug, coffee grounds and filter. She was kidding herself. No amount of caffeine would make this day bearable.

Somehow, she'd made it through the rest of her shift at Rustic Hearts yesterday…and also managed to avoid Cal. On her way home, she'd dropped in on her folks and done her best to pretend nothing was wrong. She'd gone through the motions of joining them for a cup of tea and holiday gingersnap cookies and, more genuinely, sharing in her mom's relief that her dad was none the worse for having taken a tumble with that Christmas tree. Then she'd returned to her silent house, decided she couldn't face making those six-dozen cookies and cuddled in the dark with Holly for hours. She'd let any phone calls go to voice mail—they were all about that children's Christmas Eve play, anyway—and hadn't turned on the lights on her Christmas tree or anywhere else. The tree lights would've reminded her of Cal, and cocooned in the darkness she felt safe and apart from the world.

But in the bright light of morning, there was no such refuge or safety. She had to face the truth. She'd handled things badly with Cal, so what was she going to do to try to fix it?

After pouring boiling water into the coffee filter, she checked her phone again. He hadn't sent her a message. Not that she'd expected one after she'd said it was a mistake for them to get back together. Her face burned. Cal had caught her at her worst. She'd been worried about her dad and stressed about the line of customers, the play and those cookies. So she'd lost her temper like she had all those years ago.

She'd also talked about her family's legacy. She could hardly have said anything to hurt Cal more. His lack of family was where he was most vulnerable, and in a way she'd used it against him.

How would she get through the next two days, let alone Christmas Day itself?

Josie. Laura. Before she did anything else, she needed to call them. They'd be there for her. They always were, but she'd never needed them like she did now. She tapped a message into their group chat.

Are you guys around? I've got kind of a situation & could use company. I'm at my house.

A situation. It was a whole lot more than that. A situation was a leaky faucet or a problem with the furnace. Things she could either fix herself or call in a professional. When it came to a broken heart, especially one that was her own fault, she was on her own. Alana stared at the screen, willing one of them to respond.

Josie was first.

What's up?

Me and Cal... Hot tears pooled in Alana's eyes. After last night she'd thought she was all cried out, but evidently not. It's over. Even typing the words made Alana's stomach drop and cold sweat trickle down the back of her neck. On top of everything else, was she coming down with that flu bug Anne Sullivan had?

Farm-Hers emergency. Already in town. Be with you in a few. Josie was the one who'd come up with the name "The Farm-Hers" because the three of them worked in agriculture. However, that name was when their friendship was new. Now, it was only used as shorthand for a crisis.

See U soon. With a ping, Laura joined the chat. Only a block away.

A few minutes later, her friends were at Alana's front door, and as she let them in, they both wrapped her in a hug and made soothing noises.

"So what happened? I thought everything was going great with you and Cal." As Laura stepped away from the hug to unwrap her scarf and take off her coat and boots, she worried her lower lip.

"It was, but..." Alana paused until Josie had removed her winter gear and the three of them were settled on the living-room couch with Holly snuggled on Alana's lap. "I ruined everything."

"I doubt it." Josie patted Alana's hand atop the cat's head. "Like my grams always says, few things are so bad they can't be fixed."

Like Josie and her grams, Alana usually tried to think positively but not this time. Not when she thought of what she'd said. "I was wrong. I said some awful things to Cal and he—" She choked back a sob.

"Well, admitting you were wrong is the first step." On Alana's other side, Laura rubbed her shoulder.

"I was angry and emotional and I must've hurt him." As the story poured out of her, Alana cried some more.

"Here." Since Alana had emptied the living-room tissue box the night before, Josie dug in her purse for more and handed over a bunch. "From the sounds of it, Cal was pretty upset, too."

"Maybe, but I started it." Alana patted her face and blew her nose. "I want to fix things with Cal, but how?" When she'd lain awake in the darkness for most of last night, she'd not only faced some truths about herself, but also put herself in Cal's shoes back then and now. How torn he must've felt between his loyalty to his brother, that promise to their mom and Alana. How unhappy and confused. And with her flying off the handle, he couldn't explain. She likely wouldn't have listened if he had.

"First of all, don't be so hard on yourself. He caught you at a bad time. Your dad falling would've been scary on its own, and with the store so busy? It'd be a lot for anyone," Laura said.

"But usually I can handle everything." Alana sniffed.

"You're human, not a robot. We all get overwhelmed." Laura's half smile was wry. "Believe me, I've been there."

"Likewise." Josie smiled, too. "Both you and Cal have some talking to do. Some apologizing as well. Don't forget listening, truly listening to each other. That's been a big one for me. Still is, actually, but me and Heath are working on it."

"Trevor's mom says that if you want to be married for a lifetime, you have to keep working at it for a lifetime." Laura folded her hands on her lap. "It's good advice. Saying 'I do' is only the beginning."

"Cal and me… We hadn't talked about marriage." Not this time, anyway, but if she'd read the way that Cal had looked at her correctly, they'd been heading that way and soon.

"But marriage is what you want, isn't it?" Laura nodded as if answering her own question.

"You've always wanted kids," Josie added.

"I have. I still do, but…" Another wave of grief rolled over Alana. "I thought I was happy in myself and with my life, but then Cal came back here and everything got mixed up."

"Do you love him?" Laura's brown eyes were wise. Knowing.

"I do. So much." And Alana always would. Did that realization make things better or worse?

"Then that love is all that matters." Josie clapped her hands. "I bet you already know what you need to do without us chipping in."

"I need to apologize but why should Cal listen to me?" Alana gestured to her phone. "I could try calling him and if he doesn't answer go over to Mrs. Barrett's. Oh, no. I have to work at Rustic Hearts in a few hours, and I need to bake cookies and there's that play at church, a dress rehearsal and costumes and my dad and the farm and—" She dropped her head in her hands, almost as overwhelmed as she'd been yesterday, when Cal had wanted to talk to her.

"Stop being a people pleaser and put yourself first for a change." Laura's tone was brisk. "Take it from me, folks can manage without you if you give them half a chance."

"I'm not a people pleaser. Am I?" An uncomfortable thought struck Alana. When had she last said "no" when anyone asked her for something? She always replied "yes" and that's why she'd gotten roped into helping with that play and baking cookies. "Maybe I am." But she liked helping others. Most of the time.

Laura already had her phone out. "Go have a shower and get dressed, and we'll make those cookies for you."

"You two can't drop everything for me and—"

"You'd drop everything for us. In fact, you've done so before." Laura waved away Alana's objections.

"You're also calling in sick at Rustic Hearts. You're in no state to deal with customers, and you need time to figure out what you want to say to Cal." Josie had her phone out as well. "A couple of my casual farmhands are looking to pick up extra work. If they go to Hansen Farms, that'd free up your mom to be with your dad or for the two of them to help in the store. As long as your dad doesn't carry any trees, he should be okay. His accident was the talk of the special holiday assembly at my girls' school earlier."

Alana glanced between her friends.

"It was also the talk of this morning's chamber-of-commerce breakfast." Laura's eyes gleamed. "Small-town life." She laughed and Josie joined in.

"If my folks can't be in the store, there's a college student who sometimes helps us out. I could give her a call. She's home for Christmas. I saw her a few days ago." If Alana hadn't been so churned up, she'd have come up with that idea before.

"Excellent." Josie made notes on her phone.

"As for the play, since Bella and Lottie are taking part, I should be the one taking Anne Sullivan's place," Josie said. "I'll already be at church for the dress rehearsal, so it's no problem for me to supervise the kids backstage."

"And I can deal with any last-minute costume issues," Laura added. "Danny's involved as well." Laura's expression softened as it always did when she spoke of Trevor's nephew, now more like a son to them both. "Alana shouldn't need to step in, especially because between the music director and youth minister, the actual rehearsal part's already in hand."

What felt like an enormous weight lifted off Alana's shoulders. Thanks to her friends, she had a plan. And even if Cal wouldn't listen to her at first, Alana would keep trying.

Love. The simple but oh, so powerful word curled itself around her heart. If she and Cal loved each other, surely they could work things out. However, love was only part of it. This time she had to fight for their relationship like everything depended on it. Because for her it did.

"GET YOUR COAT and boots on and come with me." Mrs. Barrett came out of the kitchen carrying her purse.

"Come with you where? I need to replace my phone." Cal gestured to the device and its dark screen. His cell had stopped working yesterday before his shift at Rustic Hearts and, as near as he could tell, whether due to a virus, system crash or something else, it was beyond fixing. He'd intended to tell Alana, but then everything had gone wrong and a broken phone had become the least of his worries.

As he'd done since getting out of bed after a largely sleepless night, Cal continued pacing around Mrs. Barrett's family room. The furniture had changed and the TV was also new, with a comfy sectional sofa and shelves holding books, games and movies, but the room was still as comfortable as when Cal used to hang out here as a teen.

Last night, as soon as he returned from work, he'd told Mrs. Barrett the whole story about the fire, seeing Jesse and what had happened between him and Alana. As always, she'd listened without judging, only nodding occasionally to support and encourage him. But when Cal reached an especially hard part, she'd taken both his hands in hers and held them tight.

Alana. Cal wanted to go to her but he couldn't. She'd made it clear she didn't want anything more to do with him. It was like being an unwanted foster kid all over again, hoping someone would choose him and then, when they finally did and he started to feel settled, he'd be moved on again. Deemed not good enough and be right back where he'd started.

No, that wasn't true. He still had a future, even if it was without Alana. He'd regroup, but he'd have to do it somewhere else, not Strawberry Pond. A different school and course. A different apprenticeship. An entirely new place to try to fit in and belong.

Boston was the logical next choice. Except, he wanted the trade-school course he'd chosen. He wanted to work at Strawberry Pond Automotive with Brad Johnson and his team, and pitch in at Hansen Farms with Alana and her family. He still wanted Alana, but how could he get her back?

"Are you expecting any urgent calls?" Mrs. Barrett's voice yanked Cal back to the present.

"No." Alana wouldn't be calling him, and since his phone already wasn't working properly when he was in Boston, Cal had given his brother Mrs. Barrett's landline number.

"Does the name Mandy Blanchard mean anything to you?" At the door leading to the garage, Mrs. Barrett put on her outdoor clothing and motioned to Cal to do the same.

"I'm not sure." In the recesses of memory, faint recognition flickered. A dark-haired woman at his mom's funeral who'd hugged him and Jesse and said she was sorry. Christmas and birthday cards with crisp five-dollar bills inside. Writing thank-you notes for his foster parents to address and mail.

"Mandy was a friend of your mom's." Mrs. Barrett checked she had her car and house keys. "At the time your mom passed, Mandy wanted to take you and Jesse in herself, but she couldn't, so… Well, she always tried to keep an eye on you two from a distance. There was a statement from her and contact information in your foster-care-case summary file."

So why was Cal only hearing about her now?

"From the little Mandy told me at the time, she was in a bad place back then but, well, when I called her earlier, she said she'd like to see you." Mrs. Barrett held the door open. "Mind you, I told her it might help for *you* to see *her*. She only lives forty-five minutes or so away. Over the mountain."

"But what…? Why…?" As Cal followed Mrs. Barrett to her car and got into the passenger seat, he couldn't figure out which question to ask first. Or even how to ask it. Cal had put away memories of his parents—his mom especially, and everything to do with her—deep inside and made sure he never revisited them. He and Jesse had talked about their folks, but Cal had been careful to keep the conversation about fun stuff, not the bleaker moments. And definitely not their mom's death and being taken into foster care.

Three quarters of an hour later, after a mostly silent ride across a narrow road that snaked alongside a mountain, a church, general store and scattering of houses came into view. After turning right at the church, Mrs. Barrett pulled up in front of a gray bungalow with white shutters. Although it was only early afternoon, the short December day was already drawing in, the weak sun beginning its dip behind the snow-covered mountains that encircled the village like a hug.

"I'll leave you to it, shall I?" Mrs. Barrett glanced at him and kept the car running.

"No, please… Can you come in with me?" Cal was a grown man, but now, Mrs. Barrett was the closest he had to a mom, and he needed her.

She nodded. "If it's what you truly want."

"It is." Want. Need. Right now, the difference didn't matter.

"Okay." Mrs. Barrett gave him a reassuring smile and then they left the car and walked up the path to a front door decorated with a pine-cone-and-red-ribbon-wrapped wreath.

As if she'd been watching for them, the door opened and a woman's face framed by short, wavy dark hair popped out. "Callum?"

"Yes, ma'am." Reaching the door, Mrs. Barrett a few steps behind, Cal stood straight, almost at attention.

"Oh, Callum." The woman's voice caught and then she opened the door wider to invite him in. "You look so much like your mom as I remember her."

For an instant, Cal stood stiff in the front hall, unsure what to say or do.

"Come in, come in. I'm Mandy." She gave a light laugh. "I didn't mean to make you uncomfortable. It's...seeing you again. I never thought this day would come."

In the flurry of taking off winter coats and boots, Cal studied her. It was a long time ago, and his memories of his mom's funeral were blurry, but maybe Mandy *was* the same woman who'd hugged him and Jesse that day. As she led them into a living room where a gas fire flickered behind glass and a screen, Cal sat in a deep armchair and took in what must be family photos on the table at his side. A young woman in a wedding dress, a serious man in military uniform, as well as several young kids with gap-toothed grins.

"Tea, coffee or a soda?" Mandy paused in the arched living-room doorway. "I made snickerdoodles."

Cal swallowed. His mom used to make those

cookies, and as a small child the chewy, cinnamon-flavored rounds were part of Christmas.

"If you show me where everything is, I'll organize drinks and such." Mrs. Barrett, who'd hardly sat down, got to her feet again. "I expect you and Cal have a lot to talk about." She sent him a loving but meaningful look before disappearing with Mandy.

In a few moments, Mandy was back and she sat across from Cal on the sofa.

"So." He cleared his throat. "How did you know my mom? Did you go to school together, or…?" His voice trailed away. The living room didn't have a Christmas tree, but a red poinsettia sat on the coffee table and a teddy bear in a Santa suit was perched in a rocking chair by the window.

"I met your mom in a patient-support group." Mandy's voice was low. "She was sick for a long time, even before she told you boys, and, well, we got close." Her smile was bittersweet. "I made it through but she… She didn't. I used to feel so guilty. Why was I still here but she wasn't? I never had kids, and my husband left soon after I was diagnosed, but your mom was all you and Jesse had."

"You shouldn't have felt guilty." Cal's mouth seemed like it was stuffed with cotton batten. "Mom wouldn't have wanted that. She was…"

He stopped again. His mom had been everything. How could he sum up what she'd meant to him?

"Your mother was kind, loving and the most generous and unselfish person I've ever known." Mandy clasped and unclasped her hands. She was petite, like Alana, but also like Alana, there was an inner strength to her. As if no matter how life buffeted her, she would bend, not break. "No, she wouldn't have wanted me to feel guilty but I still did."

"So what changed?" Cal sat forward. Despite meeting and talking with Jesse, he still carried his own guilt about his brother.

"I realized that since I was lucky enough to have my life, I needed to live it. For myself as well as your mom." Mrs. Barrett came into the living room carrying a tray and set it on the coffee table. "And no matter how much guilt you might feel, you can't change the past. So if you're thinking about that past, then you're stuck in it, and you aren't giving yourself a chance to change your future." Mandy gestured to a mug for Cal to help himself.

"My mom asked me to look out for Jesse. I promised her I would, and I tried but… I always thought she'd be disappointed in me. I couldn't keep us together or keep Jesse out of trouble. He's doing great now, but I failed Mom. It was a deathbed promise and I…" Cal put a hand to his mouth to stop himself from saying anything else. Where had all that come from? He hadn't even told Mrs. Barrett but the words had spilled out to a woman who was pretty much a stranger.

"Disappointed? Failed?" Mandy stared at him as she shook her head. "Your mother adored you and Jesse. But she also knew that while you were responsible and reliable, Jesse could be a handful. She worried more about him. She'd never have wanted you to feel guilty. As for you promising to look out for Jesse? She said the same to him about you, she told me so, although she also said it went right over Jesse's head. He was too young and even so, unlike you, he was immature for his age."

"She did?" It was as if Cal had always looked at life in one way and the different pieces, which he'd thought were static, were shifting and rearranging themselves into a new form.

"Your mom knew she was dying, and she also knew it was awful for you. She wouldn't have wanted to put anything else on your shoulders. I'm sure you did your best for Jesse. You were that kind of boy. Your mom wouldn't have expected anything more. That's what the promise was about." She held out a plate of snickerdoodles. "Cookie? I made them with your mom's recipe."

Cal took a cookie and bit into it, tasting Christmas, home and family. For years, he'd longed to have his mom's snickerdoodles again and wondered what recipe she'd used because none of the cookies he'd bought, or tried making, were ever the same. And here it was with Mandy, a woman who'd given him cookies and so much more. "Thank you."

"It's my pleasure, truly." When Mandy smiled, it was as if the last bits of guilt, confusion and feelings of unworthiness seeped out of Cal, as light and airy as snowflakes melting on a sunny windowpane. "Now, tell me about yourself and Jesse. I also have some old pictures you might like to see of me and your mom."

"I'd love that." Cal rubbed a hand across his eyes and blinked back unexpected tears. As a boy of ten, he'd trained himself not to cry or show any other kind of what he'd always considered weakness. It'd been part of packing his emotions away and keeping himself safe. But Mrs. Barrett was crying softly and tears also rolled down Mandy's face. Cal didn't need to be embarrassed. His emotions were honest and heartfelt, and it was more than time he acknowledged them.

He stood and opened his arms, first to Mandy and then Mrs. Barrett. He didn't have his mom by birth, but he still had other women in his life to love, support and guide him. He only had to reach out and, from now on, he'd keep them close. He'd keep his mom close, too, unlocking those precious memories and opening his heart to them like she'd want him to.

He'd also try again with Alana. He had nothing to lose, but maybe, if he was lucky, everything to gain.

CHAPTER TWENTY

ON CHRISTMAS EVE morning after taking the previous day off sick, Alana had to get to work at Rustic Hearts. There was lots to do before the store opened. However, here she was sitting in her car with the engine running in front of Mrs. Barrett's house. After last night's storm, the front walk and step were still piled high with snow, the only footsteps Alana's. Nobody was home. They hadn't been yesterday, either, but a neighbor said she'd seen Mrs. Barrett's car heading out of town.

Cal also wasn't answering his phone, although Alana had called once yesterday afternoon and then again in the evening. There was no point in leaving a message. What she needed to say couldn't be captured in a brief voice mail.

With one last look at the house, where a jolly life-size inflatable Santa ornament on the front lawn seemed to mock her, she drove away. It was the last day selling Christmas trees for the season. Since she wasn't working the postholiday store sale, it was also her last day at Rustic Hearts for the year. Soon, another Christmas would have come and gone. Instead of her "best Christmas ever," it was shaping up to be the worst, and she had only herself to blame.

If only she'd listened to Cal, truly listened, and tried to understand where he was coming from. But she'd been distracted, caught up in everything else but him. *Them.* Her heart gave a dull and painful thud. She hadn't thought about "them" at all, only herself and her family's legacy. She'd handled everything so badly and wanted to make it right but how?

Cal had said he'd leave Strawberry Pond the day after Christmas. Had his plans changed? If so, why would Mrs. Barrett have left town as well? Driving through the quiet early morning streets and then picking up speed as she reached the county road that led to the tree farm, her thoughts circled. All the could-haves and should-haves ended up in the same place. Regret. Usually calm and measured, she'd lost her temper like she'd done the first time she and Cal had broken up.

However, she wouldn't stay stuck wallowing in that regret. As Alana drew into the snow-cleared lot at Rustic Hearts, parked beside her mom's pickup and cut the engine, she made a promise to herself. Somehow, no matter how hard the next few days were, she'd keep moving forward. Although she hadn't been able to reach Cal so far, she'd keep trying, but she also wouldn't let herself hope for happily ever after. After getting out of her vehicle and locking it, she went into the staff room, where, from the kitchen area, the scent of coffee brewing infused her senses.

It was a warm, welcoming and home-like smell, but apart from hanging up her coat, Alana didn't linger, instead going through to the store. While she'd resolved not to ruminate over Cal, that staff room, the place where she'd last seen him—broken up with him again—was too raw.

"Mom?"

Topped by a Santa hat, her mom's head emerged from behind a decorated Christmas tree. "Alana. Oh, honey."

In an instant, Alana was wrapped in her mom's arms and also enveloped in the unconditional love, understanding and support her mom had always given her. "You heard?" Despite herself, Alana sniffed, trying not to give in to more tears. "About me and Cal?" Even saying his name hurt.

"No, I guessed." Her mom held her close. "I knew something wasn't right when you dropped in at the farm the other night, and when you called in sick but didn't call me, well, I was sure of it."

"I'm fine, or I will be." Alana tried to smile. "I guess it wasn't meant to be. Second chances and all that are only for books and movies, not real life. I tried to find Cal and talk to him but he seems to have already left town."

Her mom made a harrumphing sound. "If Cal Paquette *has* left Strawberry Pond, he must've had a good reason." Her mom's keen brown eyes studied Alana. "I couldn't sleep so I got here way too early. We're ready for opening and have a bit of time. Do you want to tell me what really happened between you and Cal?"

"I'm sorry you didn't sleep well." Deflecting her mom's question, Alana gripped the edge of the counter, wishing she *had* braved the staff-room kitchen to get herself a coffee.

"I never do rest easy when one of you kids is troubled." As if she'd guessed Alana's thoughts, her mom took an insulated coffee mug from beneath the counter and passed it to her. "When you were small, it was easier to make things right. Nowadays, the problems are bigger and harder to solve, but that doesn't mean I stop being your mother and worrying over you."

Alana sipped her coffee.

"I should've told you about me and Cal, what's been going on with us these past few weeks."

Why hadn't she told her mom? It wasn't because Alana was embarrassed but rather her relationship with Cal, such as it was, had seemed fragile. It was also new and for both those reasons she'd needed to keep it to herself. "Things happened fast. It's only been what, five weeks or so since Thanksgiving and Cal came back to town? I told him I'd give him another chance and after some initial bumps, we were getting along great."

More than great. She'd fallen in love with him again, although if she was honest with herself, she'd never stopped. Except, in the past weeks, that teenage love had grown and deepened, no longer a love between a boy and girl but between a man and woman.

"So it seemed." Her mom pulled a stool over to the counter and sat, busying herself tidying a display of tree-care products. "We all saw how well the two of you were getting along. Your dad thought I should talk to you, but I said no. You'd tell us when you were ready. *If* you were ready."

Alana nodded and curled her cold hands around the mug. She'd always considered herself lucky that her family never tried to run her life. For good or bad, she'd been allowed to make her own choices and learn from them. "Everything went wrong when Cal told me..." She hesitated. Keeping secrets didn't do anybody any good, and her folks needed to know the truth.

"His younger brother was responsible for the fire that destroyed our barn. Cal was there, too, but he covered for Jesse. It's complicated, and Jesse didn't start the fire on purpose, it was an accident, but Cal thought he had to protect his brother because of a promise he made to their late mom. Jesse had just turned eighteen and been released from the state's care. That's why Cal left so suddenly to join the military. Because his brother planned to enlist. From the sounds of it, Jesse's really turned his life around. He's a firefighter in Boston. He's married and he and his wife have a baby."

"I see." Her mom's hands stilled on a plant food container. "A brother. Cal never mentioned Jesse."

"No, but like I said, it's complicated." Cal's shame, embarrassment and guilt, and how the brothers had drifted apart, were private and not for Alana to share.

"At the time, the police and fire chief said they thought that fire was caused by vandalism." Her mom's forehead creased. "They even questioned your dad and brothers in case they'd set the fire deliberately. Everyone knew Hansen Farms was struggling, so I suppose—"

"Neither Dad nor Jordy nor Ben would've done such a thing," Alana interjected, her heart pounding as if she'd run a race. "Not ever, no matter how badly the farm was doing."

"True. We all knew that..." Her mom turned the plant-food box over in her hand as if she didn't see it. "The fire chief apologized to your dad for asking the question, but we understood why he had to. In the end, everything worked out. We got the insurance payment and we rebuilt. It was a hard time but we made it through. In a way maybe that fire was a good thing. Not that I thought so at the time, but afterward."

"How could it be good?" Alana stared at her mom in astonishment. "Everything we lost. The farm stand. Where Granddad carved his initials on the beam. Those apple seeds."

"We lost *things*, but we still have the memories of them. We also didn't lose any people or animals. That would've been a true tragedy." Her mom gazed into the distance as if reliving that time. "Our family's still our family and that fire, devastating as it was, helped us start over. Looking back, we built a new and better foundation for Hansen Farms on the ashes of the old."

Alana had never thought of it like that. She'd been so caught up in what they'd lost, she'd never considered what they might have gained. "So knowing the truth, you won't hate Cal?" Her stomach clenched. The truth supposedly set a person free, but she hadn't realized it could also make someone question what they knew about themselves and their family. "I have to tell Dad and—"

"I'll tell your father, but why would either of us hate Cal?" Her mom's mouth quirked into a gentle smile. "That fire's past history. There's no sense in dragging it all up again now. I assume Cal apologized?"

"He did. He also said he tried to stop his brother from fooling around with matches." Everybody made mistakes. The most important thing was learning from them. That's what her folks had always said to their kids, so why, when it mattered most, hadn't Alana lived by it?

"There you are, then." Her mom patted Alana's hand. "If Cal's the man I think he is, he'll be wanting to talk to your dad and me directly." Her smile widened. "It's Christmas, remember? A time of hope. No matter how dark things may seem, we need to look for the light. It's usually there somewhere, even if it's hard to find."

As her mom went to turn the sign on the front door from Closed to Open, Alana double-checked the cash in the register.

Everyone's life had hard times, but Cal had experienced more of those than most. She didn't only need to *tell* him what he meant to her. She also had to *show* him. With a quick glance at her mom, who was now welcoming the first customers into the store, Alana locked the cash drawer and darted to the aisle with locally made Christmas ornaments.

Light. Hope. And love. They weren't only words and feelings but choices. A way of living life, no matter what. Maybe it was good Cal hadn't been at home or answering his phone earlier because Alana hadn't known exactly what to do or say. But now, she did.

BEFORE CAL WENT to find Alana, he had to do one more thing. After clearing the front walk and steps of snow, he put the shovel back in Mrs. Barrett's garage. It was lucky the town had plowed the back alley before they'd returned to town. Otherwise, they wouldn't have gotten her car into the garage. Since the storm had blown up suddenly, and it was too snowy and windy to venture out, they'd spent the night at Mandy's.

While Cal had wanted to return to Strawberry Pond—and Alana—as soon as possible, it'd also been good to talk longer with Mandy. In learning more about his mom, he'd also learned more about himself, Jesse and their family. And after Mrs. Barrett had gone to the guestroom, and Mandy had set up Cal with pillows and blankets on the pull-out sofa in the family room, he'd lain awake looking at the twinkling lights on the Christmas tree. Thinking, dreaming and planning how he wanted his life to be. Not only with Alana, although she was part of it, but also, his whole life. One he'd live as best he could like his mom would've wanted.

On the drive back to town, new resolve filled him. Coming into Mrs. Barrett's house and taking off his outdoor clothing, he sniffed the air filled with cinnamon, ginger and other spices. She must be making the spice sugar cookies Cal remembered from every Christmas Eve he'd spent here.

"Hey." He came into the kitchen, where Mrs. Barrett, wearing a red apron, stood at the counter, wielding a wooden spoon in a big mixing bowl and singing along to carols on the radio.

"Oh." She looked up and grinned. "You caught me." She turned off the radio. "There's something about holiday music that makes me want to sing."

"I remember Mr. Barrett playing his guitar and you and your sons singing." Although Cal hadn't recognized it at the time, music was one of the ways the Barretts connected as a family and they'd included him. "I still can't carry a tune, you know." He laughed and sat on a kitchen chair.

"That doesn't matter." She returned to her mixing. "When you became part of our family, we wanted you to join in with us whether through music, game night or whatever else."

"You made me feel like I belonged." After bouncing between foster homes every few months, Cal had been wary, loathe to become involved with the Barrett family because he'd been sure he'd soon be moved on. It had taken time for him to feel at home, but they hadn't given up on him and so earned both his love and trust.

Mrs. Barrett scraped the bowl. "You *did* belong, and like with all our foster kids over the years, Gary and I wanted to treat you like one of our own." Her voice caught. "It's my first Christmas without him and I… Well, having you here is a blessing. My boys felt so bad they couldn't get leave for the holidays, but really, Christmas is only a day, isn't it?" Her bright smile didn't mask the grief in her eyes.

"Nevertheless, it's a day that brings a lot of memories." Good and bad, but Cal was trying to focus on the better ones.

"It sure does. Here." Mrs. Barrett gestured to a plastic box holding cookie cutters. "Choose a few for me, will you?"

Cal nodded. Mrs. Barrett knew he found it easier to talk when he was doing something practical. Working with his hands, even on a simple task, soothed and centered him. "I wanted to ask you something." He rummaged through the cutters, choosing a tree, angel and star shapes.

"Go ahead."

"Mrs. Barrett, I—"

"I've said you can call me Donna, remember?"

"I know, but I can't. It doesn't seem right so… I was wondering if… I've been thinking about it a lot, maybe I could call you 'Mom Donna' instead?" Cal held his breath.

Mrs. Barrett dropped her spoon with a clatter. "Oh, I'd be honored. I'd never think of trying to replace your mother, but 'Mom Donna'? That's perfect."

She'd been like a mom to Cal for years, and he shouldn't have waited so long to tell her how he felt. As he hugged her, his mom by choice, Cal felt he belonged even more.

"It's also a wonderful early Christmas gift." Releasing him, also knowing that Cal had never been one for prolonged hugs, Mom Donna gave him a loving smile. "My dad's family was German so we always opened our presents on Christmas Eve. When Gary and I got married, we combined traditions in our own family and added new ones as well."

Family. Memories. A legacy. All the things Cal had never thought he had, when, in fact, he did. First with his folks, and Mandy had only started telling him about his mom, and then here with Gary and Donna Barrett. He also now had Jesse, Maria and Lucas and could be part of their family celebrations. Jesse had mentioned connecting with some cousins of their dad's, so there were likely Paquette stories and traditions, too.

Cal wasn't alone. He was part of all kinds of families, both birth and chosen. Once, he'd also been part of Alana's family, and he wanted that again.

"Go on." As Mom Donna—he'd thought of her that way in his heart for months, years even—wrapped cookie dough to chill, her smile turned tender. "Rustic Hearts will be closing soon. The store and tree farm shut early today. I noted their hours the last time I was in. You should be able to catch Alana on her own while she's closing up. After a quick shower and change of clothes, you can be on your way. You might want to wear that gray shirt with the red trim. It's festive but not too much and the soft gray color brings out your eyes."

"Okay." Cal was happy to take her advice because it was what a mom would offer and came from a place of love. The same kind of love he had for her.

But now, he had Alana on his mind. Would she listen to him? He wouldn't know unless he tried. He also had a special Christmas present for her. One he'd worked on for ages. And one he hoped would show her he was all in and wanted, needed, a future with her.

CHAPTER TWENTY-ONE

"MERRY CHRISTMAS." ALANA USHERED the last customers, a couple around her age, out of the tree lot and locked the gate behind them. The man carried the miniature pine they'd chosen and held the woman's arm, while she cradled her pregnant belly, the gesture both loving and protective.

The Christmas Eve rush was over. Everybody who wanted a tree either had one, or they'd left it too late. Ditto anything else that might be needed for Christmas decorating. Alana went back into the store and locked the side door as well. All morning and now in the early afternoon, each jovial holiday greeting fell flat. For the first time ever, she dreaded Christmas.

The other staff had already left. Her mom, the high-school students and then, only a few minutes ago, Ted. All of them were going home to spend time with their families. Like Alana should be doing. Gathering together on Christmas Eve afternoon was a Hansen family tradition. They'd have a meal at the farm before attending the early church service. Then Jordy and Ben and their families would go home, while Alana and her mom made final preparations for Christmas Day.

Turning off the holiday music, which had given her a headache, she glanced around the quiet store, where lights glowed on the artificial trees, and one last candy cane sat at the bottom of the green bowl. That candy looked as lonely as Alana felt.

Both Ted and her mom had told her not to stay late, but she didn't feel like going home. Not when along with Alana's overnight bag, her mom had picked up Holly to take the cat to the farm to join the Christmas Eve fun. But would the farm be any better than an empty house? Her nieces and nephews and sisters-in-law would be there, with her brothers joining them after finishing farm chores. They'd be one big happy family, which Alana usually loved, but now, she'd rather not be around so much holiday cheer.

She could go back to Mrs. Barrett's house but despite her earlier resolve of continuing to try to find Cal, when she'd called him during her morning break and lunch, he still hadn't answered his phone. Was he trying to avoid her?

Maybe she should start getting ready for the postholiday sale. Updating prices and putting out their Special Offer and Clearance signs. She could also unpack some of the new inventory that had come in. While the tree farm was seasonal, they'd begun to open the store with limited hours at other times of year. Next up was Valentine's Day. Her stomach lurched. Sorting through unwanted Christmas decorations was bad enough, but Valentine hearts would be much worse.

She picked up the candy cane and tugged at the wrapper as tires crunched outside in the parking lot. Whoever it was, they were too late. As far as Alana was concerned, Christmas was over and from now on, she'd only be going through the motions.

A vehicle door slammed and then the front door, which she'd forgotten to lock, opened.

"I'm sorry, we're closed." She manufactured a professional smile and focused on her candy. If she didn't make eye contact, hopefully they'd go away.

"I know you're closed but it's important."

At Cal's voice, Alana's head jerked up and she dropped the candy cane back in the bowl. "You…what're you doing here?" She blinked in the bright sunshine that flooded through the store windows. It was him. For real. Standing there with his parka open and the backpack he often brought to work slung over one shoulder.

And everything she'd planned to say and do went out of her head except for the most important. "I'm sorry."

"I'm sorry, too. For everything." He reached the counter in several steps and leaned across it to take both her hands in his, tugging off his gloves as he did.

"I lost my temper." She stared at their entwined hands, his so much bigger than hers and with a raised white scar on his index finger knuckle. How had he hurt himself to leave such a mark? There was so much about Cal she still didn't know, but maybe she'd have time, years even, to find out. "Like when we broke up before, I was so mad. Then, I thought you were ruining my life. Two days ago, it was because you as good as lied by not telling me about the barn fire."

While she tried to deny it, that still rankled, but if she'd been in Cal's place, would she have done anything different? As someone who tried to avoid conflict, she might not have told the entire truth, especially if it was to protect one of her brothers. A people pleaser. That's what Josie and Laura had called her, and there was a lot of truth to it. Did Cal have those tendencies, too? He'd said he'd tried "to be the perfect foster kid to fit in."

Fresh realization dawned. That must've meant

he ignored what he needed because he wanted a home. He'd also likely covered up Jesse's bad behavior long before the night of the barn fire. And he'd sacrificed himself and his relationship with Alana for his brother. Which was excessive, but seen through the lens of Alana's new understanding, it made sense.

"Well, in a way back then I ruined both our lives." Still holding her hands, Cal's voice was low and laced with regret. "But I had a lot of growing up to do."

"You weren't the only one." She squeezed his hands, trying to show him she understood even if she couldn't find the words to tell him exactly what she meant. "But you were the bigger person. You did what you thought you needed to for Jesse."

"I did but that's another thing." Cal's eyebrows drew together. "Even when I first covered for Jesse about the fire, I knew it was wrong. We both should have gone to the police and your dad, and been honest about what'd happened. Right away, no waiting. However, I thought I was responsible for my brother."

"So you said. Because you promised your mom."

"I thought it was a promise. A deathbed one but it wasn't, not really. Mom asked me to promise to 'look out' for Jesse, that's all. It was me who took that idea to an extreme. I convinced myself she meant I not only had to protect him like I'd always done because he was my little brother, but also 'look after him.' In a way become a parent to him." Cal grimaced. "I tried to keep Jesse out of trouble, but I couldn't. What I didn't really see or accept until recently is that Jesse was responsible for his own choices. Like we all are."

"You were only ten and you'd lost both your parents." Cal was an orphan and must have felt so abandoned. Alana's thoughts whirled as she considered what Cal had said. The false belief that had kept him stuck long after Jesse no longer needed him. "Jesse was even younger. I can't imagine how awful it was for the two of you." But along with everything else, that experience had made Cal who he was. The man she loved with all her heart.

"It was bad, but there were good times as well. Especially here in Strawberry Pond. With you." He took one hand away to pull up a stool and sit across from her. "Along with the Barretts, you and your family helped me have an ordinary life. A good one. Until Jesse turned up again."

"The fire." Would it always be between them, an insurmountable barrier that reared up at times of stress? No, Alana had to ensure it wasn't. "I wanted to make things right. Yesterday and again this morning, I tried to find you. I went to Mrs. Barrett's house, but when I rang the doorbell nobody answered. I also called you a few times but your phone always went to voice mail. I thought you'd left town, and I'd never see you again." Her voice cracked and tears threatened once again.

Cal stared at her, a telltale sheen in his own eyes? "Even though you said us getting back together, our feelings for each other were a mistake?"

"I was wrong to say what I did. You, us, we were never a mistake. I was also wrong to talk about the family legacy. I know I hurt you, but I didn't mean to." Her face was hot and she longed to take back every word. "I love you, Cal, and I always will. Please believe me."

That was all she could say. She'd put herself out there, heart, soul and everything she had to give. Open, raw, honest and vulnerable, like she'd never truly been with anyone. Whatever happened next was up to him.

"You came after me. You tried calling me." Cal spoke slowly as a mix of emotions rushed through him. Awe, relief and a love so powerful it made his chest tight and his breath stutter. "And you love me, despite everything?"

"Absolutely, I love you." Alana's face was

bright red, and she took her hands away from his. "I never stopped."

"I love you, too, Lanie, and I have since we were kids. Maybe even from the first moment I saw you. You were the prettiest girl I'd ever seen, and you still are. Woman, I mean." His own face warmed. "But it's not about how you look. That's only on the surface. It's who you are inside. All of you. Your goodness and caring. How you accepted me. A foster kid."

"I didn't see you as 'a foster kid.' You were only ever Cal. The boy, and now, the man, I love."

Cal's heart squeezed. He could hear Alana say she loved him every day for the rest of his life, and it still wouldn't be enough. "I'll never take that love for granted, but I have to tell you some other stuff as well. It's not bad, but I didn't see you'd called me because my phone broke and I haven't been able to replace it yet. I checked my voice mail but—"

"I didn't leave one." Alana's voice was small. "After what I said, I thought you'd probably not even listen to it or delete any message from me."

"Never, but I get why you thought that way." Cal scrubbed a hand across his face. From minor miscommunications to much bigger issues, the two of them had a lot to figure out. "When you thought I'd left town, I did but I was always coming back. I went with Mrs. Barrett—Mom Donna, that's what I'm calling her now—to visit a friend of my mom's. She only lives over the mountain, but with all the snow last night, it wasn't safe to drive back so we had to stay over."

"Mom Donna." Alana's voice was warm. "That's beautiful and right."

"It is." One day soon, Cal would tell her about talking to his foster mom, but first things first. "Speaking with Mandy, that's my mom's friend, was healing. She helped me see and really understand what my mom would've wanted for me." He paused and took a deep breath. "I was the responsible kid, but I got so caught up in Jesse, I lost sight of living my own life. Then, when it all came crashing down with that barn catching fire, I didn't know what to do except keep on being responsible for my brother."

"That makes sense." Alana nodded, encouraging, supporting and wanting the best for him like she always had, even when Cal hadn't seen or understood it.

"In the end, Jesse turned out okay. He became a firefighter because he felt so bad about what he did. Now, he gives talks to kids like he once was. Tries to head them off from making the mistakes he did." Cal swallowed and worked moisture into his dry mouth. He wasn't used to talking, and in the past few days he'd done more than ever before. "He, we... We both want to fix things with you and your family. We have a lot to make up for."

"I already told my mom what happened." Alana's gaze caught Cal's and held. "She didn't react badly at all. I was surprised, but something she said made me think. Not only about the fire, but you and me. Us."

"And?" Cal held his breath. Alana had said "us."

"Mom said although the barn fire was devastating, it also helped her and dad start over. At the time, Hansen Farms was struggling more than they'd ever let on to me or my brothers. But in a way that fire gave them a clean slate, so to speak. A big part of the family legacy was gone so they had to look to the future. In thinking about us, that's what we have to do. Together."

"Together." Cal liked the sound of that almost as much as hearing she still loved him. "About that family legacy—"

"Like I said, I was wrong to mention it," Alana interjected. "So wrong and—"

"It's okay, really." Cal stopped her from apologizing further. "I didn't understand what a family legacy meant because I thought I didn't have one. I still don't, not one like yours, anyway, but I have memories of my parents. I have Jesse and Mom Donna and now my mom's friend Mandy, too. But I also hope I'll have you and us, and you'll help me understand what a family and its legacy truly means. So I'll know why a farm stand made by a grandfather's important, and how you cherish marking a kid's height on a barn door because it's part of them growing up in a family. And in a place where they have history and roots and a bunch of folks who care about them."

"I—I… You will have me. If you want that. You'll also have my family. And we can…learn from and help each other." Alana's voice was thick with tears.

"Want you? I've never wanted anyone else." Cal slid his backpack from his shoulder and then his parka, letting the parka drop to the floor, but he kept hold of the pack. It was the most important moment of his life and he didn't want to mess up. He came around the counter to Alana and opened the backpack. "I made you a Christmas present, and despite what happened, I didn't quite lose all hope of giving it to you." He rummaged in his pack and took out the miniature artificial Christmas tree wrapped in holiday paper that he'd bought and decorated for her. "Here." He set the parcel on the counter. "Open it."

"It's… Oh, my." Alana's eyes widened as she took off the paper and saw the tree and ornaments Cal had made out of scrap metal, wood, wool, fabric and paint, working in his bedroom at Mom Donna's after his shifts at Rustic Hearts, sometimes late into the night. This tree had been his special project, a labor of love, and he'd kept it private. For Alana's eyes only. "It's beautiful and..." She touched a tiny cat in brown, black and white wool. "Is that Holly?"

"It sure is."

"There's your football jersey with your team number. My first car. A strawberry for Strawberry Pond. Oh." She sucked in a harsh breath and her fingers stilled on the most important ornament of all. It had been a last-minute addition, maybe even impulsive, but it also felt right.

"Fifteen years ago, we talked about getting engaged at Christmas. I meant it then and now... Well, once again it's Christmas. Will you marry me, Alana?"

"Yes." When she looked at him, her eyes held all the love he'd ever wanted. Ever imagined.

"Then I hope you'll wear that ring. It was my mom's engagement ring, and I'd like you to have it." He took the small solitaire diamond in its yellow-gold setting off the tree branch.

"I'd be honored." Alana held out her left hand, and Cal slipped the ring onto her wedding finger. "It fits, almost." She looked from the diamond to him. "Or it will if I put some tape around it before we can have it resized. I want to wear it for Christmas. For you."

"I'd like that." While she could wear the ring on a chain around her neck, it meant a lot that she'd think of a way of fixing things so his mom would be part of this moment, as well as their journey through the years and seasons of life together.

"This truly is my best Christmas ever, but..." Alana put a hand to her mouth. "I have a gift for you, too. I almost forgot." She reached under the counter and retrieved a small box tied with red ribbon.

Cal's fingers trembled, and she helped him with the ribbon and they lifted the lid together. "Oh." He recognized a similar silver-colored heart-shaped disc ornament to the one she'd helped him choose for Mom Donna. Obviously by the same maker and although just as meaningful, it held a different message.

"It's true." Alana traced the engraved script before wrapping her arms around Cal's neck. "I loved you back then. I love you still and I always will."

When she kissed him, his already full heart almost overflowed.

There was only her. Only ever had been her because there'd never been anyone else who'd touched his heart in the same way. Whom he'd wanted to be a family with. His very own family, which he'd look out for and look after, now and always.

When he returned her kiss, he knew that it was his best Christmas ever, too. One embodying the true meaning of the holiday season and its enduring messages of love and forgiveness, reconciliation and second chances and, above all, hope.

EPILOGUE

EXCHANGING GREETINGS with family and friends, Alana left the church after the early Christmas Eve service and went out into the cold, crisp air, where stars lit up the soft darkness. With Josie and Laura stepping in at the last minute, the children's play had gone off without a hitch, and several members of the Strawberry Pond Knitters had thanked Alana for the cookies she'd contributed to their cookie exchange. Cookies, she'd been sure to mention, that Laura and Josie had helped her make.

Once again, she glanced at the engagement ring Cal had given her a few hours earlier. The single diamond sparkled like both a smile and a promise. A link with Cal's beloved mom and already more precious to Alana than any other piece of jewelry she owned.

There'd been lots of congratulations this evening. And from her mom and dad and brothers to Mrs. Barrett, everyone at church and an excited phone call with Jesse and Maria, Alana and

Cal had been enveloped in love as they started on this new path as an engaged couple.

"Alana." Mason and Noah ran up to her, followed by a man who must be their dad. "Did you see us being sheep?"

"I sure did. You were fantastic." She glanced at the man. "Is…" Alana stopped. She couldn't ask about Heather, not in front of her children.

"I'm Kyle." He introduced himself. "Heather told me about a job at Hansen Farms? Cal Paquette did as well when he came to see me a few days ago. He's the one who got the boys involved in the play tonight. Last-minute, but it was fun for them." Kyle cleared his throat. "Thank you for your kindness. The town's been good to us and the kids, and Heather's doing better. Her doctor's started her on a new treatment and, well, we're hopeful."

"I'm so pleased to hear about Heather, and I'd be happy to talk to you about a job." Alana's throat was tight. Life didn't have guarantees but choosing hope was powerful in facing problems and keeping going.

"Dad took a video of us for Mom." Mason's voice was low. "I wanted to stay home with her, but Mom said I'm a kid. I should be here."

"Cal also arranged for a volunteer from the Pond Pantry to visit Heather so I could bring the boys to take part in the play." Kyle adjusted Noah's beanie so it covered his ears. "Lots of folks have been offering to help. I guess word got out."

"It's the Strawberry Pond way. Together, we take care of our own. I'm sure a job with us will work out so go celebrate Christmas and try not to worry."

"What a year." After Kyle and the boys left, Laura appeared at Alana's side. "I mean that in a good way," she added with a soft smile. "I got married, and now, you're engaged."

"And a first wedding anniversary for me." Josie joined them at Alana's other side. "Who'd have thought it?"

"I certainly didn't. When it came to me getting married, anyway." Laura's laugh was self-deprecating. "Here." She tugged Alana to a quiet area on one side of the wide steps and Josie followed. "I need to tell you both something." She glanced around and lowered her voice. "So far only Trevor and our moms know, and I want to keep it that way for now, but you two are my closest friends. I also know I haven't been myself lately. It's because…" She hesitated and spoke in a whisper. "Trevor and me… We're… I'm having a baby. Next summer if all goes well. I didn't know it was possible to be so happy and terrified at the same time."

"That's wonderful news." Alana hugged her

friend, although mindful of Laura's privacy, she tried to contain her exuberance.

Josie echoed the congratulations and grinned. "Happy and terrified sounds about right. For pregnancy *and* being a mom." She laughed, and Alana and Laura joined in. "I'd never trade it, though."

"What wouldn't you trade?" Heath came up to them with Trevor and Cal.

"You, of course." Josie winked at her husband and then wrapped an arm around him.

Trevor took one of Laura's hands with a worried look. "Should you be out here standing in the cold?"

"I'm fine," Laura reassured him. "But I'm kind of tired. Let's find Danny and head home."

"We should head home with the girls, too," Josie said. "Although it's Christmas, I still need to be up for early milking tomorrow. This one's learning." She nudged Heath in the ribs. "But he still needs supervision."

"You just like spending time in the barn with me," Heath teased her back, amusement lighting his eyes.

"Lanie?" As her friends left, and several choir members started an impromptu carol singing on the way to their cars, Cal stepped forward. "I need to take Mom Donna home, but we'll both join you at the farm tomorrow morning. It's really great of your folks to include us."

"You're family now." She tucked her left hand with its engagement ring into his. "Hopefully one year, Jesse and Maria and Lucas can join us, or we can celebrate Christmas with them."

"I'd like that." Cal squeezed her hand. "Hey, you're not wearing gloves. Your hand's freezing."

"I didn't want to hide my ring." She smiled up at him. "See you tomorrow?"

"And every tomorrow after." Cal's expression turned serious. "I know we've only gotten engaged, and there's a lot to plan and details to figure out, but I don't want to wait too long to get married."

"Me, neither. After we say 'I do' you can move into my house." They'd already waited fifteen years, and Alana wanted to get started on married life. Her gaze drifted to Trevor helping Laura into their vehicle, and Heath doing the same for Josie.

"Really? Live with you and Holly?" Cal's eyes widened.

"Why not? It's close to the garage for your apprenticeship as well as the library for me. You can use the den office to study for your college course. I also have a guestroom for when Jesse and his family visit. It makes sense, doesn't it?"

Alana's voice faltered. She'd thought that Cal moving in with her after the wedding would be a foregone conclusion.

"It's a wonderful idea. I… Your house, it'll be—"

"Our home." Aware of onlookers, Alana stood on her tiptoes to give him an all-too-brief kiss. "For our family."

"I like the sound of that."

"Me, too." Warmth filled her and, as her folks, Ben, Jordy and their families and Mrs. Barrett joined them, Alana glanced at the carolers whose high voices still filled the air, and others who'd lingered to listen to the joyous music.

Her house was home and Strawberry Pond was, too. But the home she truly needed was the one she'd make with Cal. Her first and forever love.

* * * * *

For more Strawberry Pond romances from Jen Gilroy and Harlequin Heartwarming, visit www.Harlequin.com today!